FORCE

by Kindle Alexander

Trademark Acknowledgements

The author acknowledges the trademarked status and trademark owners of the trademarks mentioned in this work of fiction.

Dedication

Kindle, I love you forever.

Perry, you're missed.

Robert, I know the reason.

Table of Contents

Part 1   1

1. 1: The Birthday   2

2. 2: The Meet the Family   10

3. 3: The Slide into Fourth   18

4. 4: The Celebration   29

5. 5: The Grind   41

6. 6: The Tiny Dancer   49

7. 7: The New Heights   59

8. 8: The Himalayans Dash   69

9. 9: The Unknown Beau   76

10. 10: The Chaos Beau   87

11. 11: The Did It Happen Beau/Dash   98

12. 12: The Old Man Beau   106

13. 13: The Recovery Beau   113

14. 14: The Overdo Beau/Dash   121

15. 15: The December Dash/Beau/Dash   132

Part 2   143

16. 16: The Huff Dash/Beau   145

17. 17: The Every Good Deed Dash/Beau   156

18. 18: The Anniversary   166

19. 19: The Clients Dash   179

20. 20: The Boots Beau/Dash   190

21. 21: The Backyard Dash   198

22. 22: The Out of Town Beau   207

23. 23: The Investigation Dash   218

24. 24: The Shred Beau/Dash   226

25. 25: The Lon Beau   236

26. 26: The Free Fall Dash   245

27. Books By Kindle Alexander   255

PART I

1: The Birthday Dash

July 3, 2019
Sea Springs, Texas

Something as simple as a roll from one side of the bed to the other had become a complicated deal for me these days. I'd been in this predicament every time I tried to sleep for almost three years. The primary culprit: pajama-fucking-pants.

What numbnut invented something so pointless? Clearly, they had no feeling in their nuts. Every time I moved, I cut off essential blood flow to the region, which woke me up repeatedly. How could something made with good old-fashion American ingenuity have such a glaring oversight?

Then, as if that weren't the most awful thing in the world, my pride added a fatal blow, preventing me from swapping these ridiculous pants for comfortable form-fitting athletic shorts like Beau wore. In the beginning, when clothes in bed became a thing, I chose pajama pants when Beau thought I should wear shorts. Now, he slept like a comfortable baby while I generally stared at the back of his head, not even his face, though I doubted that would help pacify my frustration after all this time.

For the sake of my current pity party, I usually avoided the truth: I was too damned hard-headed. I put these pants on every night, no one forced them on me. My husband of almost four years, Beau Richmond-Brooks, had taught me a good lesson about being too focused on things that weren't near as important as him. Nowadays, I reserved my argumentative nature for the courtroom or for situations like this, where my defiance to admit I was wrong only led to my own discomfort, no one else.

As I lay there, staring at my husband's broad shoulders, I counted his long, measured breaths while my thoughts slipped to other things. Despite our challenges, Beau and I still squabbled over our minor differences. The same ones we'd had from the beginning, nineteen years ago. They typically revolved around something I wanted that veered off the course Beau set for himself. In our current life, Beau never bent. But he had a unique ability to capture my attention and steer me back onto his track.

Silently, yet with a touch of drama, I rolled over. My pants stayed in their previous position, cutting off more circulation than before. I stared at the dark ceiling, manifesting new thoughts about how much I loved my life.

As I rested my palm on my shirtless chest—noting that was how my whole body should be—I rubbed at the sweet ache of insurmountable joy there.

Fortunately, I didn't need much sleep. I lifted my head, catching the first rays of morning sunlight peeking around the sides of the curtains. In peaceful moments, I reflected on all the victories I had accomplished over the past four years. This perfectly sized, cozy bedroom was one of them.

We had managed to build a replica of Beau's ancestral family home, making only a few minor adjustments. While I didn't override Beau's vision, I made tiny enhancements. I couldn't resist incorporating a few elements from my Dallas home. For example, this bedroom suite was much larger than the previous one. That oversized, open concept followed throughout the entire home. I installed a few smart options in all the first floor rooms. Mood lighting and a sound system helped nourish my soul. Beyond the curtains in our room were the same floor-to-ceiling retractable windows that we'd had before. They led to a private section of the nice-sized swimming pool in our backyard.

Many nights, Beau and I would sneak out for a private swim, sharing conversation and simply enjoying being in each other's company. Those memories stayed vividly trapped inside my heart, truly special moments for me.

When sneaking outside wasn't an option, we'd take refuge in the en suite bathroom built for a king, or two guys who really liked to spend time alone. Bubble baths were a new addition to our private time. The oversized, luxury bathtub was everything to me. I cherished holding my guy in a cozy embrace, surrounded by warm, temperature-controlled water with tight bubbles floating on top. My cock firmed underneath my pajama pants, the material not stretching to accommodate the additional space. I ran my hand down my chest to travel under the waistband and grip my cock.

I tugged in measured movements, continuing my mapping of the first floor of our home. The bedroom opened into the furthest side of the living room. A dining room and spacious kitchen were all there in an open concept, making the downstairs feel enormous. But while christening our home, I demanded each of those spaces be considered separate. I fucked my guy over the kitchen island, the dining table, and every piece of furniture in the living room. My fist gave a hungry stroke down then up again, until the whispers penetrated the room.

The sound came from the baby monitor on my nightstand. "Livie, wake up," Ava said quietly to her sister, unaware that we could hear every little sound coming from their second-floor bedroom.

"The sun's not up," Livie whispered, bringing a smile to my lips.

"Mia?" Ava said.

"Paw said we have to stay in bed." Mia had a way of drawing me into her sweet charm.

Our identical triplets. Who would have ever guessed that was a possibility with in vitro? It was a shocking discovery during an early ultrasound.

Where Mia believed in being happy, she teetered between right and wrong. Livie followed all the rules. If there were no rules in place, she created them to remove any potential chaos to her day. Ava, well, we had trouble there. She enjoyed breaking all of Livie's rules. As a parent, Livie was a dream child. As someone watching from a distance, Mia and Ava had all the fun.

I tuned out the whispers, confident that Amelia would handle them. She loved and cared for those little girls as much as Beau and I did. She'd become their beloved *abuela*.

The damned hospital gave us a false sense of assurance and confidence, making their care look effortless. They handled our daughters like they were footballs—flipping them front to back, side to side while changing their diapers and swaddling them in their blankets. Even during their neonatal stay when they were barely the size of my hand, those nurses were fearless with their care. Yeah right. There was no way Beau and I could have managed the trio alone. Three crying babies in a home of two men who had never been around children... Hell, we'd been outnumbered from the minute we were told there were three.

In the end, they survived the baby stage, and so did we.

Beau counted it a win for the parents side, which included his influence. So the win was his.

We had no difficulty getting pregnant. It wasn't a consideration not to have all three once we got over the shock of the idea. A week shy of their third birthdays, our little girls continue to bring unbelievable depth to our love and lives. They could be quite bossy, and entirely too smart to accept simple answers to their constant questions of "why," and they were good big sisters to our infant son, Weston. His baby monitor came with a video screen and sat next to the girls' walkie-talkie-type listening device.

"You have to be quiet," Ava said.

"Stay in bed until the sun comes into the window," Livie said, repeating Beau's directive.

"The sun's up, Livie," Ava whispered. "Come on. It's Daddy's birthday."

"We can surprise him," Mia said with pure joy.

The only downside to having three little girls was the collective noise that stacked until it echoed through the house. In hindsight, renovating two of the four bedrooms on the second floor into one large space to let the girls share a room together might not have been the best idea. At just two months old, Weston, who we called West, had barely slept through the night. In another small renovation, Amelia left the third floor suite to take the bedroom between the girls and West. Maybe it was going to help or maybe not, only time would tell.

Even if Amelia didn't intervene, the girls weren't going to get far. Where the back spiral staircase used to be, we'd installed a small elevator to help Amelia get around with ease. The girls couldn't access that. At the top of the main staircase was a professional-grade stair barrier. No chance they could get past that locking system.

Turning quietly to face Beau once again, I took a moment to rifle through the blanket to find Beau's warm body. This was my last possible chance for my good morning birthday sex. I hooked my leg around his thigh, positioning myself against him head to toe. Duke stirred in his bed just a few feet from ours. I lifted a fist, giving Beau's command to motion him to the bathroom's doggie door. After a good shake, he lumbered out with Dixie reluctantly following.

"Your body's hot," Beau murmured. I took it as a tease and pressed a kiss on his shoulder. Beau remained a fine specimen of a man, muscular and hard, and buried under a summer blanket to keep him warm under the icy blast of cool air I required to semi-sleep. A wicked smile formed as I contemplated the idea of keeping him warm instead of this cold, unfeeling fabric. I pushed away everything separating Beau from me as he turned to face me. My guy was more awake than I'd initially suspected.

Even with having to steal moments to be together, I was always ready, anytime he wanted me. Like right now.

"Happy Birthday," he whispered. "They're gonna work their way into our room."

Beau had chopped off his long hair, keeping it close cropped these days. This new look, including a slight mustache and beard, made him a tad bit more handsome. That wasn't something I thought was in the realm of possibility. His strong jaw resembled a steel trap, and the jewel tones in his amber eyes sparkled brightly.

"I love my life," I whispered, propping myself up on my forearm as I gazed down on him.

"Me too," he responded in that sultry tone that curled my toes. He cradled the back of my head in his hand, gently pushing me down for an early morning kiss. I kept it light and sweet, always preferring to brush my teeth before we kissed, despite how often Beau teased me about it.

"Do you think Daddy and Paw are sleeping?" Mia asked in that same hushed whisper.

"Put your house shoes and robe on," Livie said.

"Dixie's outside. Paw's awake. He'll come get us," Ava said.

As far as I was concerned, a quickie wasn't out of the question. A birthday blow, maybe. Beau was like a Hoover. He could easily pull it out of me in a few minutes.

"Suck me before West fully wakes. I'll have a better day if you do." As I spoke, I swiftly shoved my pajama bottoms down. My heavy cock, much like a heat-seeking missile, sprang free from its cotton prison. I circled the shaft, my hips arching closer to my guy's mouth. "Put me in your mouth, Beau."

"You're a wicked man," Beau murmured, bending toward the small bead of pre-come clinging in my slit.

A quickie blow was decidedly un-wicked, but the fantasies I had for the remainder of this weekend were next level naughty. The only gift I asked for was a couple nights away at a new Houston luxury resort with my husband spending dedicated time working me over until my muscles quivered under the assault... The thought vanished as my heart gave a violent stutter of excitement against my rib cage. Beau swatted my hand away, taking my hard, ready cock into his fist. He licked his way up the side of my shaft until he swiped his tongue at another droplet at my tip.

Truthfully, I loved watching my guy love my body. Beau's knees moved between my spread legs, giving me a tight rub from base to tip then back down again. Every so often, he twisted his palm, sending jolts of pleasure shooting this way and that. I groaned, loving that move.

"Is this what you want?" Beau breathed huskily. His warm breath cascaded down the length of my cock. A bolt of excitement shivered up my spine.

Fuck yeah, that was exactly how I wanted him.

Beau rolled his shoulders and swiveled his neck, tightening the grip on my cock. Those sexy, alluring eyes lifted to my face. The intensity in his gaze promised something fantastic, even if it was short lived.

"Don't fight it," he instructed. "We gotta be fast."

I didn't mention that he was the one causing delays. Instead, I mostly closed my eyes and fisted the sheets beside me. I tucked my bottom lip between my teeth as I let go of any control I had. The depth of my arousal soared to the stratosphere.

"My God, you're stunnin'," Beau whispered over my wet cock, his hand gliding over my stomach before moving to my chest. He swallowed me whole while his sinful fingertips tweaked my nipple, pleasure thrust my hips forward, sending my cock further down his throat.

Beau needed to either quicken the pace or take it down a notch. Both options appealed to me, but I opted for the latter, gently lifting my hand to cradle his chin.

"I love you forever." My tone was laced with the reverence and devotion I felt to my core. Joy and contentment bloomed, mixing with a combination of lust and love swelling within me.

"Baby, I can suck you," I offered as he took me into his mouth. Such driving need always urged me to give him the same pleasure I received. "I think it's your turn," I whispered, skimming my fingers through the short strands of his hair. My gorgeous husband leaned into the touch.

I heard an audible pop. The air conditioning floated over the skin he'd made warm and wet.

"It's not my turn. I'm five down. Concentrate, baby. We don't have too much longer."

He was right and again licked up the side of my cock.

"I like licking your ass like that." Due to him, my life was perfect. I never wanted it to change. "Go slow when you put me back inside your mouth. I want to remember this moment throughout the day." The thump of my heartbeat drowned out all other sounds as he did what I asked and slid me into his mouth.

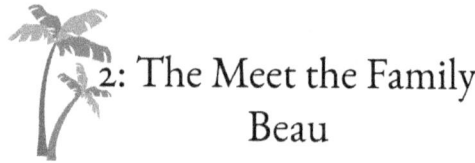

2: The Meet the Family Beau

Dash wanted a show. Why did I even pretend to let myself believe we could make this a quick sexy time? We no longer went at it like rabbits. These days we cherished our alone time. I dipped to take him back in my mouth. When the burst of tangy pre-come hit my tongue, I knew Dash's best efforts to slow this down were fizzling fast. For me, I coated my mouth with his essence, savoring Dash's undeniable pleasure.

I caressed the fingertips of my free hand against the soft skin of his thigh then on to his sac, fondling the weight in my palm. With a lick around his base, I glided up to his bulbous head, priming to take Dash's cock deep down my throat. It wouldn't be much longer than that. The sensual groan that followed had me giving his balls a pressured tug. The action was one of his favorites, and his body reacted in kind.

"Damn that feels good. It won't be long." I followed the guidance of the only man I had ever truly loved, the only one I had ever experienced intimacy with. I'd had the best, nothing compared. I swallowed him whole, my lips sliding down the velvet steel I'd just made wet.

"Fuck," Dash murmured. My gaze rose to meet his. I wasn't sure when the end would arrive, but I sensed it was drawing near. The blunt tips of his fingernails scraped across my scalp as I pulled completely off his rigid length.

"Pick up the pace, baby," he breathed above me, beginning to work his hips with my thrusts.

I swallowed him to the back of my throat.

"Fuck, Beau-baby." Dash was so damned long I couldn't take him too far down my throat, but I was going deeper each time. In that effort, I pumped Dash's cock in and out of my mouth, managing more each time.

My airway blocked. My mouth watered, helping to take him even deeper. My eyes bulged, yet I kept going. The idea of enhancing Dash's experience, giving all I could give, turned me the fuck on. The heady lust had my heart hammering as my dick swelled, and my toes curled. My fist followed my mouth, rising and falling with each pass. The entire time, I pinched and tugged at his sac. My reward was the deep sensual moan, his hips driving his cock further down my throat. I was doing exactly what he wanted.

Oh yeah. This stolen moment of good-morning sex caused me to piston my head up and down, seeking oxygen where I could, and finding the rhythm that was all us.

"Damn, loosen your jaw, baby. Make today the day," Dash hissed, his thumb tenderly caressing my jaw. I tried to do what he asked, relaxing my mouth and swallowing deeper. It worked, I took Dash to the root. This time, the tip of my nose mingled in the soft thatch of hair.

What a rush. Breathing didn't seem to matter. His balls seized, drawing tightly up. Psychedelic swirls became my vision. Haze clouded my thoughts. My throat tightened as he gave an abrupt pitch of the hips. "My fucking God. Beau-baby, I'm close."

His release exploded with his cock still lodged down my throat. Today was an all-time first for us. How did this feel so damned good? The wet slurping sounds were even a turn on, causing me to grip my cock, squeezing tighter. Dash's hips slowed, his unintelligible words encouraged me to stay the course. I'd never imagined anything this sexy. I was dominated by everything Dash.

A magically sated feeling rushed through me as I tumbled to the mattress. I took a deep inhale that felt exhilaratingly wonderful.

Minutes passed in this euphoria. The only sound that broke through the daze was hearing West stirring in his crib. He was such a sweet-natured little guy. It'd take a few minutes for him to cry for attention. The other noises indicated the calm home was moments away from chaos.

With a burst of energy that came from a hidden secret reserved stash for moments like these, I launched myself out of bed, shaking the sated fog from my head. A quick look over my shoulder revealed that Dash was still coasting on the high of his orgasm. A smile tugged at my lips. That must have been spectacular for him. Usually, he'd be the first one of us out of bed, ready to do mornings with the kids.

I entered the bathroom just as Dixie burst inside through the doggie door. Duke was on her heels. They generally competed to see which one could get through the opening first. Dixie won nine times out of ten.

"Mornin', you two," I said. Their tails wagged while they pranced at my feet. That excitement used to be reserved for me, but now they were telling me to open the bedroom door so they could greet their children. Even West enjoyed the play time they shared.

I quickly splashed cold water over my face and swished it through my mouth. I'd have to rub one off as soon as I got the chance. In a calculated move, somehow managing to keep the chuckle on the inside, I reached for one of Dash's pretty decorative towels and ran it over my face. They were reserved to make the room pretty, a prop like a picture on the wall, a concept he explained to me regularly. I reached for my robe, putting it on as I went to the bedroom door, the dogs making it there before me.

"Do you hear West?" Dash asked, his voice husky and sated. When he used our little guy's name, Duke and Dixie went on full alert, positioning themselves in the direction of his bedroom on the second floor. Now that the dogs had a focus, nothing would stop them. Once the door opened, they'd bolt through the house, prancing around the base of the stairs, waiting to get past the child safety gate to greet the children good morning. Dash was still where I left him, pants pushed down to his thighs, his limp dick still content from my fantastic blow job. An arm hung over his eyes.

"Do you think our sex makes the dogs sad?" Dash asked.

My eyes narrowed at the silly question and it burrowed into my brain like a pesky earwig. Now I'd be wondering about it all day. I didn't like the idea of my dogs being down in the dumps due to all the crazy good sex I received. Dammit. I tossed the edge of a blanket over Dash as I passed by. "I don't know. Maybe. I'm about to open the door. Why does every day have to begin at sunrise in the morning?"

"Wait for me. I'll come with you." Yet, he didn't budge an inch.

"Meet us in the kitchen." As I opened the door, our girls with their house shoes and robes on, blonde hair springing free from their braids, were running toward me, giant smiles on their faces. Only the placement of their birthmarks distinguished them.

"They're awake," Livie yelled like it was Christmas morning. Duke sprang forward, rocketing toward them like a furry missile. The collision was a daily occurrence, sending all three tumbling while somehow creating a fluffy cushion to absorb their falls. It felt like a reunion after ages apart, not a few nighttime hours. Duke's tail wagged happily, thumping against the floor until everyone was upright again. Ava's shoe had mysteriously ended up between his teeth. Dixie let the chaos happen, sitting on her haunches, waiting for the scene to end.

Even though we were going on three years with the girls in the house, about eleven hundred days, I was still taken by their excitement with life. Their mom was blonde like Dash, pretty in the same ways he was. The girls shared all of his great traits, including the bright blue eyes.

"Daddy's still tryin' to sleep," I said, waving a hand toward our bedroom. "Go get him. Tell him happy birthday and tickle him."

"Dammit." Dash let out a disgruntled groan, and the bedroom sounded like a wildlife observatory. I couldn't hold back a grin as those bedcovers rustled, and Dash's body thrashed about. I knew he was rocketing those pajama pants on faster than a speeding bullet.

"I'll get him, Amelia," I called to the real superhero in our house. She flashed me with a warm smile while I tightened the knot on my robe and let out a yawn. The signs of age had begun to settle on her face, and I genuinely wished for her well-being. She took care of us as if we were the joy of her world. I hoped she felt the same love from us.

"His bottle's ready." As if West tried to hurry us up, he burst out with a small infant cry.

I didn't know how long we'd have that newborn cry, but it warmed my heart as I took the bottle and pivoted to the foyer, and up the sweeping staircase, two steps at a time.

"Scott's pulling up."

"Tell him I'll meet him at the office after we have breakfast," I said. Ever since the kids arrived on the scene—and our three girls arrived almost immediately after we moved in—the house had been babyproofed in every way. Back then, Dash and I went way overboard, making me now have to climb over an oversized gate at the top of the stairs while holding my cock and balls to keep from getting pinched like so many times before.

"Shh, West," I murmured as I gently pushed open his bedroom door. Overall, he was a good little guy. His tear-filled eyes met mine, curiosity flickered over his face, wondering what I was about this morning. As if he hadn't just called me up. I placed the bottle on his dresser and moved to the side of the crib, smiling down at my son. "Good mornin'. How'd you sleep last night? It had to be at least four hours this time. I'm proud of you."

He stretched his tiny arms over his big head. Well, at least he tried to. His fists actually reached his hairline. I patted his diaper, checking what needed to be done there and lifted him into my arms. "I told your sisters to tickle your dad for his birthday. All those little hands coming at him at once. Someday you'll appreciate these stories," I said, lifting his fist for a high five. "Maybe I should've told them to jump on the bed. That always drives your dad crazy."

"Beau!" Dash called from the first floor as I began to change West. Our gazes connected. He had a way of looking into the deepest, most peaceful parts of me. If old souls existed, West surely had one. He regularly overwhelmed me, drawing out a sense of contentment I didn't know was there.

Just as I snapped his onesie back together, I heard the girls squealing, their footsteps pounding down the hallway. Dash was on their tail, moaning as if he pretended to be a zombie. Another set of feet—booted this time—stomped up the staircase. I went for West's bottle, waiting for everyone's entry.

"He's in here, Daddy." The girls' laughter and shrieks filled the room as they ran to hide behind me, presumably to avoid being eaten by the zombie hot on their trail. Dash made it around the doorframe, looking adorably disheveled with his arms stuck out, head rocking back and forth, making grunts and groans. Screams bounced off the sheetrock as they ran past him to get away. None of it bothered West who cooed happily in my arms.

Dash dropped the act. The days of him always having perfect hair and immaculate style were harder to find. I loved this new Dash and the precious moments he created.

"Amelia sent me up," Scott said from the doorway. The girls gathered around his legs for protection.

"Uncle Scott's here, Paw," Livie announced as if it weren't obvious.

"Happy birthday, Dash," Scott muttered, looking down at the girls.

"I'll meet you at the office after breakfast, unless you wanna stay. It's Amelia's famous pancakes," I said, gently brushing West's lips until he opened for the bottle.

"We'll be out by then," Scott replied, grinning as he lifted his gaze to mine. "We scheduled our charter an hour early today."

Dang it, I'd forgotten. The day was rearranged to get me home by noon to spend the rest of the day with Dash. We had an entire day and night of celebration planned, including

Amelia, the kids, and Scott's family. I quickly transferred West to Dash without my little guy losing his meal.

"Paw's late for work." I smiled down at Livie, giving a play by play for anyone who didn't understand what was happening.

"I gotta go. I'll be home early. Be good and be ready," I said to their upturned faces.

Amelia was a real pro at the hair braid, but nothing could hold together through their tossing and turning at night. Factor in tickle time, and their tendrils of curls sprang out every direction, making them cuter than normal.

"I'll have the boat ready for the firework show tonight." As if they had only just heard the plan, all three began bouncing with excitement. They absolutely loved our boat trips, and I'd done my best to foster a love of the ocean. Even so, they were strangely girly considering the strong masculine presence in their lives. I suspected, as they grew older, Mia would be the one to accompany me on my adventures. We'd see.

Dash's brows knitted together. "I liked the idea of you being home all day. Let me see if Amelia's started breakfast. Maybe we could go to the café while Paw works this morning."

"Amelia's plannin' to have a birthday breakfast on the patio. Lauren's bringin' their kids. They want to swim," I explained, maybe delivering more bad news. There were ten kids between both of our families. Dash was always the center of attention, playing tirelessly until either he or the children gave out. "Y'all be good for Dad," I said, and bit the bullet to the conversation. By law, Scott couldn't take the charter without me on board to help, or someone there. We couldn't hire anyone, because we weren't even paying for ourselves yet. On my way out, I leaned in, giving Dash a quick kiss on the lips.

"Lauren wants me to remind you of the reservations at Chuck E. Cheese so the animatronics can sing happy birthday to Dash," Scott said, yawning to a jaw-cracking effect. The girls responded with another round of excited bounces. "We'll meet y'all there."

"I can't tell you the joy," Dash deadpanned, but I knew he was genuinely excited about the time spent together.

I bent for a peck and left the room. Dash and the girls followed.

"We need to get dressed so we can eat, play, then swim." At Dash's pronouncement, the girls walked more subdued. They'd have to endure hair brushing before braiding again. Their least favorite thing. Though I wasn't sure if it was the brush or sitting patiently they actually disliked more.

"Give me five minutes, and I'll meet you at the dock," I said, hearing Amelia coming up the elevator to help Dash. I went the other way, following Scott over the gate.

"I'm grabbin' a thermos of coffee. Meet me there. They're probably waitin' on us." He cut to the right toward the kitchen. I went left to our room.

"Take a Red Bull for me. If there are cinnamon rolls, take a couple, and I want one." I'd forgotten how much Dash enjoyed the TikTok cinnamon roll recipe. Amelia made them twice a year. Today was one of those times. I might grab one too. The devious plan made me smile. Dash believed six of the rolls were for him. He'd be frustrated with me for taking three, meaning our kids wouldn't eat, or that I won. I did a triumphant fist pump, keeping my excitement close to my chest.

3: The Slide into Fourth
Dash/Beau

Dash

Through the good and bad times, I held on to the memory of Beau shifting my birthday by a day to give me my own twenty-four hours to celebrate. His sweetness and consideration, especially when he preferred not to make a fuss over his own birthday, had me absently bringing his knuckles to my lips for a kiss.

The July heat and humidity lingered throughout the day and into the night. The scent of heavily applied sunscreen clung to us as we enjoyed the last few hours of the night by poolside. Scott and Lauren were snuggled together on one lounger facing the pool. Beau and I sat side by side in Adirondack chairs, closer to the trickling waterfall on the outer edge of the pool. Our backyard was a carefully planned oasis where we spent most of our free time. The perfect outdoor setting for the entire family.

Having bought all of Beau's grandparents' land, and the property next to it with the thick thatch of forestry where Beau and I shared our first kiss, we had ample space for a swing set, treehouse, and a safe jungle gym built before any of the children arrived. I eventually wanted the girls to take tennis lessons. I had a space on the property reserved in my mind for a court when money freed up.

Between there and here was a lovely, fenced-in swimming pool, built-in waterfall, and a dedicated shallow end for the kids. A large, covered sandbox was nearby. We'd built a privacy fence around the majority of the property and installed expensive as hell landscaping and loads and loads of flowers to help tie it all together. I always had ideas to improve our living space, but for now, with the cost of private school starting in the fall, we spent a lot of the money we made.

Why was I thinking about that right now? I lifted Beau's hand, kissing it again. His head rested against the back of the chair, and at my gestures, he swiveled to face me with a questioning gaze. "I was just thinking about the picture the girls gave me. I loved it."

Beau's brows crinkled. "Amelia gives you a picture of them every year. It couldn't have been a surprise."

He was a rock when it came to reality, never getting lost in the whimsical fairy tale I spun about our life. My fingers tightened around his. "This year's picture is the day we brought West home for the first time. We're all in the picture. Our family's complete. West looks so much like you."

Beau nodded and closed his eyes. "It's late."

"It is late," Lauren Lee agreed, getting to her feet. "We need to go home. Tomorrow mornin's comin' quick."

Scott, Beau's childhood buddy and Lauren's husband, kept his hands on her body. How she held him captivated after so many years of marriage was inspiring. It was the same way Beau held me. Scott rose too, circling her waist. "You're gonna have to get me home," Scott said. "We have a long walk. Ten feet at least."

The joke never grew old. Scott bought the vacant lot next to ours. We saw at least one member of the Lee family every day. Our kids were fast friends. Scott focused on the charter service full-time, while Lauren became a cosmetologist, having a successful career at the only high-end salon in the area. For me, life with a talented stylist next door was everything right in the world.

Amelia set up a slumber party for most of the kiddos in the living room. I didn't know for sure, but suspected Daisy Mae and Dolly, Scott's two oldest girls had gone home. Their young teenage selves took the whole hormonal, bad attitude as a way of life. They could barely tolerate us anymore.

"Whoever's asleep, let them stay," Beau said without moving his head or opening his eyes. My brows knitted together. It was my birthday night. We'd never be quiet enough not to wake up Scott's kids. My fingers squeezed until Beau glanced at me. "What? That's what happens at a slumber party. And you got yours this mornin'. Tomorrow's comin' where you'll get more."

"Hmm," I murmured as I manifested laser beams shooting from my eyes.

"I sense tension," Scott said, happy to jump in the middle of any possible disagreement. He was loud and full of humor.

"Good night, Lee," Beau said dismissively.

"We should probably stay too," Scott said, unfazed by Beau. "It's late and a risk to get home with how much we've had to drink…"

"Figure it out," Beau said, finally sitting up and paying attention to his surroundings. "Lauren can get you home. It wouldn't be the first time."

"Har, har." Scott tucked an arm back around Lauren and turned to leave. "He's always testy these days. Remember when he used to be a nice guy?" He didn't wait for an answer before adding, "It's hard for me to remember too."

The never-ending banter between those two left me hiding a smile. When I turned back to Beau, he bent over the arm of the chair to be right in my face. "You know, we could take off to Houston tonight. Amelia said Belle's arrivin' first thing in the mornin'. She'll be here until we return on Monday afternoon."

"How did Amelia respond to the idea of additional help?" I whispered. Amelia was quite protective of the children and preferred to keep other adults out of the house until they were properly vetted. No one ever passed her tests.

"I sold it to her as a present for the girls. She's comin' as Belle from *Beauty and the Beast*. She'll stay in character for the length of the stay," Beau reminded me. "I showed her all the background tests she passed from Care.com."

"Ahh, yeah, I remember now. She's costing about three hundred dollars, right?" I asked. When Beau started to move away, I locked an arm around his neck, keeping him close. "That doesn't seem like a lot for two days of Belle."

"I didn't think so either," he said, giving a giant yawn in my face. "Let's just leave tomorrow. Come to bed with me." Of course Beau broke my hold and drew me up with him, walking side by side to our bathroom entrance. "She reduced her price because she's lookin' for a part-time job with us. She's bringin' a Disney library to read. The girls are so smart, they're gonna have fun. She's plannin' a tea party in the treehouse."

I pushed open the door, and cold air blasted us. Beau slipped inside first. I got the peck I expected as he passed by. "They're so curious. I bet that's how you were growin' up." He gave me another kiss with a giant grin while he descended then retreated. "At their age, I was flingin' myself off the end of the boat dock. I never learned not to do it. They had to jump in and save me several times until I figured out how to save myself."

"I love you," I said, locking us inside the house before edging past Beau into the bedroom. "I'm going to check on the kids and shut the house down. I'll be back to lay in bed and talk about nothing until you fall asleep on me."

"I'm leavin' shorts on the bed for you. The pajama pants have to go," Beau said, disappearing into our closet.

"I can't let you win," I confessed, heading back to the bathroom.

"I know it's hard on you," he said with his head poking out of the closet. He was relaxed and still grinning ear to ear. He must have enjoyed the day. Those bright smiles he was throwing out were reserved for only the best of times. "Don't worry, I won't count the win. Consider it a birthday present."

I lost him to the closet once again while I did my part to secure everyone inside the house and setting the alarm. As suspected, Scott's two older children were gone. The rest of the girls were asleep on sleeping bags all over the living room furniture and plush rug on the floor. Both dogs were sleeping near them. Amelia dozed in her recliner. West was knocked out in a smaller rocking crib near her. He'd had a huge day. These scenes always filled my emotional bank until it spilled over. I vowed to never take any of this for granted. I flipped off the overhead light and started for my bedroom.

Beau

Since we married, Dash and I established a new anniversary tradition: we took turns planning the celebration. This year fell to me. Dash gave me the odd years due to my personality. He thought that joke was hilarious. Me? He needed to leave humor to those who knew how to deliver a joke.

This was our first anniversary alone since the kids arrived. In the theme of "go big or go home," I'd splurged on a junior suite at the newly opened Escape Resorts, a luxury hotel on the west side of Houston. I aimed to wine and dine my guy. I envisioned medium rare T-bone steaks, artery clogging loaded baked potatoes, overflowing bottles of wine, and loads and loads of carnal sexcapades. We'd make up for every time our responsibilities thwarted our sexy time.

Instead, I discovered my anxiety was still right under the surface, and it made me insecure as hell. Over the last few years, I thought I'd managed to carve out a compatible, healthy space in Dash's life. The problems in our past never actually reached me anymore. The country boy, me, and the socialite, Dash, found a cohesive existence to live our lives. *Pfft*. A night in Escape Resorts, or better said, a reservation at Reservations fine dining and nightclub, proved I still hadn't integrated well with the wealthy. From the clothes I wore to the callouses embedded on my palms, I still didn't fit in the crowds Dash was born to thrive in. I had donned a suit that was made at least ten years ago while I tried my hand at romance and seduction. Yet all my preparation had me feeling like I was the lead character in a remake of *Hee Haw*.

I gave a humorless laugh. Clearly, I was the funny one.

The table was spacious and ours for the evening. We tucked into the half circle booth, sitting side by side—nowadays, the closeness provided better ease for me to finish Dash's dinner when he'd had enough.

The evening was a 'culinary' experience. A multi-course meal that lasted over three hours. Slowly, I unwound from Dash who pressed himself close to my side. Thankfully, I remembered the basics of etiquette I'd learned when we lived in Chicago. Well, until it came to the actual eating of the main meal. When I tasted the deliciously seasoned thick cut T-bone, I trailed the next bite with its juices dripping toward Dash for a try. Good fortune must have smiled on me because Dash was deft in his napkin skill, dodging the juices and still managing to take the bite.

Honestly, I felt like Dash was digging the vibe I tried to create. As the clock struck ten, the restaurant opened to the dance club next door. A gay nightclub. A first for me in a very long time, but clearly not Dash who strutted and danced to the other side of the building while holding his glass of wine.

I wasn't sure which one of us plied the other with alcohol. The culprit might have been simply the time of year; it was damned hot outside. Another option was the hard, tight twenty-year-old waiters who wore tiny speedo uniforms and nothing more. Their bright, flirty smiles encouraged more and more cocktails. Maybe it was the way they kept our drink glasses full, and our dance floor space was next to our reserved high-top table.

My bet landed on the way Dash undressed me while dancing suggestively against my body. First, he removed my tie, the dress shirt followed, the belt was shimmied off, and the button of my slacks was left open causing them to hang low on my hips. How did he continue to arouse me so thoroughly after all this time?

A drunk Dash was a beautiful thing. From our seven o'clock reservation for dinner to about an hour ago, somewhere around midnight, my guy had finally stopped chatting about where the girls were going to start preschool, or their meticulously planned birthday event next weekend, or whether West should begin eating cereal now.

Finally, he moved on to more important topics: sex-talking to me in a dirty, filthy way that turned me the fuck on.

Another thing that caught my eye was that most of the men here waxed their chests. With age, I'd developed a pretty good coating of fur. How often did I have to get waxed to keep a bare chest? Did I have to do it myself or was it better to pay someone? What did that cost look like? Did waxing really hurt like they said it did?

Then Dash gave me the come-hither look, stripping off his dress shirt. I liked that move a lot, and barely laughed when he carefully placed it on his seat. Some things never changed.

We were back to the hither, Dash was on me. His hands slid over my chest, roaming freely. I locked my arm around his waist, drawing him tightly against my body. The music popped as we took it to a sultry sway. What a great experience. I understood why the club required all the privacy paperwork before accessing the fun environment.

"Drink," Dash encouraged, tilting us toward the table to gather my cocktail glass. He pressed it to my lips as his palm rubbed the length of my hard cock. When I took the glass to keep it from trailing down my chest, he lifted on his toes to press those plump lips against my ear. I wished he'd whispered something to do with fucking me senseless, but he didn't. The music was too loud, and he required help to stay on his tiptoes. "I love you. We should get a membership here."

Right. He and I had recently set a budget for our finances. I didn't know, because he didn't let me know, but suspected cash was tight. He worried endlessly about the cost of a good private school for the kids. Based on what we were seeing, he and I weren't Reservations nightclub wealthy. "You think?"

His face came within inches of mine, hands on each shoulder to stay steady. "I think you're the hottest guy here."

I burst out a laugh right in his face then tried my hand at the compliment. "You're the hottest guy here."

Something raced over his expression. His body went still. "That means you think I'm old, don't you?"

What? Wait. Did that mean *he* thought *I* was old? Fuck, I halted movement too. Dammit. Old was a gay man's nightmare. My eyes narrowed, taking a closer look at my husband who might be divorced on our nineteenth anniversary. Was this one of his workarounds? A devious trap that I regularly fell for? He was master level good at those.

"Why aren't you answering?" he slurred and tipsy swayed until I righted his position.

"How do I answer? Of course you're not old. You're still the hot guy that made me tumble over my handlebars." I gave a single nod, proud of my off-the-cuff response. "Do you think I'm old?"

"Yeah," he said as if the answer was obvious. "Of course you are. You have to know that."

Divorce proceedings began to take shape. My chest bumped him several steps away into other dancers. I glared my meanest look, which he found hilarious.

"I'm younger than you, lawyer-man." I let out a shout loud enough to draw stares, which only made Dash cackle like a damned hyena.

"By eleven months," Dash said, sashaying closer with a wink and a twist. "If we weren't older..." The beat dropped to a thumping anthem making Dash have to climb my body to say what he wanted me to hear. I didn't give a single inch of height to help him reach my ear. "We wouldn't be celebrating our nineteenth anniversary if we weren't old!"

Then, in a daring move, his tongue darted straight into my ear, swirling there until reaching the outer edge. His tongue lapped around the shell. He reared maybe an inch away, puffing a teasing breath over the skin he'd just made wet.

"I want another hundred more years." He caressed my cheek with his palm, tilting me so he better captured my lips, kissing me roughly. Instantly, tongue and teeth battled for domination.

As suddenly as he stole the kiss, he edged back, our gazes colliding. Those mesmerizing blue depths held me captive, waiting for whatever he wanted to reveal. "You ready to go to our room?"

Always. But that thought stayed locked in my head. Instead, I nodded and kept him firmly in my hold. I gathered our clothes, tossing them one right after another toward Dash. He scrambled to keep each article from hitting the floor. I extended my hand above my head in hopes of gaining our waiter's attention. Dash had other plans, clasping my arm and darting stealthily through the maze of dancers, ending at the bar.

He paid, of course. I never did, although we shared accounts. Our walkout was just like any other... Dash strutted ahead of me, pulling me along like his loyal sidekick. But this time, Dash didn't hold all my attention. The scenery was seriously handsome men. I'd never been around this many gay men in my life. I might not ever think about life in the same way again.

Once we made it to the hotel's hallway, the soft, bright lighting was blinding. "What did it cost?" I asked. The handhold we shared swapped hands when Dash turned to face me, walking backward now.

"Guess?"

"Two hundred and fifty dollars," I said, exaggerating my answer.

Dash slowed his roll and cocked a brow. "Four hundred and seventy-five dollars."

I rooted in my spot. Dinner was charged to the room. That alone was a few hundred dollars. "Six hundred dollars for the drinks we had at the club?"

"Yeah," Dash grunted, finding something funny. He tugged at my hand to get me moving again. I reluctantly did.

Damn, that dumb club looked a lot less appealing now. Membership was out of the question if a single night of drinks cost that much.

"So this weekend's costin' us a couple of thousand dollars?"

Dash let out a hearty laugh. I didn't find the joke.

"I've got my work cut out for me next year. Topping this anniversary won't be easy," he said, and I couldn't help the unguarded *tsk* at the very idea. First, we weren't having additional anniversary celebrations because I just spent all the money from now until forever. Second, everything Dash did was over-the-top. Him trying to beat this one meant we'd have reservations on the first flights to the moon and back. As a family, we took family vacations all over the country. This year, the girls' birthday party was on a seven-day Disney cruise with our entire family. That was scheduled a mere four days after we returned from this anniversary weekend. Dash promised me the cruise was my mom's idea, and she was paying, but I didn't believe that lie. He'd never let someone else pay for us, he envisioned it as his job.

Dash created our epic family gathering and parties, not for bragging rights or to constantly outdo himself, he genuinely wanted to create lasting memories while building a solid loving base for our family. He was good at it even if I did have to bring my lunch everyday... I was dumb. Such a cheap way to save a little bit of money.

"You'll crack that code, I'm sure," I said, dragging my feet while Dash practically pulled me along. His ass was still a thing of beauty. The extra weight he'd gained—nothing crazy, a few extra pounds here and there—only made the way he filled out his clothes better. His ass was a double gripper, the perfect bubble butt.

At the elevator doors, he pressed the button, and said, "Can we go up—" He turned to me, dislodging my stare, drawing me out of my daze.

"What'd you say?"

"Were you just checking out my backside?" Dash teased, flipping around for me to look again. And I did. Watching him might be my favorite pastime.

"That baby blazer you wore lets me see both the front and back. A bold strategy since I'm a sure thing." I shrugged because it was the truth.

"You're making this trip to the room harder than it has to be, Casanova," Dash said, walking into me, tilting his face up for a smooch. "I wanted to spend time with you in the room, talking, just being together while alone and uninterrupted." He caressed my cheek, his thumb skimming my lower lip until the ding of the elevator startled him, sending his thumb directly into my eye.

I shoved him into the open car, not hard but enough, rubbing my inverted eyelashes from underneath the lid. Whatever about quiet time. My guy drank too much and was feeling the high. We only had so long before he crashed, passing smooth out.

4: The Celebration
Dash/Beau

Dash

"Hmm. Yeah, it's an intriguing development. File a motion for continuance on Monday. Handle it on your own. I'll be back Tuesday morning. Let's meet with the client then. Have Stone rearrange my schedule accordingly. It'll substantially increase the bottom line. Do a preliminary cost analysis. Have it to me Monday evening," I said to the newest member of my team, Mason Taylor, a highly driven third-year attorney who actively sought me out for employment. My cell phone was stuck to my ear, a full bottle of wine in my other hand. I hustled naked from the living room back to the bedroom where Beau was waiting.

"Should...wait. Changing directions. Is the client required to attend court with me on Monday? Will his presence be an advantage to his case?" Mason asked.

"No," I said with a shiver. "I have to go. Send me the cost analysis. I need to be prepared for Tuesday." In a fluid move that I'd mastered years ago, I swiped my thumb absently across the screen to end the call as I expertly dove under the edge of the blanket Beau held up for me. Not a drop of wine was spilled. Clearly not the first time I'd made such a maneuver.

Twenty-four hours into our anniversary weekend and we'd eaten two delicious buffets, spent time together sipping fruity cocktails while baking under the sun, had a sixty-minute couples massage then back to the room for ass busting sex, twice. I loved that the direction of Beau's plans brought us back to the hotel room every few hours.

Now, we were finally alone in the suite with the temperature of the AC turned down as low as it could go, requiring Beau and I to cuddle together under every blanket we found in the suite. During the dive, I tossed my cell phone in the middle of the mattress, pressing my icy body against Beau's warm one.

"It's seriously cold out there. Maybe you should go turn the AC up a few degrees, so we don't freeze to death," I suggested cheekily, taking a decent-sized pull from the wine bottle.

"If I go, I'm takin' the blankets with me," he said with all certainty. His hand reached for the bottle before it properly left my lips, splashing a drop or two on my chest. "I can't handle the cold like I used to. You might have to scoot over to your side. Your body's makin' me shiver." My guy actually tried to shove me away from him.

Yeah right. When that didn't work, he scooted the other direction. Beau was smarter than that decision. I smirked as I followed him, landing in the space he'd made warm with that big body. Perfect.

"How did we endure Chicago?" Beau seldom spoke about the dark period we barely survived.

Of course I didn't respond, knowing that our difficult years were entirely my fault. "Stop moving and take a drink. If we don't get you drunk, how can I take advantage of you? If you're aware of what's happening, that's called having consensual sex. We do that regularly."

"Not that regularly," he hissed and lifted the bottle, taking several hearty gulps. I tucked pillows behind my back before getting another crack at the wine. Beau settled in around me, throwing the blankets over our heads.

"Is my guy missing our intimate time together?" I teased, cherishing the way he made me feel loved and adored. I also agreed with him, having children really put a dent in our naked alone time. I missed us like this too.

"Yeah, I am. I wish we found a way to fit it in more," he said, scooting farther down under the duvet, tossing a leg over mine. His lips pressed against my chest. The kiss was light and nibbly, the perfect foreplay for things to progress.

"You have to know that I regularly think you're naked under all those clothes you wear," I said, doing my best to hide a smile. It took a second before Beau's gaze lifted, glancing questioningly at me. I managed to hold my tongue as he worked through my tease.

"You're dumb," he finally said.

"I've been waiting to drop that joke," I said, laughing while braving the cold to place the wine bottle on the nightstand. As I decided we'd had enough foreplay, and it was time to make amends for our lack of sexual activity, my cell phone's irritating ringtone indicated the call came from home.

It was shrill and loud, designed to capture my attention. It did its job.

"Why do you have that ringtone? Make it stop," Beau complained, peeking out of the cocoon he'd created. It wasn't his fault that I misplaced my phone, but I still took the blankets with me while I hunted for it on the bed. Luckily, I found it on the fourth ring.

"Hello," I said, swiping upward to connect the call. I leaned back on my ass, expecting Beau to absorb my body weight. He wasn't there, so I toppled to the mattress while he ripped the covers away and headed toward the thermostat.

"Daddy," Ava said, sounding bothered and irritated.

"Ava, how do you know how to call me?" I asked by way of a greeting.

Three days shy of their third birthday, and this was a first from any of them. Of course, I knew they were smart, likely on the higher end of intelligence, but understanding the process of calling us directly was going to change everything. My concerned gaze lifted to Beau who sat on the edge of the mattress. I scrambled toward him, trying to share his body's warmth.

"Daddy, don't be mad at me," Ava started. "I remember your number from Paw's phone. Abuela won't let Dory spend the night, and Mia and I want her to. Will you tell her to let Dory stay here?"

"Daddy," Livie said in the background. "Abuela's head hurts, and Belle says we need to be nice and quiet, and her hands are full with the four of us." Her last words were said with scorn at Ava's selfishness.

"I didn't say you wanted Dory here. Just me and Mia do," Ava shot back.

"What's goin' on?" Beau asked, tossing the cold end of the duvet over me. His hard body was finally at my back.

"Ava's figured out how to call me, she learned the number from your cell phone and wants Dory to spend the night. Amelia has a headache, and told her no."

"Huh," Beau said, clearly absorbing this new turn of events. "They aren't told no very often, so when it's said, they need to listen, or otherwise they go on the naughty list. And they can't call you unless it's an emergency. You're too busy for that. And bein' told no isn't an emergency."

"Daddy, that's why I called you, because Paw always says naughty list, naughty list, naughty list!"

I pressed the speaker option so I didn't have to be the heavy. Beau was by far the stricter parent. But Ava wasn't wrong. The naughty or nice list was a regular concern in our home, causing my smile and Beau's frown. I pointed to the wine bottle which was now closer to Beau, needing more to get through this conversation.

"And four of us means me, Mia, Livie, and Dory," Ava said.

"No, four of us is us and West. Four. One. Two. Three. Four," Livie answered, being our good girl.

"You girls are too smart for your age," I added, proud of those math skills.

"We know," Livie said. "Some of our friends don't know the alphabet."

"Where's Belle?" Beau asked, taking the phone.

"Belle's feeding West, and we're hiding in our bathroom. I think you're mad," Ava responded.

"Girls, Dory isn't comin' over, and yes, I'm frustrated. You know better than to challenge Abuela. When she says no, that's your answer. I want you to be quiet and helpful and only call us if it's an emergency. This is not an emergency," Beau explained, moving to hand me the wine bottle. I gulped it like Kool-Aid.

The silence on the other end lasted maybe ten seconds before Livie said, "Told you."

Beau handed me back the phone.

"Take the phone back to wherever you found it, and please be as good as I believe you are," I added, receiving two thumbs-up from Beau.

"Okay, bye, Daddy. If you change your mind, call Abuela," Ava said. "Bye, Paw," they chirped in unison. The phone disconnected.

"So that's new," I said, putting the cell phone on the nightstand within easy reach.

"They're too smart for their age," he said. I rested my palm on his thigh, fingertips trailing a caressing path. It'd take some time to regain that spark of romance, but I was up for the challenge. I edged closer when his cell phone dinged. "They better not have figured out how to text."

"Of course they have." I fell to my back, feeling like the world was trying to ruin our alone time. "I was just priming you to make my move. Let's make love then order room service then go back to the dance club and have thirty-dollar cocktails served by handsome waiters. There were some really pretty men there. Did you think so?"

Beau ignored me as I followed his thumbs deftly moving over the small keyboard. A return text showed a picture of a handsome, buff, middle-aged rock climber. "Who's that?"

"A new lead in the club," Beau murmured distractedly. "He's finalizin' the arrangements for the Himalayas. He's ordering our meals on the plane."

Rock climbing attracted a certain kind of guy, but they were rarely that attractive. This guy met Beau in stature and looks.

Shockingly, I had a momentary lick of jealousy, emotions I'd only had a couple of times before. It was incredibly hard to tamp down.

"When's the climb?" I asked, lifting to a sitting position right beside Beau to read the texts. Wow. He had a beard, more substantial than the growth Beau wore. And had a fuck-boy hairstyle that I couldn't properly pull off, but looked natural on him.

My heart gave a twist of concern. I wasn't the young man I used to be, and got to my feet.

"Late October into early November. It's a couple of weeks. I put it on the shared calendar." Beau lifted his gaze to mine and didn't focus on my cock that was eye-level. I didn't turn hard either. What the hell? "You were invited to go. You haven't been to that side of the world."

No, I hadn't. I wasn't a fan of camping. I preferred climate control and flushable toilets. More importantly, the thought of both of us being so far from home didn't set well. I lost his gaze to the phone again, his thumbs moving over the keyboard. He barely texted me, but this guy... Suddenly, he clicked off the phone and placed it next to mine on the nightstand.

"What did you say you wanted to do?" Beau asked, and still hadn't touched my penis.

"I'm jealous," I stated honestly. The only thing I wanted to do was to ride in on a white stallion and drive a saber through this sports climbing guy's heart so he couldn't go on the trip with my love. It seemed a fair option.

"Jealous of what? The trip? You can go..."

No. He was purposely being vague, and I cut him right off, not playing his games. "The guy you're texting is nice looking."

"What are you talkin' about? Most of the guys in the club are attractive," he said, as if that helped the situation in any way. My silence, due to being dumbfounded, had a perplexed expression knitting his brow together. "Jesse has a wife on the team. She's goin' with us. You'd like him and her. He's a doctor of somethin' smart, not a medical doctor, doctor. We can invite them over so you're comfortable around 'em."

His words soothed me. My jealousy vanished. If Beau didn't genuinely understand where I was coming from, then I had to be off base. I let it go.

"It gets really chilly in here," I said by way of an answer. "But the room loses it fast. Do you think that's on purpose?"

I received the *'you're silly'* head shake from my guy, which was probably deserved. "How about dinner, dancin' for an hour or so, then marathon sex until it's time to leave in the mornin'," Beau suggested.

"How about a fast shower with sex, then dinner at the sushi place downstairs. We'll decide about dancing. I might want to walk the complex. There's a lot going on here."

Beau's handsome face scrunched slightly, knowing I really wanted to stop by the Kellus Hardin art show. He was local to the Dallas art scene. And Beau wasn't a big fan of my favorite Asian meal, but he'd get something to-go from another restaurant, and we'd meet to eat together.

He nodded and rose, heading to the bathroom. "You bottom in the shower and I'll get a hamburger from the grill."

I followed, watching him strut in front of me. "We'll see." He gave me a sly glance over the shoulder, meaning the competition was on.

Beau

Four Days Later

Dash was on his A-game with Livie by his side. She was hypnotized in delight at her daddy's adherence to complicated schedules and remarkable organizational skills. Mia held my right hand, Ava had my left, and West was snugly bundled on my chest. In a show of love and devotion, Livie lifted her hand to tuck into Dash's as he pointed his other finger this way and that, instructing the porters who gathered our luggage and assorted baby and children's contraptions from the car to the cruise ship.

Our coordinating outfits were another Dash induced reality. He found Disney character fabric and had most of our clothing made. The girls donned matching sundresses and sandals, their long hair in braided pigtails, and sunglasses on. The only way to tell them apart outside of personality, was the placement of birthmarks along their arms. West wore the same fabric onesie paired with a baby cap.

Dash commissioned two Hawaiian-style button-ups in the same material as our children and khaki shorts. My ball cap was new, and turned backward, not a Disney hat, but color coordinated with the rest of our clothing. Watching everyone else in their normal clothes, I felt like we may have gone overboard.

Today marked the start of their official birthdays. Tonight's special dinner was private and princess-themed. They each planned to wear different princess costumes. Our girls were three years old and on their very best behavior.

"Beau!" My mom's voice rose above the sea of people trying to board early.

"Gigi!" the girls sang in unison. At that moment, that "very best behavior" they'd been excelling at went out the window. They broke the handhold and bolted in the direction of my mom's voice. I'd trained the girls in the same manner I used with Dixie and Duke, and I was seconds away from whistling them back when I spotted my mom busting through the throng. She jogged toward them, meeting in the middle with a near collision.

Dash and I also started that direction. I was amazed at how much my kids adored my mom and Wesley Carter. Even with all the miles between us, we'd somehow managed to make a functioning family. Kailey, my nine-year-old sister, was still as sweet and kind as always. She loved being with my kids and wore a matching dress. So did my mom.

"Happy Birthday!" Mom exclaimed from her knees, squeezing the girls in a giant, four-way hug. "I missed you. Now stand in front of me so I can see if you've grown taller." Mom barely gave them space, and they lined up side by side. Ava was already giggling, knowing where this was headed.

Mom stood, her expression serious, eyes measuring the trio. "You have grown! I told you to stop growing so you'll be my little grandchildren forever." She feigned anger, hands fisting on her hips. The girls erupted into laughter, insisting they had no say in the matter. It was sweetness and giggles as they piled back into warm hugs. Kailey included.

"Hi, Beau," Kailey said, separating from the girls to hug me tight before doing the same to Dash. "Hi, Dash. Dad's coming. He's getting something for the room."

As if waiting in the background for his cue, Carter started for us and the girls zoomed toward him, mimicking the scene with my mom. Carter had somehow wormed his way past my barriers and into my heart. Mom glided over to me, not to hug me or even to say hello. She wanted to see West.

"Hi, Linda," Dash said before dashing off to join Carter. Those two were practically joined at the hip. They spoke every day, sometimes multiple times a day, and saw each other as much as possible.

"Oh, Dash, he's wearing a matching onesie," my mom cooed over West. "It's so cute, Beau. You all are adorable." I finally got a side hug. "Can I hold him?"

"He's sleepin'," I hedged, not quite sure why I played defense. She was unfastening the straps, gathering him into her arms. The little guy in his blanket didn't wake in the transfer. Yesterday's flight adventures really knocked him out.

"Let me see my namesake," Carter said, balancing Ava and Mia on each hip. Livie flailed her arms for Dash to pick her up.

"Dad, his name is Weston, not Wesley," Kailey chimed in, adding to the other running joke about the similarity to his first name.

"He's sprouting like a weed," Carter said, ignoring her. No amount of effort ever changed his mind, convinced we named West after him. "He's doubled in size since we saw him last. He's gonna be a big guy."

"The Carter, Richmond-Brooks family?"

The collective gasps and sudden turns of the girls' heads, including my mom's, might have changed the jet stream of the area. Elsa from *Frozen* waved hello, greeting us. Livie's eyes went wide, her legs instantly went board straight so Dash would put her down. They all hit the ground, running the few feet to Elsa.

Regardless of Carter being the official patriarch of the family, and this being a present to the children from their grandparents, I suspected Dash had wrangled Elsa to meet us at the entry. Of course, I didn't know the cost. Everyone understood how cheap I was, but watching our girls being over-the-top excited was worth everything.

Elsa waited for the rest of the family to catch up, speaking directly to the girls like a pro. After the briefest acknowledgement to the adults, she turned, asking the girls to clasp hands. Our official tour for the arrival had begun.

Dash and I followed behind, coming in last. He clasped my hand. I side-eyed him, but his huge grin said it all. He was as happy as I was. I intertwined my fingers with his.

"Paw, I'm not sure," Ava said, clutching my neck in her version of a death grip.

"I got you. I promise not to let you go. Trust me," I said, moving the next step forward in line. "You've been itchin' to do this since your dad showed you the ship." Her head rested on my shoulder, and I did my best to run a hand over her head. It wasn't easy with the life jacket and floaties she wore. In theory, Ava was the bravest of the three, but that didn't say much in the face of the slide. "Think about somethin' else. It's gonna be fun. Next time you can go on the bigger slide because you're gonna love it. Did you like your birthday presents from Gigi and Pop-Pop?"

Her face sparkled as she pulled back to look me in the eye. "Paw, she gave us all the Disney toys and princess dresses and stuffed animals. It was so much. I'm wearing my Minnie Mouse dress and ears to dinner."

"I thought you planned to be Ariel?"

"No." Her head swung back and forth until it didn't. "Maybe. I don't know."

I couldn't help but chuckle as the attendant lowered our raft into the entrance of the tunnel. The lifeguard gave a once-over, scanning Ava's life vest. "Keep your arms to your side." She dropped her elbows against her side to show Ava.

"Okay." Ava tucked her elbows in when I put her on her feet.

The little kids slide required a parent and took us over the main part of the swimming pool to a shallow edge where the rest of our group waited. I took a seat on the raft and reached for Ava. She misunderstood the seating arrangement and ended up face-to-face, arms tight around my neck.

"Baby, I'm gonna turn you around. Hang on to my legs, and I'll hold you." Once she flipped, I held her securely in place with one hand. She took my other arm, wrapping it around her too. "Make sure you look through the tunnel and grin big at Daddy." My amusement turned to laughter as she did exactly what I instructed, grinning big through her worry. "You're brave, Ava. Kailey won't ride a slide. She's afraid."

"1, 2, 3, go." We got a slight shove, and Ava screamed, her hands clutching my forearms. A trickle of water guided our way. Ava easily found her groove, the water swishing and swirling around us. All three girls had taken swimming lessons.

"There's Daddy and Gigi! Wave." She took her greeting job seriously as Dash snapped a picture then waved as big as Ava. "Get ready to hold your breath." Moments later, we popped out of the tunnel with the smallest free fall. A lifeguard and Carter were there waiting. The girls and Kailey stood cheering Ava on. The great thing about this cruise was the excitement everyone shared with each other. The staff and guests alike applauded her accomplishment.

I hoisted her up by the back of the life jacket, dragging her through the shallow water to deposit Ava with the others.

"You should try!" Extreme excitement laced Ava's words. "I was scared and then I wasn't. It was fun! Paw's strong. He'll keep you up if you go," she said, adding a little jump at the end.

"Beau!" Kailey called when I was about halfway to our table. "Can you take me on the medium size slide?"

What? Was she braving up?

"Sure," I said, not questioning or teasing her for fear she'd back off. "Let's go on the other slide. The bigger one's not that big, and the rafts are larger. It'll splash more water." I rambled, glancing at Carter and our mom. "I'm takin' Kailey."

"You going again?" Dash asked, jogging to me.

"Yup, she wants to try," I said, grabbing her life vest. "She's bravin' up. Put this on. I'll make sure it's cinched up in line."

"Good job, Kailey." Dash lifted his hand for a high five. "I'll take pictures and wave. Watch for me."

He followed, chatting with Kailey to help her nerves. I had such a stunningly beautiful life.

# 5: The Grind Dash

October 2019

Some folks might raise a brow, Beau also fell into that category, but these days I truly genuinely dedicated at least eight hours a day, five days a week, to my law firm. The success I built was sweet, and the connections and friendships I forged added sprinkles to my well-rounded life, making it all the more precious for me and my family. But, man, nothing could beat the liberating feeling I got in the late afternoons when I caught a glimpse of my home on the same street where Beau and I started our love affair. Inside that cozy haven was my family—a miracle after everything Beau and I had lived through—waiting for me to arrive.

All right, for the sake of truth, they probably weren't pacing the floor, waiting for my arrival, but I was ready to be there with them again. I wasn't quite sure if I knew if Beau was home already. The farther I went down the street, I saw Duke and Dixie running freely in the fenced yard. They were still incredibly well-trained. Beau worked with them all of the time. Taking them on any trips where we drove. As I got closer, I spotted the edge of a swing, small tennis shoes kicking out before descending.

Everything about my life was vastly different than where I started in Southlake, Texas. Thank goodness for that.

Beau ran his and our lives in the same way he treated the German shepherds. The tough love guy, who always monitored everything in our lives. He helped Amelia cook healthy meals, cleaned the house, gave baths, and bought an Audible account to read to the girls every night. I, on the other hand, had a regular supply of Drumstick ice creams, Snack Pack puddings, and real sugar Dr. Pepper drinks waiting as my after-dinner treat. It bothered the hell out of Beau when he caught me splitting my desserts in four ways.

I hardly gave a second thought to the whistle Beau used on either the dogs or the girls, but I was certain it worked like magic. It always did, regardless of how other people judged his techniques.

Once I passed the small cluster of trees, I spotted West's swing near Beau's generously oversized workshop, the little guy's hands moving as if capturing the air. Again, Beau would throw a fit if I mentioned West being his biological son, because he was both of ours, but it was obvious. Besides looking like him, the little guy loved the sunshine and was at home being outside.

I'd quietly worried that I might not feel the same bond with him that I did with my biological children, but boy, I'd gotten it wrong. He was my little buddy. I often volunteered for nighttime duty. Neither West nor I were big sleepers. The hours I spent alone with him in the middle of the night were precious moments I cherished. He and I had long conversations and reading sessions, mostly about my work. I even shared secret information, but he never spilled the beans.

Also, West didn't judge my reading glasses that no one else knew I wore. They made me feel old, but West loved me no matter what I looked like. He probably thought I was his favorite father.

The turn into our circular drive brought a sense of anticipation. I never took a single moment for granted. If I'd managed to hang on to a bad mood to this point, being here made life right as rain again.

The home was stately, the exterior and interior represented both of us. We went with red brick, light and dark trimmings with a large wraparound porch, I'd insisted on that add-on. Three large rocking chairs and four smaller ones sat to the left of the door. I liked to eat my ice cream Drumstick while watching the sun set in the evening.

Amelia enjoyed sitting with me and seemed as appreciative of this life as I was. My love and respect for her had only grown over the years. She barely left this house, superstitious of everything these days, but I was glad she found contentment. She was such a loving, nurturing person.

As I put my SUV in park—Tahoe large enough to fit us all—I spotted the fence gate opening and three blonde heads running toward me, Duke and Dixie bolting along with them. I shrugged off my suit coat before opening the SUV's door, hoping to keep the dog hair to a minimum.

Both dogs came to an abrupt skidding halt, Beau didn't allow either to jump on people, but they whimpered, wagging tails, prancing all over the place. I bent to pet them while the girls reached me, all trying to hug me at once.

I groaned when the dogs leaped inside the car, why had I left the door open? They were always eager for a ride. It took seconds for them to be seated in the furthest set of backseats, where they'd stay in wait for hours if we left them.

"Daddy, Paw picked us up early from school and took us fishing," Mia said, pushing a stray piece of hair out of her face. "We caught so many fish. He knows all the good spots."

"Oh, you're lucky," I replied, standing after our hugs. "You got to ditch school *and* go on the boat."

"Yay," Ava shouted, giving a leap into the air.

"I like school," Livie said, glancing up at me. Everything about her was in perfect order, not a hair out of place, not a speck of dirt on her. Even at three and almost a half, she'd mastered reading and carried a book tucked under her arm everywhere she went.

"But, Livie, Paw showed us how to skip rocks," Mia interjected. "Daddy, his grandpa taught him on Dog River. My rocks skipped, but Livie's and Ava's sank to the bottom. They have to practice more." She shoved the stray piece of hair back again.

"He said he was the Dog River festival skipping champion. Right?" Ava said, glancing back at me for verification.

"Yeah," I said. Ava gave me a crooked, proud grin, turning to walk backward, and still face me.

"He was the champion for two years," Mia said. "Paw told us you skipped years in school because you're so smart. I think Livie's gonna do that."

"I hope not," Livie said. "I wanna go to school every day."

"Ava, flip around so you don't fall." At the gate, I glanced back at Duke and Dixie, still inside the SUV, now in the front seat watching us go.

"Paw didn't take Duke and Dixie with you?" I asked, allowing the girls into the backyard first, leaving the gate propped open for the two rascals when Beau whistled.

"They came with us," Mia answered first. "They rode with Paw to pick us up."

"What's Paw doing now?"

"Getting ready for his mountain trip," Mia answered again. If her exuberance said anything, she must have had a great time today. "He's gonna miss me, but he says not to miss him because he'll be home in two weeks, but his days are in the future. So it's at least one more, or one less..."

"I'm gonna miss him," I said, heading slowly toward Beau's shop. "Did he tell you what day he's coming home?"

"That's all he told us," Ava shot out from over her shoulder, still feet ahead. "His friends wanna see something else while they're there so he's staying longer than he wants to. I think the rainforest. Then he's coming home."

"He's going to India," Livie added. "He showed us on a map."

Beau stepped out of the shop about the same time I made it to West, lifting him from the swing. He was a little chunk these days. On the ninety-fifth percentile on everything physical.

"Ugh," I teased, raising him high enough in the air to look into his eyes. We'd been warm this fall. West wore his sporty athletic shorts and an oversized sweatshirt. His feet were bare, never really feeling the shoes we chose to cover them, but loved to wear one of Beau's ball caps.

"The dogs made it inside the Tahoe before I shut the door," I said, tilting my head for a kiss.

Beau whistled. Not the loud shrill one, but enough that I heard the two animals scurrying across the concrete toward us.

"Why do y'all kiss so much," Ava said, feigned yuck in her voice.

"We're married. That's what you do," Beau said and kissed me again.

"They told me you picked them up from school early. It upset Livie, but overjoyed Ava and Mia, and took them stone-skipping."

"And fishing," Livie corrected.

"And fishing," I said to Beau, who grinned. "You caught a lot of fish."

"But we can never keep them no matter the size," Mia said before taking off for the swing set, Ava on her heels.

"Paw, tell him about the dance school," Livie said, wrapping both arms around my leg, clinging tightly, me being a life preserver in her sudden traumatic storm. Whatever the problem, I was on her side.

"Sweetheart, I told you that's gonna have to wait until I get back. Classes are on Saturday and your dad has too much to do while I'm gone."

Livie's sad eyes bore into mine. "But Daddy, if I wait, I can't start until after Christmas because of the practice for the re...re..."

"Recital?" I guessed, my hand reaching for her hair, loose today, and I caressed down. "I should be able to take them. It's not a problem. We're talking a couple of Saturdays."

"It's in Houston," Beau explained. "It's close to their school, and the other two aren't interested. Saturdays are usually Amelia's days to catch up on her shows. She needs that down time."

Hmm. That did make it more difficult. I glanced down at Livie who instantly sprang a leak in her eyes with big silent tears. She understood the problem, but apparently was wanting an identity outside of her sisters. I read about this. I handed West off to Beau, and bent at the knee, rubbing my thumbs under her eyes, to help dry the sadness. "We'll make it work. Is it ballet? You'd be a beautiful ballerina."

She nodded, a hiccup heaved her chest. "And tap. And I need a pink leotard and two different shoes, but they sell them all inside a special bag. Me and Paw saw it."

"Do your friends go there?" I asked, drawing her into my arms. She nodded and hiccupped again. "So your heart's set on that particular dance school and not one closer to the house." She nodded again, giving a giant sniffle.

When we chose a highly-rated school that was also LGBTQ-friendly, of course, I understood we'd be driving quite a bit for various projects and friendships. It wasn't a surprise.

"All right. We can get you started this weekend. Maybe take a class and see if you like it."

She gasped with joy, launching toward me with a giant hug. "Thank you, Daddy." After I was given the proper amount of love for my decision, she bolted toward the house. "Abuela, he said yes like you thought he would! I get the pretty bag, and I'll wear it over my shoulder."

My happy grin faltered as I stood and faced Beau. "You don't have to agree to everything they ask for. We're two months from the end of the year, and that would have made a great holiday gift for her."

All very valid points.

"At some point you're going to learn to tell them no without my input," I said. "I'm a sucker, and their tears destroy me. Maybe if you'd given me a heads-up." Of course, I was teasing him. I gathered West in my arms again. "Hi, buddy... No, don't look at Paw, only me."

I heard a heavy sigh, but Beau didn't push it further. This wasn't the end of the discussion, but a break for him to gather his thoughts and come back at me.

"I'm makin' hamburgers on the grill. We stopped by the grocery store and grabbed baked chips and apple slices to go with them. Amelia's back is messin' with her. She doesn't like to leave the house anyway. I told her to take it easy before it becomes a thing," Beau said, walking side by side with me toward the house.

"Are the hamburgers real red meat?" I asked, crossing my fingers hopefully.

"No." Beau shook his head as if the mention was absurd. "How was work?"

Disappointing. "I took another pro bono immigration case today. It'll be difficult, but I'm looking forward to the fight."

Beau gave me a side-eye glance, giving a side-grin to match. "You're doin' what you always wanted to do," he said with the same sense of accomplishment I experienced. My younger self had only wanted to get a law degree to do legal aid and pro bono work. The adult me recognized that making money had swerved me from those goals. Maybe now I could toss in a few cases here or there.

"Joy called today," I said, switching gears. "She's pregnant."

"That's great. She needs to come for a visit or we go there. It's been too long since we've seen her," Beau said and gave another whistle while opening the back doors to the house. Everyone in our family came running, Dixie making it to the door first, busting through ahead of anyone else. They always had to be first everywhere we went.

"Stop laughing at them," Amelia said, sliding between me and Beau. "He whistles for you too."

My brows instantly furrowed.

"Of course, you don't come when I call." The way he said it made my brows scrunch tighter together. Beau trained me like the animals. "Did she say anything about your family? Are they still not talkin' to her too?" Seconds passed as I absorbed the blow of information. "Stop lookin' at me like that. West is smilin' at you."

The little guy in my arms did make it better. "She said Carter posted pictures of the kids with him on the Disney cruise. He's certain my parents have seen the post, but I'm not sure they'd have the reaction he suspected. They'd never take a cruise like that. It's too 'working man' for them."

"Huh," Beau said, clasping my shoulder to turn me toward the house when Mia bumped into me.

"I won," Mia said, managing to get past me.

"I wasn't racing," Ava said, clearly racing Mia, and the apparent loser in the contest.

"Yes, you were," Mia shot back. "I run fast."

"No fighting," Amelia called, handing Beau a platter of raw, not beef, burgers. That was also a new development in the home. Once school started, the girls learned all about arguing. I didn't like it a single bit. "Paw's cooking on the grill. Everyone grab something and let's eat on the patio."

"What about your telenovela?" I asked, teasing her.

"Someone needs to close Dash's car door, and probably needs to lock the gate, Beau. And Dasham, take your son upstairs and change his diaper. I got my shows recording. Don't you worry about me." Her sassy way made me follow her directions so I didn't get in further trouble.

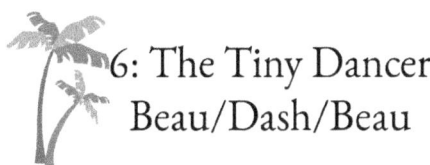

6: The Tiny Dancer
Beau/Dash/Beau

Beau

October 2019
Saturday

"There's no world in which they're going to eat that," Dash scoffed at the double pack of frozen veggie crumbles I tossed in the cart. But I was on a mission.

We had thirty minutes before Livie's dance class let out. I continued to scan the frozen food behind the glass doors, looking for healthy alternatives to fill our freezers. Amelia and I worked in tandem to instill healthy eating habits in our children. Veggie crumbles presented as taco and spaghetti meat... Oh yeah, veggie burgers and hot dogs. I grabbed a large box of each.

"They've figured out those aren't real hot dogs."

"No, they haven't," I shot back, rolling my eyes, refusing to give him my attention. They loved ketchup and that masked everything. I glanced over my shoulder to say just that, but I was struck speechless. I turned to stare as my husband let our baby son, West, lick on his ice cream cone.

I shifted my hopefully accusatory gaze from West's mouth to Dash's grin.

"He likes it."

Of course he liked it. The ice cream was pure sugar and tons of chemicals created with the sole purpose of making you like it. Just put his one foot in the grave. Luckily, the immense explosion happening in my head didn't include me slapping the cone from his hand. Before the kids came on our scene, we studied every parenting 101 book and course we could find. Every one of the experts agreed on the importance of teaching children how to eat properly and exercise regularly from an early age. Then literally, since they had arrived, Dash had turned into a sloth. The only time he hurried was running to the freezer for whatever processed treat he wanted next.

"What're you doin'?" I asked. Dash finally realized that we weren't all having a grand time. His gaze lifted to mine. I could see the gears turning, connecting the dots.

"You're mad."

No shit.

"I know we agreed, but theory and practicality don't always intermingle in the real world. Good food's a joy. I want them to have a balanced life, Beau."

The pads of my fingers smashed to my eyes as I wrestled for control. Those decisions weren't his alone to make.

"Dash, we made a commitment to each other to do our best by them. That ice cream's full of additives and chemicals. They want you to be addicted. At the very least, give them real food. Make homemade ice cream as a treat. Maybe we could do that tonight to celebrate Liv's first class."

"What time is it?" Dash asked, ignoring me. He and I both set alarms before entering HEB so we wouldn't be late for Livie. We were on a tight schedule over the next two days until I left for the Himalayas. I was in full-on mission mode, determined to make life a little easier for Dash and Amelia while I was gone.

As I stared at him, he lifted the cone, taking a long lick in a circular motion to prevent a sticky meltdown on his fingers.

My dick turned hard in seconds.

"You just did that to try and avert my attention," I accused irrationally. Wait. "Did you send me on this trip to get me out of town?" Anger and arousal created chaos in a person.

Dash let out a hearty burst of laughter that echoed down the aisle. If the previous argument hadn't drawn all the stares, Dash's eruption did the trick. He maneuvered the cart with his elbows. West's mouth was wide open for another bite.

I hesitated for a moment but eventually followed as he wheeled the cart to the automatic sliding doors in the front of the store. He didn't glance back at me or utter a single word while unhooking all the straps to West's seat device and lifted it and him out of the cart. The cone flew to the trash, the groceries left in the cart, and he started toward the parking lot, signaling that he intended to finish the conversation in the privacy of our vehicle. His long stride ate up the parking lot.

Fuck it, I was ready for the fight. I wasn't the one in the wrong. I spent the majority of my life following the instructions of all the experts, which included Dash. I mean a ridiculous amount of time trying to give my best to those I loved. Life would be a breeze if I plopped a Happy Meal on the table every night, but we chose a different way. We made a pact. He needed to do his share.

Dash

My quick hustle out of the store slowed on the approach to the Tahoe, taking plenty of time to buckle my little guy into his high-tech seat. Then I used several wipes to clean the muck off his face and hands as well as my own. The entire time I worked, I took deep centering breaths, holding them for several seconds, hoping my irritation dispelled on the exhale. It didn't, even with Beau's hard body looming by the passenger door, waiting for me to finish.

Call it undealt-with baggage from our past or maybe straight-up selfishness, but I lived on a tightrope of Beau's expectations. I balanced his demands while trying to be a super-parent and provider.

I had never aspired to be a circus performer.

This time, I couldn't shake it. About once a year, I allowed myself to have an emotion that Beau didn't control. It generally started a disagreement, but this time, I wanted to stand up for myself. I stared at my little guy in the eyes.

"Wish me luck," I murmured. I stuck his pacifier in his mouth, which made him ridiculously happy, and shut his door securely closed. The barrier between Beau and I was gone, and I barely acknowledged him.

"Get in the car. I don't want to embarrass us anymore than you already have," I said with petty disdain and rounded the back of the Tahoe toward the driver's door.

"I don't want to argue in front of West," Beau called, causing my eyes to dramatically roll. When I lifted on the side step, I glanced at Beau and his defiant position.

"Then don't." That was good enough. I dropped down on the seat, shutting my door firmly, and started the engine. We had at least fifteen minutes left before we had to be across the street at Livie's dance school.

Stubbornness, something Beau did exceptionally well, had him taking a few minutes before hoisting his body inside. His door wasn't fully shut before I voiced my thoughts in a calm, reasonable tone. "Give me hell about anything. You're ridiculously talented at that. But don't ever say to me again that I'm trying to free myself of you. You've put me through too much over the years to say those words idly."

Remarkably, all the bad language on the tip of my tongue, managed to stay unsaid, and I reached over to press the radio button with the children's song to keep the conversation from West.

"That's absurd," I stated with finality. "I'm regularly on the wrong end of your decision making." Beau waved his hand dismissively. "I've always prioritized you above everything else. You can't say the same thing. I spent the majority of my twenties virtually alone, waiting for you to remember me and your commitments to me."

"Am I destined to be reminded of my epic failures for the rest of my life?" I shot back, my voice not much higher than a low sizzle from my crushing anger. My grip tightened around the steering wheel, my heart thumped violently against my rib cage. He was pissing me off. "You've always been the one who tosses me aside without a second thought. You literally came to my office one time, jumped to crazy conclusions, and put me on notice. The very next thing you did was leave me. We never have a discussion on anything, that's why I don't try anymore. It's only you jumping ahead and deciding what's best for all of us. It's not right, Beau. I've always wanted this to be a me and you thing. Something we accomplished together. I'm not perfect, I make mistakes, but I know you're the love of my life..."

"This has nothing to do with that. We committed to a certain way of raisin' our children." His hand popped out, palm upward, suggesting something obvious, meaning what? Who knew? I was tired of trying to figure him out. "Why do you always go to the past instead of dealin' with the life happenin' right now?"

I dropped my forehead to the steering wheel, thumping it several times. He wasn't wrong, but his callousness toward my feelings triggered me.

"Look, I spoke out of turn," Beau continued, that hand still stuck out, now turned toward me. "I understand you didn't buy me the climb to get rid of me. It was a thoughtful birthday gift, but this argument that we're actually havin' has been brewin' for a while. We're no longer aligned in the biggest responsibility of our lives. What we're doin' matters. We have to get it right because our fathers didn't. Hell, we technically shouldn't have even been able to have babies."

In my peripheral vision, I caught the moment when he turned, facing forward again. That hand tucked back inside his crossed arms.

"And I didn't know you were still twisted about the past," Beau added. "I'm sorry I hurt you, but I did what I had to

do because I became a borin' afterthought for you. If I hadn't
had stood up for myself, we wouldn't be right here, right
now. I'll be more careful with my words, but you know that
you're the only person I've ever been with either emotionally
or physically. You can't say the same thing. You detached
from me for years before I finally left you."

Fireworks suddenly erupted inside my head. "Jesus, Beau.
Chandler—"

His dumb hand thrust between us again, halting my
words. His voice rose to penetrate past the fury causing my
cheeks to heat. "It wasn't just Chandler. It was everything to
do with your firm. Your boss, Lon, was your ally and best
friend. Your assistant replaced me as the person you shot
ideas past. In the end, we spent many days not havin' any sort
of contact. You looked at me like I was an embarrassment. I
felt your censure to my core." He took the wind out of my
sails, and I fell back against the seat. He wasn't wrong, but
we'd dealt professionally with his feelings, and ultimately, I
quit a job I loved to follow Beau here. "Forget it. I'm over it."

"Yeah, right," I shot back, delivering my own version of our
past. "What you put me through to ensure I never removed
you from the girls' lives speaks a different story. Seeking third
and fourth legal opinions on the very clear and contractual
agreement between the two of us. We had to hire another
attorney for you to adopt them. I didn't put you through
any of that when I adopted West. I trusted you when you
promised you wouldn't leave me ever again."

Minutes passed in silence. My heart hurt. I suspected his
did too.

"Clearly, we have unresolved issues with our past," I
started. "But I'm here. It's not always easy with my father's
name on the biggest building in the city, but I ignore
it, because I love our lives. I'm proud of what we have
accomplished. It hasn't been easy, but I've tried my very best
for you."

We sat in silence again. Beau didn't speak so I continued.

"I know what we said before they arrived, but as we've
raised our children, I've found that I want them to enjoy life.

Being disciplined is important, but I also want to teach them spontaneity and guilt-free days have merit."

"You should have told me you wanted to change things up. It's essential that we're on the same page. We need to improve our important conversations. When Livie expressed interest in joinin' the dance club, it was reasonable to wait until next year when I had more time available. Now, Mia's enrolled in a pottery class. Ava's takin' a karate class. It doesn't matter that those are at the rec center. You'll be pulled in too many directions while I'm far away. I'll be worried the entire time I'm gone."

"Beau," I said and put the truck in drive. The last five minutes of the dance class allowed parents to watch through a special window. We needed to be there on time, Livie was sure to be watching for us. "I know you don't see it, but you're making decisions by yourself that I should be a part of. You hired Belle full-time. That should've been discussed. Did you check her driving record since you plan for her to take the girls to and from school?"

Beau didn't answer as I parked in front of the dance school, and left the truck.

The emotional gap between us was palpable. We made it inside, Beau carrying West and his diaper bag. My anxiety double-timed while watching Livie's effort to follow along with her more experienced classmates. She did her very best, and we'd practice at home to catch her up. The joy pumping through me had me reaching for Beau's hand. He flicked it away, putting West and the diaper bag on that side of his body.

When class ended, Livie burst out with a giant smile, stealing my heart in her new pink leotard and tights. Her long hair was tied in a bun, black tap shoes on. She waved excitedly at us before running to her cubby, changing her shoes while chatting with her friends, and tucking everything in her bag. She came out with her duffle and sweater dragging the floor.

She darted for me, not Beau, and hugged my leg tight. "Thank you, Daddy. I loved it so much."

If Beau noticed the singular appreciation, he didn't say a word. His palm caressed over her shoulder. "You did really great, Livie. I need to change your brother's diaper." If the tension between us eased, I didn't sense it. "I'll meet you two in the truck. Remember your Powerade. We need to keep your muscles hydrated after all that hard work."

She lifted a fist for him to bump. Another incredibly sweet moment.

Once Livie was in her car seat, chatting endlessly about the class, my guilt set in. "Hand me the buckle, babe."

Both hands cupped my cheeks, turning me to face her. "Guess what? The teacher said she's going to teach us how to create a dance on paper. On paper, Daddy."

I had no idea what she was talking about, but I nodded my encouragement. "You like for things to be written down on paper." We were forever writing her to-do list and schedule for the day. She watched closely as we wrote each letter then tried to mimic our handwriting. She nailed it every time.

"I do." Her hands suddenly fisted, her body shook with sheer excitement.

"Watch a show for me," I said, handing her a tablet. "I'm gonna talk to Paw in front of the truck for a minute."

"Okay." She began navigating the iPad like a little professional. I shut her door and went to the front of the vehicle to wait for Beau. The warm sun worked its magic. I'd deal with whatever I was going through privately. I leaned my ass against the hood and slid my shades on as a gaggle of moms and their mini-mes strolled by. I detected interest, at least by one. They'd figure it out soon enough.

Beau

I was always so damned rule-oriented, holding myself and everyone around us accountable for what? So I could defeat myself in the end? He wasn't wrong, but I wasn't either. We might have created a momentary truce of unresolved issues, but we needed somewhere quiet to talk this out and solve our problems before it began to fester.

But who wanted to talk? Look where talking brought us to.

I pushed through the dance studio's door and saw Dash standing in front of the Tahoe. His extraordinary appearance never faded or aged. He'd moved past always having to look perfect... Well, sort of. Now, he wore his hair in such a way that it didn't take a lot of effort. His clothes were all handmade from his days and salary in Chicago. He had a classic style, not trendy. I did a lot of laundry each week, yet I wasn't allowed to touch his clothes. Only Amelia, who had handled Dash's idiosyncrasies since birth, was given that authority. And I felt sure he had actually guided her since his birth. The modern, trendy sunglasses and bracelets made him look wealthy and runway ready.

Like normal, he drew every eye around us. The dance moms stared too. Before his pretty charm affected me, I glanced away. Dash was too astute at reading people. In not too much longer, he'd have me apologizing, and I wasn't ready to do that. Kind of shitty, but still true.

Four steps later, I felt his gaze riveted on me, and I had no other option than to look at him. Neither of us said anything as I passed him, until he pushed off the grill and followed me to West's side of the car.

When I locked my little guy in the car, Dash was standing in front of me. Arms crossed. Immoveable. "It's my fault. I broke the agreement. I'm sorry. I was way off base with the other things I said."

And there I stood, ready to sabotage the things I held dear because Dash showed me a small amount of favor.

"You said what you meant. It's not a new argument. You've used some variation of it several times before." My words had nothing to do with the real reason we began to fight this afternoon. "We'll have to deal with that when I get back. We probably need to call our therapist. You definitely need to. Until then, if you wanna change somethin', tell me. It's fine."

Dash's smile said lots of things, the biggest was he didn't believe a word I said.

I rolled my eyes then my shoulders. The tension there made the muscles ache. "We need to get home before West wants a bottle."

"I don't have resentment about our past." Dash reached for my forearm, taking hold to keep me in my spot. The touch helped soothe the ache in my heart. So much of my healthy mental well-being centered in my guy. "I love you. The disagreement hit differently for me in the store. I was pretty proud of your birthday gift. Whether you know it or not, I put a lot of thought into gifts for you. You do so much for all of us. You do more than your fair share, and you work two jobs. I want you happy."

I stared at him, silently. He didn't understand where I was coming from. We tackled life together, nothing was a burden if we did it with one another. The concept had changed the fiber of my entire world. Dash and I were a team. It felt incredible when it was performed correctly.

"My immigration case is messing with my head. If it hadn't dropped in my lap..."

I cut him off before we slid into another tendril of diversion that didn't hold weight in our actual argument. "No, the case matters. That family needs you," I said, and shook my head. "We need to find a better balance and figure out why you keep going back to when I left Chicago, but not now. I leave in a couple of days. I'll be gone and I don't want to worry about home." I let that be enough and gently twisted out of his hold. I meant the words, but I lied when I said I wouldn't carry the problem with me. I'd think about it until I came home from the trip and then concede my side.

"All right. If it's what you want," Dash said, defeat in his tone.

I didn't respond, not to be petty, I just didn't know what to say that hadn't already been said. I took my seat and concentrated on the kids. Livie was good with West, she kept showing him the screen, and talking him through the game she played.

It was still a long ride home.

7: The New Heights
Dash/Beau/Dash

Dash

Monday
George Bush Intercontinental Airport

It didn't take a kindergarten diploma to realize my partner was still upset with me. Perhaps "upset" wasn't the right word. Sulky might capture his mood better. He was certainly temperamental. Eerily quiet too. I took the turn into the George Bush Intercontinental Airport, following the directory signs for Turkish Airlines.

"You have a layover in Istanbul?" I asked, feeling increasingly frustrated. The only sound interrupting the stillness was an occasional sniffle I let out due to my allergies. The damn trees were trying to kill me.

I needed to carve out time for a doctor's appointment. Sudafed wasn't cutting it this year.

"Yeah, they adjusted the itinerary to include some sightseein' there. I updated the calendar," Beau said, tilting his head to better see the lit directional signs against the dark night, guiding us to the proper drop-off.

At least he answered me this time. It seemed like a step in the right direction. I wish he'd come around enough for a quick blow job to tide me over until he returned.

Man, my guy could hold a grudge.

"Remind me when the climb begins," I said.

He turned his head in my direction. I could feel his eyes rolling. He wasn't wrong. I did remember the entire itinerary. Of course, I did, but I wanted him to talk to me before he left.

"We had too much goin' on, I don't remember the exact dates, but I marked it in our calendar. I believe Friday's when we begin. We're sightseein' for a couple of days, so maybe the climb begins Thursday. No, I don't think that's right. Probably Friday." Even through the moodiness, I could hear his excitement. The corners of my lips tugged a grin free.

"It's a perfect trip for you. Send me pictures when you can. I'll show the kids," I said, voicing the request so the girls could see what he was doing in real time.

"They won't be excited about starin' at a bunch of rocks." he said, gesturing toward the gate. There were ten or so members in his group waiting at the entry doors to the airport. We may have been the last ones to arrive.

"It's your first time in the Himalayans. It's exciting. I've never been there. Maybe we can go back together," I said, pulling to the curb just beyond where the team stood.

"I guess."

Yippee. We were back to the ambiguous two-word answers. I put the gear shift in park as he started for the door handle.

"Remember, I love you, and I'm here waiting for you to return."

Beau's questioning gaze pinned me. "'Course. I love you too. That's why I want you to eat better so you'll be here as long as you can."

The worry bugging me began to ease. "So being abnormally quiet with no effort to make love before you leave means you love me? Because I didn't like any of that treatment."

"I'm sortin' through everything in my mind, but I can't let go of you and the kids eatin' better foods. It's nonnegotiable for me, and you won't stop with the junk food no matter what we've talked about. You make me look like the bad guy all of the time. I don't like it. So we'll talk about it and everything else when I get back."

"Okay, I agree. We'll wait until the day after you get home to have the discussion, no longer."

He grinned and nodded, probably for my benefit more than his, but I took it.

"Sure." Anything else said was lost when someone yanked his side door open, allowing all the airplane and airport noise into our vehicle. James and Ben, two of his climbing buddies, grinned from ear to ear.

"Come on, big 'un. We're waitin' on you." James, with a firm grip on Beau's forearm, tugged him out of the SUV. Ben opened the back door and removed Beau's efficiently packed gear. The damn thing was heavy, and he carried it like it was nothing.

"Kiss him goodbye when you get back." Ben, a longtime friend of Beau's, cackled at his own joke. Of course, I couldn't just let Beau go without a proper farewell. The group met Beau between the sliding glass entry doors and our Tahoe. Knuckle bumping and other greetings took place. Beau subtly glanced over his shoulder, hopefully to see where I was. I stepped out, following Beau.

Tucking my hands into my slacks pocket, I walked to the group. "Y'all have a good time."

Beau took his backpack from James and mounted it on his back. At least, that's how I described the fluid way he carried the heavy bundle. I leaned in, he did too. I'd expected a kiss, but he bypassed my lips for my ear and said, "Take care of our family, and make sure Duke and Daisy get their runs in. Otherwise, they'll get restless and make everyone crazy.

Good luck with your case." He brushed his lips against my ear, sending a sudden happy shiver down my spine.

"Call us when you can," I said. He nodded and stepped away, waving a hand in the air as he walked backward, again trailing behind the group.

"Remember the phone rings both ways." It was a phrase he always said when headed out for a climb.

"Be careful what you wish for. Our phone plan says we can talk internationally."

Beau grinned brighter at me before ducking inside the airport. Through the windows, I tracked him to the check-in counter. I wanted to wait for a few minutes, be available if he needed anything or left something in the SUV, but the security guard's whistle knocked me out of my Beau-induced trance. Beau glanced at me one last time and waved.

My mountain man. He'd come home with a longer beard, shaggy head of hair, and weathered skin crinkling the corners of his eyes. I couldn't wait.

I climbed in the Tahoe and put it in drive, and sighed as I pulled away. It looked like vegetables were in my future. I'd do it for him until I'd had enough, and we'd have this conversation again.

Beau

I put my head in my hands, my thumbs circling my temples, trying to relieve the low-level headache I couldn't shake. My inner being held on to a heavy sense of unease that had nothing to do with the flight I'd boarded. The idea of leaving while in a disagreement with Dash made me edgy. With each mile this airplane flew away from my family, the worry escalated. Whatever had driven me to continue with my vacation needed to take the wheel. Otherwise, I was turning around when we hit the ground.

Think about the positives. I understood that I regularly turned to a negative place to protect what I held dear.

A cool thing? I'd upgraded my airfare for a bigger seat. It wasn't that big, my body still had to scrunch to fit properly, but it was better than economy. The treatment from the in-flight staff was excellent. The interior of the plane was dark, the lights dimmed. I should be sleeping. With my head against the headrest, I stared out the window at the night sky. No amount of redirection worked. Mere seconds later, I rose from my aisle seat, waking the person in the seat beside me. The antsiness that I couldn't shake required movement, so I began to walk the aisle of the plane again.

"You doing okay?" a flight attendant asked as I passed by the galley.

"Yeah. Can't sleep," I muttered.

"I can help with that." Her smile brightened, and she pointed in a direction behind me. She guided us to a hidden set of stairs at the front of the plane. My shoulders touched each side of the small stairwell, opening to what I assumed was first class with many empty seats.

"We've watched you try to get comfortable. The flight crew agreed to seat you up here until it's time to deboard, but it's our secret. Take a seat wherever you like. We have free internet up here." She whispered all of this quietly then winked. I nodded in appreciation, but didn't understand the wink. "The code's on the remote control. Do I need to bring you anything?"

I shook my head, and quietly mouthed *thank you*. For this flight, she'd just become my favorite person ever.

"Blankets are in the cupboard. There's a water bottle for you. We have about nine hours left until Istanbul. Rest up."

She left me, trotting down the stairs. I clocked the location of the restroom and chose a seat about halfway down the aisle. I stretched out in the reclining chair with the water bottle on the small table inside the mini cubicle. This was what I thought I'd paid for. I dry swallowed a Xanax from my pocket, one of a few tablets my doctor gave me for the flight. Maybe it'd kick in this time.

I turned down the brightness of the phone screen to not disrupt those around me and entered the internet code in my cell phone, feeling the anxiety slipping away. Probably because

I was texting Dash in the middle of the night with zero regrets of waking him.

"*What are you doing?*" I typed.

Instantly, the dots on the bottom of the screen bounced away. Of course, he was awake. It baffled me how he managed to function without sleep.

"*I'm with West. He's unsettled. Why are you awake?*"

Seconds later, a picture of my little guy and Dash appeared on the screen. Dash's bed head was epic. He wore a face mask, probably due to the cold he was developing, and our baby was cradled in his arms, drinking from a bottle. Dash had no idea I knew how much time he spent with West in the middle of the night. He muted the volume on the baby monitor so he wouldn't bother me, but the screen showed the time he spent in West's room.

"*They gave me a halfway decent seat, but I couldn't sleep. I was walking the plane and a flight attendant took pity on me. I'm in first class now. Did you know airplanes have an upstairs?*"

The dots drummed again. I waited patiently, knowing he was using one hand to type.

"*Yeah. I've seen that before.*" The dots reappeared. "*I miss you already.*"

Yeah. I missed him too. He held me captivated even during the difficult times.

"*I miss you too,*" I replied and lifted the phone to take a photo of me stretched out on the recliner. Out of nowhere, the bottom of the seat popped out, bringing my legs up. No matter the cost, I planned to always fly first class and added that to the message, attaching the photo before pushing send.

"*Jealous. Looks comfortable,*" Dash said. I stared at the screen, lost to the picture of Dash and West together. He and I used the same surrogate, wanting the kids to be related by blood, but my genes had marked West. He looked like me. All of our children were taller than average. The girls had bubbly personalities. They experienced a range of emotions all the time, but West was a serious little man. His brows knitted together regularly as he watched everything.

"*You still there?*" Dash asked.

"*I am. Are you ready for trial?*" I asked. His pro bono case went to trial tomorrow. I hoped the clients knew how fortunate they were to have found him. Dash was tackling an immigration case that he'd spent countless hours preparing his arguments for. He also knew how to navigate the system, calling in favors to get assigned a judge who regularly sided with the immigration laws.

"*I am. It's probably not the time, but I'm sorry about what happened. I don't like you leaving without having everything settled between us. You're right, our health matters.*"

I snapped another photo of me grinning like a Cheshire cat. I sent the photo as my reply and counted it a second win that kept me from saying *I win*.

"*Is that grin because you love me beyond reason? Or the fact you won the argument?*"

"*Probably the second one,*" I teased. "*I'm ready to apologize too. I do tend to make decisions without involving you. I'd be pissed off if you did that to me. This is where you win because I do get how the kids need a treat now and then. But I want them to learn that healthy food tastes good too.*" I sent the text that felt like the size of a book. Maybe the largest text I'd ever sent.

"*Thank you. I agree. I should've approached you instead of going around your back, but talking to you can be like hitting a brick wall. People say I'm immovable but I'm a pushover compared to you.*"

"*We still need counseling, maybe me more than you, but you're clinging to some resentments that I thought you were over. Maybe the same past keeps me twisted up too. IDK. We need to work it out. It's gonna take time.*"

"*Deal. I really wish you'd had this epiphany six hours ago. Then I could've gotten a quick blow in the parking lot of the airport.*"

My smile was immediate. He knew I wasn't into PDAs. We exchanged quick pecks here and there, but it wasn't often. We both feared how the parents of the girls' friends perceived us.

"*Maybe I needed the blowjob,*" I countered.

"Yeah right. That's never going to happen. The bedroom's the only place we're allowed to have sex. Remember when we used to do it everywhere. There wasn't a restroom in Chicago that we didn't have sex in." Dash typed in two back-to-back text messages.

"Yeah, right. The swimming pool says something different."

"Changing subject, because I'm turned on and you're not here to deal with it. Do you ever look at the moon and wonder if I'm looking at it too?" he asked.

"Of course not. I'm always home with you when the moon's up. I'm going to sleep. The pills the doc gave me are kicking in." A giant yawn had me pausing before I finished the message. *"Thanks for talking to me. It's already hard enough to leave you without throwing in a disagreement."*

"I feel the same way. Go to sleep. I am too."

"Good luck, tomorrow." I decided that was enough. I felt lighter. Maybe it wasn't the past that got me twisted, but the fear of losing the great life we'd created. Who knew for sure. I placed the phone on the table and stared at the ceiling. This was probably my final climbing trip. My heart liked that idea a lot.

Dash

Three Days Later

"Girls, pay attention to Amelia, or you'll be late for school," I said between labored breaths through our Alexa devices in the house. From what I could tell, my sinus issues had escalated into something severe that was getting worse by the day. Given the aches and pains throughout my body, whatever was going on with me probably needed a doctor's visit.

"Daddy, I wish I could see you," Ava called from the other side of my closed bedroom door. "I'm wearing my Maleficent costume from the cruise. We're gonna wear the Tinker Bell costumes when you and Uncle Scott take us trick or treating so no one will know which one of us is which."

"Babydoll, I don't want you to get sick. That's the only reason I'm keeping you out of here. Tell Amelia to send lots of pictures," I managed, my eyes closing, feeling like those few words exhausted me. In what may have been a first in my career, I had taken the last two days off work to give my exhausted body time to heal. It hadn't helped. "Go to school and enjoy your Halloween party. You have all of next week off. I'm sure I'll be better."

The following sneeze was a neck-jarring, brain-rattling explosion inside my head. Fuck, I felt bad. In the last forty-eight hours, I'd slept about thirty-five. The rest of the time, I stared at the ceiling, truly feeling like shit. It was such a bummer. After the court victory, I missed all my client's family celebrations, knowing there would be delicious home-cooked meals. At least she had her partner and children with her, which made me feel good, sort of. I barely held any malice toward her father who'd shared this cold with me, or I guessed that was what had happened.

"Dash," Amelia said from the other side of the door. "Do you need anything?"

"Yeah," I said. "For Beau to come home and take care of me. He owes me."

"You don't sound any better," she said, concern in her voice. "You need to see a doctor before the weekend. I'll call them. They make house calls."

Another bout of hacking coughs made my chest concave, at least in theory it did. Stars filled the blackness in my head, pounding violently in pain.

"I'm calling them," she said.

"Give me until Monday." Whether I actually said the words aloud or not, I didn't know. Pain zipped through my head like a cannonball.

Silence followed, suggesting she either heard me and chose to ignore what I said, or she was in fact gone. I had forgotten about the house call, I just wished I'd have a magical turnaround without causing any more stress to Amelia.

I hadn't heard from Beau since the flight to Kathmandu. Being so far gone in such a dangerous sport made me worry. Even more than that, for the last five years we had spent every night together. I should've gone with him. I dragged his pillow to my chest and curled in around it. Seconds later, I fell back to sleep.

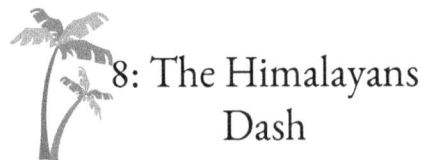# 8: The Himalayans
Dash

"How long have you been not feeling well?" Jane, a nurse practitioner from my primary care doctor's office, asked later that day. She stood beside the bed, with a disposable mask covering the majority of her face, and gloves on.

"About a week," I answered. "I put it off to sinuses. I struggle this time of year." I paused to take a few labored breaths before I could continue. "Now I think it's the flu."

As I closed my eyes, I struggled to open them again, but it was a lost cause. Instead, I lifted the lid of one eye with my fingers. Jane perched on the side of the bed and began to examine me. Maybe the mask seemed suspicious but the fog inside my head made it hard to think. I closed my one eye.

"Take another breath for me," Jane instructed, pressing her stethoscope against my chest. My lungs felt ravaged. Maybe I had pneumonia. I couldn't figure it out. Overthinking made my head spin. When had that happened before?

"We need to get you to the ER to see what's going on. I'll call an ambulance," Jane said.

"I just need time," I murmured.

"Dasham, she's not talking to you," Amelia said from somewhere around my bedroom door. "The decision's out of your hands. You've made a mess of things."

"His oxygen saturation levels are lower than I'd like," Jane said. She took something off my finger as the bed bobbled. Another round of spiking pain shot through my brain. Jeez, it hurt.

"Will he be admitted?" Amelia asked.

"Most likely," she said. "I don't know what this is, maybe pneumonia. We're well beyond a simple bronchitis brought on by a sinus issue. Wear a mask and gloves when cleaning the room. Disinfect well. If you or any of the children show symptoms, call us immediately. Don't wait."

"Okay," Amelia said, her tone wasn't as forceful as moments ago. "I'll call Beau."

"No, don't," I said. Another round of coughs racked my chest. It was frustrating and painful. I couldn't draw anything up. My throat was on fire. "Let him have his vacation."

Amelia *tsked*. "He deserves to know what's happening to you. He'd never forgive me if I didn't."

"No reception anyway," I whispered. "Call Beau's mom. She'll help." Sleep lulled me into its waiting arms.

I had no idea how much time passed, but when I woke up, medical professionals were talking nearby. I tried to find my bearings, but nothing looked familiar. The oxygen mask attached to my mouth made it impossible to speak. It didn't matter. I fell asleep again.

One Day Later
Methodist Hospital
Sea Springs, Texas

"Pneumonia? His condition seems far too dire to only be pneumonia. When will you know something more definitive? His family's on pins and needles to know anything." Linda's voice cut through the haze that shrouded my mind as I surfaced from sleep. A beacon calling to me even if her voice was filled with concern.

She spoke in deeper tones—low and mumbly, hard to hear. When I tried to do a self-internal diagnostic, I realized I was much weaker and likely sicker than before. Why couldn't I kick this cold? As I moved my body slightly, the weight of the medical equipment and tubes attached to me added gravity to my situation. I hadn't realized I'd even been moved. My mind struggled mightily to grasp Linda's side of the conversation, but it was futile. I couldn't do it. Another voice and shadowy figure much closer to me spoke in low ominous tones, but any words became something akin to Charlie Brown's teacher's voice, a nonsensical sound meant to convey some meaning I couldn't grasp.

"Why Houston Methodist?" she asked.

They planned to move me to Houston? Why?

My chest hurt like a son of a bitch.

"My husband wants to know why he needs a ventilator?" she asked. Now I understood why the conversation felt loopy. Carter was involved on the other end of the phone. Good, I trusted him. "Wesley, please let them explain. They appear to be as apprehensive as you are... Good... Get in your plane and fly here, but land in Houston. He's going there as soon as it can be arranged. Plan to stay. Someone needs to advocate for Dash, and Amelia needs help. Two of the girls and West are acting out. I need to be there... No, I'll handle Kailey. Don't worry."

The following silence concerned me until a cold hand touched mine, which offered a small, much needed comfort. I tried to open my eyes, but my brain wasn't firing on all cylinders. I couldn't manage it.

"Rest, Dash. Wesley's coming to be with you. I haven't reached Beau, but I'll continue trying. Amelia and the girls miss you. I know West does too. Stay strong for us." Her gentle words and reassuring tone enveloped me like a soothing blanket. "We love you, Dash. I know Beau does too."

"Beau... Love," I said into my oxygen mask and managed to squeeze her hand. The strain of listening drained me, and I slipped back to sleep.

Beau

November, Ten Days Later
The Himalayans

Base camp was a welcome sight. As I had done countless times today, I swiveled my head and rolled my shoulders. A small smile may have touched my chapped lips as I passed my team, who were loudly celebrating the end to another successful climb. I agreed with them. We did great, but I needed Aleve and promised myself to make more time to exercise in the future. Maybe. Or perhaps this was in fact my farewell climb. I missed my family something awful, and for the first time, I saw the dangers of such a hobby. One wrong move and I was toast, leaving behind everything I cherished.

I was also freezing. Despite having lived in Chicago for years and knowing how to handle the cold wind and snow, I had spent a majority of the time freezing my ass off, even in all these supposed warm clothes. They had cost a small fortune to upgrade my wardrobe. Money that could have funded one of my kids' first years of college. Dash would be disappointed that I spent my vacation missing him and our children.

"Brooks, catch." A can of beer came hurtling my way. Peer pressure had led me to remove my protective face gear when we started walking to camp, but I stubbornly refused to remove my gloves. I caught the can and made my way to the tent to layer up with dry clothes before joining the final night of festivities. Tomorrow started the long trip home.

I ducked into the tent where the wind couldn't reach me and dropped my backpack to the floor. I still had a couple of hand warmers and needed both right now.

Clearly, I'd turned into a giant wimp.

"Beau Richmond-Brooks." I paused my search through the bag and listened. I couldn't have heard that correctly. "Is there a Beau Brooks?"

"Yeah, he's in the red tent."

I continued sifting through the pockets of my backpack, indifferent to whatever they needed until I could feel some warmth returning to my fingers. I had enough warmers leftover to add to my boots when the flat of my tent flap suddenly lifted. "You have a call."

A hand thrust a Sonim tactical smartphone toward me, used in remote places like this, only for emergencies. From the time I lifted to take the phone until I tumbled back on my ass, bringing the phone to my ear, my heart raced and my chin hit my chest. A gloved finger stuck into my other ear to block the noises coming from every direction. "Hello?"

"Beau?" My mom asked, relief in her tone.

"It's me, Mom. What's goin' on?" Dread and fear closed my eyes. My entire body tensed and heated, I felt a flush crawling up my neck.

"Son, I've been trying to reach you. We need you to come home early." The tremble in her voice told me she was holding back tears, but she powered through, making me have to play her words through my head again to understand. "Dash is very sick. They flew him to Houston Methodist over a week ago. Wesley's with him. I'm helping Amelia at home with the kids. We've arranged a flight to take you home. The camp staff has the information."

"What do you mean Dash is sick?" I asked.

"They haven't been able to find the cause, but they're saying it's a severe respiratory infection. What's happening isn't making sense to them. They've got him on a ventilator and multiple antibiotics that don't really appear to be helping. They contacted the CDC to help identify what he has, to get him the right medications."

"A ventilator?" I questioned incredulously and began pushing my shit back in the pack.

The camp attendant poked their head through the tent's opening. "That's costing you about sixty-five dollars a minute.

We've called for the helicopter. They're on the way. There's a private plane waiting. It's been there for several days."

"Son, get going. Call me on the plane. Thank the camp staff. They've been incredibly supportive. Hurry, Beau. Don't wait."

The call ended without a response from me. Within seconds, I grabbed my gear and pushed out of the tent.

"What's goin' on?" Jesse asked. My team gathered around me as the whump-whump-whump of a helicopter neared. I caught sight of it as it lifted over the edge of the mountain and drowned out my ability to reply.

I grabbed Jesse's bicep, drawing him close to yell at his ear. "Dash is sick, I've got to go. It's bad." A numbness embraced me like protective insulation, keeping the shock and disbelief at a distance.

"How're the kids?" Ben asked. He had small children, and we regularly shared stories.

"Don't know." What had my mom said about my children?

The unknown answer had me hustling faster toward the helicopter, following the guy who handed me the phone. My unlaced boots loosened with each step I took. The whooshing of the rotor blades overpowered any other noise as I hunched and ran toward my ride home.

"Put on the headphones." The camp staff yelled as I climbed inside. The pilot, wearing mirrored aviators, reached around and tossed the headphones in my lap. The door shut me in. The headphones instantly quieted the roar of the engine and blades.

"We're flying you to a private airport in Bhadrapur," the pilot said through his microphone with a thick Napoli accent. He gave a thumbs-up through the split in the front seats. I mimicked his gesture. It appeased him, and the helicopter rose into the air. The campground shrunk below us. We ascended swiftly, swinging around to head away from the ominous looking snowcapped peaks. On the other side was dense forestry as far as the eye could see.

I had picked up a few words while I was here, hoping I hadn't been misled. "*Samaya*?" I crossed my fingers that I was asking about the time to our destination.

"Twenty-five minutes."

I nodded, adding. "*Dhan'yavāda*."

Who knew if I used the word properly before factoring in my thick Southern accent. I had to tamp down the worry as I leaned over and tied my boots. The warmers went back into my backpack, and my fingers unzipped my heavy jacket. Anxiety made the body warm. What could be so alarming that brought both Carter and my mom to Sea Springs?

Had Dash died and they were protecting me until I arrived home? Instant panic surged over my being, rejecting the idea. My mom would be truthful with me. Besides, why say he was on a ventilator if he wasn't. With Carter's influence, I'd have been dragged off the mountain if the worst had happened. There were so many flaws in my reasoning abilities that even I couldn't keep up. Yet, I would cling to the small glimmer of hope until I was on the plane home and had my mom back on the phone to ask these questions.

The ride was far from smooth. The chopper swayed and jolted as it maneuvered through the turbulent mountain air. I clutched the seat. A blend of adrenaline and fear kept me on edge. The scenery shifted from rugged mountainous terrain to a sprawling urban landscape. I took a deep breath, trying to steady my nerves.

Finally, the helicopter began its descent, landing as smoothly as the takeoff. The ground crew stationed nearby sprang into action, ready to usher me to the plane.

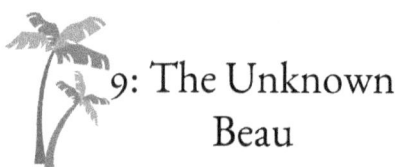 # 9: The Unknown Beau

Houston Methodist Hospital

"Carter," I called, my heavy pack in hand. Being back in civilization made me feel like a hobo after spending days and days in the wilderness. I couldn't sleep on the long flight home. There'd been a private vehicle waiting when I landed, and I'd been given directions to meet Carter in a more quiet, secluded area of the hospital where high-profile patients were placed. I maintained my quick stride as I approached him about three-quarters of the way down the hospital hall.

"How is he?" I asked, still feet away. "Where is he?" The desperation to see him ate at me until I felt I was crawling out of my own skin.

"He's stable. They've decided to begin weaning him off the ventilator. I've vetted his care team and brought in some renowned specialists. They all agree with this current treatment plan, meaning something has to be encouraging them." Carter glanced behind him and then back to me, speaking quieter. "But I don't see the improvement they apparently do. He's very sick."

"I wanna see him." I'd listened to that same update for the entirety of my flight, I had to know more. I maneuvered around Carter toward a decent size waiting area with the standard chairs, sofas, and coffee machine. My gear needed a drop-off point before I tossed it in the trash but Carter stopped me.

"He's three doors down." Carter nodded me to a room between us and the waiting area. "The window's open. I was able to pull some strings and have a suite here for my private use, keeping me close if Dash needed me."

A force drew me to Dash's room. I wasn't prepared to see my love looking like death in a hospital bed with machines and tubes hooked to his frail body. The way he breathed, his chest expanding abnormally, had my heart shattering, a dizzy light-headedness assailed. The pack in my hand dropped to the floor as I took in my surroundings. Tension tightened my neck, shoulders and upper back, locking my muscles together in instant physical pain.

Tears sprang to my eyes. I couldn't do life without Dash. My beautiful guy was being ravaged by some unknown disease. How was that possible in today's age?

I started for the room, but Carter's hand rested on my forearm, stopping me. He nodded toward the red label on the door.

"They've set up cautionary protocols. If you go inside, you'll have to be in protective wear."

I didn't give a single shit about any of that and reached for the door handle again. It was locked, keeping me from him.

"What the fuck, Carter? That's my husband. I need to be in there with him," I barked, slapping at the ache in my chest, taking my irrational anger out on the person who stayed by Dash's side, and flew me halfway around the world to be here now.

"I'm his assigned nurse." A female voice, walking stride for stride with a woman in a business suit said. She pointed toward the cart outside his door. A stack of disposable gowns, boxes of masks, and various sizes of gloves sat ready to be used. "Let's get you in there with him."

"What's happenin' to Dash? How did he get like this?" I asked as my anger found a new target. "When I left he had a fuckin' sniffle."

"His physician's on the way. He can help answer your questions," she said, assisting in the way to properly wear the gown. I forewent the gloves, my hands ached to touch my love.

The lady in the suit said, "I'm Natalie Johnson with the Houston Department of Health. I have questions for you. Can you give me a moment then I'll leave you alone?"

"I wanna see my husband," I said, my jaw tightening, my hands clenching into fists. The stern, unreasonable side of my personality became my dominant side. I hadn't slept in twenty-four hours, and all I wanted was to hold Dash's hand in mine. "I can't be clearer. And I'm about to have a big fuckin' fit over it."

I shoved the straps of the mask over each ear, as I jumped through all the hoops necessary to be with my husband. My anxiety built to crippling levels.

"The code to enter his room is 1234. He's isolated for his protection and due to Mr. Carter's presence in the hospital. Mr. Carter's been in and out of the room regularly."

"You've just flown in from India?" Natalie asked.

I refused to acknowledge her. Two could play these games. There was literally no world where she didn't know that answer. Dash, my only objective. The sterile-looking room with white walls and all the beeping and whooshing of the equipment messed with my senses. The chill in the air did too. I went straight to the head of the hospital bed. My love was pale, with a pretty significant beard forming. His usually meticulous styled blond hair had slightly darkening roots, and was dirty. He'd lose his mind if he knew what he looked like. Other than those obvious truths, his face was gaunt, and he'd lost significant weight. His body had deteriorated quickly.

"How's he gettin' his nutrition?" I asked whoever followed me in. My hand went to Dash's head, caressing gently. If I received an answer, I didn't hear it. "I'm here, Dash," I said quietly, bending to be closer to his ear. "I got here as soon as I could. What happened to you, baby?"

"Did you hear me?" Carter asked, finally garnering my attention. "He has a feeding tube."

I gathered Dash's hand in mine, heartbroken that his remained limp. "Dashing, you've got to get better for me. I can't do this without you."

As I spoke, Dash's long eyelashes flittered. My heart tripped, and I leaned in, getting closer to his face.

"Please wake up. I need you to wake up," I pleaded, my palm traveled to his nape, cupping him gently.

"They've slowly begun to remove the sedative. They explained he'd have reflex twitching, but that's the first time I've seen his eyelashes move. I think they'll consider it a good sign," Carter said from the end of the bed. "I've been moving his arms and legs like the physical therapy team showed me, but he's been fully unresponsive." Carter said. Then he sighed deeply, a heavy burden escaped his lips. "Dash is like a son to me. I love him dearly. I'll step out to give you privacy."

My gaze was fixed on Dash's face. My thumb caressed the top of his hand. Screw the consequences, I tugged my mask down past my lips and reverently kissed his cheek, right along the edge of the beard, lingering in the feel of his soft skin.

A tear fell from my eye onto his sunken cheek. "Please don't leave me, Dash. I'm sorry for being so me all the time. Our argument was stupid. You don't need counselin', I do. I was wrong. Please don't leave me. You have to be here with me."

I so rarely cried that when a second tear dropped to his face, it took me by surprise. I couldn't leave him, and leaned further in to rest my cheek against his. I memorized everything about the warm touch and feel. My breath hitched as I took his hand in mine, and placed the mask securely back on, the gentlest of touches had his finger lifting against my palm.

The hope his touch gave was staggering.

"Fight for me and our family. We need you."

"Beau, the physician's here. They need to talk to you," Carter said.

"I'm not leavin' this hospital until you leave with me," I said to Dash, knowing in my heart that he could hear me. "You can't see that I look rough as hell, but you'd love it. Carter has a room here, because why wouldn't he? I have to go there and shower. I'll be back here as soon as I can."

I swept a hand over his head again and leaned in to kiss his cheek before putting the mask back in place. The image of his frail body was all I could see inside my mind as I forced myself to leave his side.

I pushed through the door to three sets of eyes staring at me. The nurse spoke first. "You can discard all the items in this bin." She pointed toward a red container by the door. I did. Not seeing me wearing too much more of that in my future. If I could crawl into bed with him, I would. A well of tears filled my eyes again, and I used my sleeve to wipe them away. My hand followed, scrubbing over my face. This was so much to take in.

"Dr. Wells, this is Beau, Dash's husband," Carter said.

"I don't understand what's happenin'," I said, crossing my arms over my chest.

"I'm Dr. Wells and I'm a pulmonologist brought in by Mr. Carter to attend to your spouse. Your husband arrived in respiratory distress that required us to sedate him and put him on a ventilator because his lungs were exhausted. This helped him breathe without exertion. Our scans and X-rays show an uncharacteristic pattern and we've not been able to isolate the organism as of yet. We're treating with a number of broad-spectrum antibiotics. We have expedited specimens to the CDC for further testing so we can identify and treat appropriately. Until then, we'll keep him comfortable. We're trying to back off on some of the sedation to see if he starts breathing on his own. Then we'll wean him off the ventilator. We're feeding him through a nasogastric tube. At this time, we're in a watch and wait situation. I'm working with the rest of the team, including an infectious disease specialist, and we're doing everything we can at this time," Dr. Wells said.

It was so much information to take in, but sounded like Carter had really stepped up and had things moving forward to help Dash. I couldn't be more grateful for that, even if nothing I'd heard or seen so far had lessened my anxiety.

"Is there anything I can do?" I was desperate for a way to help.

"I do have some questions for you that might help us find the origin of the disease quicker and understand better how to help Mr. Richmond-Brooks. We've spoken with your family, and understand you're the closest person to him. Do you know if he's traveled outside of the country in the last few months?" she asked.

"Not for years now, other than the cruise we took in July. We didn't get off the ship or take any day trips. But we were around other passengers who did."

"Mr. Carter already gave us the cruise information and the countries where it pulled into port. Has he come into contact with anyone that recently arrived from another country?" The direction of the probe for information didn't make any sense to me, but I tried to give her everything I knew.

"He's an attorney in Sea Springs. We've traveled around the US." I glanced at Carter who nodded in encouragement. I racked my brain. "He was workin' on a new immigration case before I left town, but I have no idea about the client or the country. He doesn't cross those boundaries with me." Still, I flipped through the conversations he and I had had. Why didn't I remember more? "Dash handled this pro-bono case on his own." I turned to Carter, hoping for his input. "Where's his phone? Maybe I could access it and find the information, but I don't wanna leave him to get it. I told him I would stay." I glanced at the doctor again. "I believe he touched my palm when I was holding his hand."

"I told them about the eyelash flutter," Carter interjected. "I can have Linda bring his laptop if you think that'll help get more information. Can you access his files?"

"He handles a lot of high-profile clients. I'm not sure what info I can track down, probably nothin'. He's protective of his clients. I'm certain his laptop's more than password secured. How's any of this helpful?"

"You've provided us with a direction," Natalie said, making notes as I spoke. "I'll have my staff locate the court records while we wait for the CDC to get back with us. Here's my contact information." She handed me a business card. "Let me know if you think of anything else or have questions."

I held the business card as I stuffed my hands inside my jeans pockets, feeling useless. "Okay." My glance turned sideways to Carter. "I need to shower. Can you show me where?"

"Sure," he said. "We have a back entrance to the suite."

I went to my bag still under the window and glanced at Dash once more. My guy was ravaged by some illness the specialists couldn't even identify. How could that happen? A grunt slipped free as I hoisted the heavy backpack over my shoulder.

"It's heave-ho," Carter said as I started toward him.

"Feels heavier right now," I answered as I trudged behind him, each step heavier than the last.

Less than an hour later, I was back beside Dash's bed, holding his limp hand in mine, gazing intently at his peaceful sleeping expression. Well, as peaceful as anyone could be while hooked to many different machines and a tube stuck down his throat. Maybe peaceful meant pained.

Different medical staff came in and out, adjusting the machines and explaining everything to me, not that I understood a whole lot of what was going on. When the doctor came back in and told me that they felt like Dash was responding well and seemed strong enough to remove the ventilator, they ushered me out of the room.

Carter placed a comforting grip on my shoulder, my immediate gratitude had me leaning into the touch, as we sat in the waiting area. The nurse promised to get me as soon as I could go back in.

Even if Dash was the obvious star of this show, the fundamental base of who I was shifted again. Another turning point in the roads of my life. I'd never do another overseas trip alone again. And had I been home, he'd have been admitted into the hospital days earlier.

The nurse let us back in the room, and I went straight to Dash's side.

The medical staff had warned Carter and I of the possibility of days or even weeks before Dash woke, but what if he opened his eyes right away, or what if he died without ever seeing us again? Like every other time I'd let my thoughts drift to the negative, my inner guard rose swiftly and punched out the damaging thoughts until they were little more than a pile of ash.

"I wish he had woken," Carter said my thoughts out loud.

"The illness has taken a toll." The voice of Dr. Well's drew my attention. "He's breathing on his own, which is remarkable from where he's been. Recovery will take time. We'll continue to monitor him..."

Carter slid a reassuring hand over my back as he moved away from the bed to speak in hushed tones. Better. I only wanted to focus on Dash.

"Here, take a seat," the nurse, whose name I didn't remember, pushed a heavy vinyl recliner close to Dash's bed. I'd been awake for over thirty hours. The seat was greatly appreciated.

"Thank you," I murmured and sat. I released Dash's hand only long enough to slide it through one of the openings in the guardrail for better access.

"They're encouraged for your husband," she said, speaking softly. "The recovery's going to take time. Be patient."

"That's fine," I said my truth. "Whatever it takes."

My mom came through the room's door, wearing all the protective kit. "How's he doing?"

"Breathing on his own," Carter said, relief evident in his tone.

I glanced over my shoulder, caught my mom's eye, and she came to me.

"Son, I'm sorry you had to come home to this," she said, pain lacing each syllable. She reached around me for a tight side hug.

"I should've never left. I had all sorts of bad feelin's. How's Amelia holdin' up? She doesn't like the hospital. It has to be hard on her," I asked.

"She's a mess," my mom said, pulling up another smaller chair. "She's cleaned your house thoroughly from top to bottom. She's also made you tamales, saying they're your favorite." My mom pointed to the rolling tray that had been pushed aside, and my stomach instantly growled. "Shouldn't you be wearing protective wear?"

I shook my head no. "If Amelia and the girls didn't get sick, and if you and Carter, especially Carter because he's been here twenty-four seven, haven't gotten sick, I suspect he's not contagious. They didn't give me grief about the decision to go without. But you keep it on. If I'm wrong, you're going back to my kids and I don't want them anywhere near this. Where's Kailey?"

"She's in Sea Springs with us, doing online classes. We're staying on the third floor. You made it a nice suite for Amelia. It's been easy to transition from Virginia to here. Kailey's sleeping in the girls' bedroom at night. They adore each other. Amelia sent me with a video of West belly-scooting across the floor." My mom's hand caressed over Dash's calf as she babbled about all the important things to me. "Did the nurse say that Dash has a long road to recovery?"

"I didn't pay a lot of attention because he's gotta wake up first. As soon as he can get home, we need to make it happen. He'll recover faster with Amelia and the kids there," I said. I was fucking tired. After a few hours' sleep, maybe I could think like a normal person. "I have some money saved. Maybe the hospital has contractors that can help make our house more user-friendly for Dash. If that's even a thing."

"Most likely. Scott told me to tell you he's got everything covered and to not worry about anything. He and Lauren have been helping Amelia and Belle. Lauren's keeping the kids occupied. They're all in a karate class now. There's so many of them between the two families that they formed their own class. Kailey's been involved too," my mom explained.

"How's Livie doin' in karate?" I absolutely couldn't picture her participating.

"She brings a notebook and draws the moves so everyone can practice them at home. She was kicked one time and decided against joining directly in the training again." I grinned, easily seeing everything my mom described. "Mia's a natural. Ava has a hard time with the discipline required. She's always ready to pound her opponents. She takes as good as she gives."

I nodded. Exactly what I thought would happen. "Mom, I don't want to leave here until he does. Should I call home and talk to them, or wait since they think I'm out of town? What's better for them?" I asked. The question caused a rawness inside me. I wanted to see my girls, but I couldn't leave Dash while he wasn't able to care for himself.

We stared at one another, clearly neither of us knew the right answer. The chance of Dash waking and jumping from the bed ready to go home was growing smaller by the second.

"I say tell them the truth," the nurse interjected. "You know your children better than I do, but from what I've seen, they tend to act out when they know something's not right, but can't find the answers. You can't go wrong with the truth."

"They're pretty protected children," I said to my mom. "We don't want 'em to learn to be bad. So I'll call this evenin' after dinner, but before bed."

Mom nodded and rose from her seat. She gazed lovingly at Dash. The gentle way she touched me as if I was valued, was the way she touched Dash.

She spoke directly to Dash as she said, "Your family said we're waiting on you to return. And Amelia wanted me to reaffirm her lesson that making people wait is rude. We love you, Dash." She inhaled and exhaled slowly, her body shuddered, trying to fight the tears. "I brought everything you asked for, including clean clothes, his phone, and the portable speaker he uses. Playing his music was a brilliant idea. It's in the bag by the door."

"Thank you." I did nothing to retrieve it or even stand for that matter. "I'll set it up after I get some sleep..." The yawns were coming one right after another now. "You go. I'm gonna stretch out here so I don't miss anything. I'll set it up when there's less traffic in here. He likes his music. The girls put together different playlists and talk to him through the songs, for his birthday or Father's Day. He loves to listen to them explain the meaning of the songs that they've never heard before. I figured I'd start there." Another yawn shot out.

I suspected I had about five minutes before I crashed. The fatigue was getting the best of me.

"His physician said he hopes Dash will wake in about forty-eight hours. They'll reevaluate after that time." Only extreme appreciation made me rise to shake Carter's hand. "Thank you for being here when I couldn't. Thanks, Mom, for makin' all this happen and takin' care of our family. I'm gonna have a lifetime of guilt." Stupid tears again built in my eyes but I managed to blink them away. My mom's tears spilled silently down as she came to hug me. "Best mom ever. I always knew you were."

She placed tissues in my hand and turned away, going for the door. Carter smiled the smallest smile ever and followed after my mother. I was barely back in my seat again when the nurse shook out the blanket and put it over me.

"I'll keep an eye on him. Go to sleep."

"I'm glad it went well today," I said, lowering the seat into an almost flat surface. "Thank you."

I let that be enough, and fell asleep thinking of Dash's sweet lips on mine.

# 10: The Chaos
Beau

"Paw!" Livie said excitedly, seconds after they positioned the iPad to allow those in the living room to be viewed by the screen. I did the same with mine, leveling the tablet on the edge of the rolling table, sitting in the chair still next to Dash's bed, within his earshot. I hope that my efforts in letting everyone see me, and chatting about nothing, helped in the matter of Amelia's and the girls' anxiety. Also in reminding Dash why he needed to wake his butt up.

"Paw!" Mia's face appeared on the screen, blocking the others.

"Mia, sit down. We can't see Paw," Ava scolded from where she sat crisscross with Livie. They'd learned the new sitting position in school. Amelia and West sat beside them.

"We miss you and Daddy," Mia said, taking a step back, her gaze still on me. She shared my uncertain emotions. My gaze went back to my little loves, missing them a ridiculous amount. My grin was probably the first genuine one I'd had since I left on my trip. "I miss all of you so much."

Kailey relocated the tablet, the screen going every which way until it took in my mom and Kailey's position on the sofa.

"Hi, Beau," Kailey said. She lifted a hand in a wave as she settled next to our mom. She appeared forlorn, which meant she had to know what was going on more than my girls did.

"You're telecommutin' classes?" I asked Kailey. All three girls' heads bent toward my younger sister. The three were fascinated with her. If she lifted an eyebrow, they did too.

"Yup," she said, sounding like me. "It might be just as good as being in class, but it's hard to ask questions."

I nodded my understanding, West caught my attention, sitting on Amelia's thigh. I wanted to believe his happy clapping was for me. I held all of his attention, and he held mine. He'd grown double in height and weight, I was sure of it. "Hey, little man."

"Abuela says Daddy's getting better," Livie said. All three sets of blue eyes stared a hole through me, waiting for my answer.

"She's right. He's asleep right now. I'm stayin' with him to help him get better. I helped him do his exercises this afternoon, like you all need to be doin' by yourself until I get home. Are y'all doin' good? Did you enjoy Halloween?"

"So much," Ava said, the others echoed her feelings. "We have lots of candy, and Abuela's giving us a piece a day."

"Daddy needs to stop being sick," Livie said. "We wanted him to dress up as Peter Pan."

Oh man, he'd have hated that, but done it in a second.

Mia's hands abruptly fisted, her body gave an excited full-length shake. "Gigi said that Kailey's going to have lunch with us at school. Everyone will see our big sister."

Kailey grinned, and I didn't correct Mia. No one else did either, even Livie.

"She's coming to our Thanksgiving parade lunch too," Ava explained. "Gigi's making her costume to look like ours."

"Do you know about Thanksgiving, Paw?" Livie asked. Of course, no one waited for my answer.

"Everyone in school is dressing up like something from Thanksgiving. I wanna be a cornico," Mia said, abruptly stopping the explanation, casting a quick glance at Livie.

"Cornucopia," Livie corrected.

"The Native Americans and pilgrims became best friends and ate turkey together on Thanksgiving," Mia finished her explanation. Ava nodded along with Mia.

"We're all dressing as cornucopias with different insides because Mia liked the colors better," Ava explained. "She's the one that knows best about it. Abuela's making the costumes. Kailey's gonna sit by me and Livie, and Mia is sitting with Gigi and Abuela if she comes, but maybe I want to sit with Abuela and Gigi. Mia doesn't make the rules."

Ava shot a mean glare to Mia, causing me to jump in before a fight broke out. Ava wasn't above tackling Mia over a perceived slight.

"No fighting. I need you guys to make Daddy some get-well cards. Can you do that for him?"

"Yes," they said in unison.

"I made Daddy a vase in pottery class. It leans but it's still pretty," Mia said, proudly. "Next time, I'm making him a cup, but I don't think he can drink from it." She shrugged sweetly.

"Good and make him a card. Gigi or Abuela can help you write a message. Give your best effort," I said, hoping it would occupy them a little longer than the five minutes every project took. "I'll hang them around his room. Make him one every day. I'll read him the messages. He also likes your book reports. Listen to your books then record yourselves summarizing them. He misses when y'all read together."

"Gigi said we could make you a lunch and she'll take it to you," Livie said, her knees lifting as her hands hung on to the tips of her open-toed sandals.

"I'd like that." I had only slept a couple of hours this afternoon, but enough for right now. I was hungry, the lunch sounded great. "Make me two sandwiches and send me some of those little cakes your dad hides." The girls laughed. So did Abuela and my mom. My sophisticated husband thought he was sneaky enough to hide the Little Debbie white cakes without anyone else knowing. Yeah right.

"Abuela bought some yesterday. We'll get them ready." Livie jumped up and ran toward the kitchen.

Ava seemed fine to let her do all the work. Mia instructed from her seat, "Liv, Daddy likes the Doritos with cheese. And Paw likes those cups of mandarin oranges. He'll eat two cups. And the cauliflower bag. Get that."

"I will," Livie called.

Their accurate dissection of our eating habits showed me the girls saw more of what was happening in our home than I'd realized. My gaze refocused on West, babbling incoherently, talking along with the girls as drool dribbled from the side of his mouth. My stare traveled to Amelia. She appeared as worried as I'd ever seen her. My mom took West, with Duke and Dixie at her feet and staring at the screen.

"Hi, you two. I miss you," I said and four ears lifted. "Are you gettin' enough runnin' time? Are you bein' good?"

Duke couldn't hold it as well as Dixie did and began talking to me on the screen.

"Ava, go pet Duke. Mia, pet Dixie. Tell 'em they did good." Amelia leaned in, catching my eye. "How's my boy doing?"

"Every time someone comes in here, they feel like he's better and it's just a matter of time before he's up. Do you want to see him?" I asked the words I didn't plan to say, and sat up, briefly turning the tablet to the profile side of Dash that I had tried to make presentable. He looked better without the trappings of the ventilator. The slim fitting nasal cannula that helps with his oxygen levels was there. Also the nasogastric tube was on Dash's other side, maybe the kids didn't see it. Tears sprang from Amelia's eyes, the sudden intake of breath stopped me from showing more.

"I'm upset, Beau." Amelia hiccupped as a full cry started.

"Abuela." Mia was there first, hugging her grandmother. Ava and Livie came to her. The tears began to double time, causing the girls to cry too. The dogs got involved, mashing the undersides of their jaws on Amelia's legs, offering their love.

"I know it's not easy to see him this way, but I promise he's better. I'm doin' his exercises with him. He's lost muscle mass. When he comes home, we're gonna take such good care of him, he'll get well just to get away from all the attention we give him."

"No, that's you, Paw," Livie said. "Daddy likes us to do things for him. I rub his feet with lotion."

"She does, Paw. I rub his hands," Mia said.

"I don't do anything because I don't like it," Ava chirped. That caused Abuela to chuckle even through her tears.

"Wesley has some people from the hospital coming out to help get the house ready," my mom said.

I doubted they were from the hospital or insurance company. Based on the way Carter tossed money around, the speed of getting the home prepared for Dash wasn't anything we needed to worry about. He'd have our home completely ready in time. "Is Carter workin' from there? Are y'all bein' quiet for him?"

"He's always on the phone," Amelia injected. "I think he's going to take Dash's law office as his office. He's behind, and the kids are too loud here. Dasham's thin. We're gonna have to fatten him up when he gets home."

"Well, he'll love that," I said, chuckling. "You'll be makin' tamales and cheesy enchiladas and those cookies he loves. Buy full fat milk and real sugar. He'll be in heaven."

"And ice cream. He likes those cones," Ava added. "They're not very good, but we don't tell him."

My heart loved hearing those words.

"Paw, tell us about the first time you met Daddy?" Mia asked excitedly, running for the tablet, and bringing it to the sofa with her. They all gathered around. My mom gave Kailey her spot to get closer. The exact story was told all the time. The girls liked to hear it and of course, Dash liked to tell it, giving more and more detail each time to hold their interest.

I leaned against the chair, finding comfort. Seemed I was in for the long-haul chat.

"I was ridin' the bike my grandparents gave me for my birthday," I explained, and Ava cut me off, helping me along.

"They lived here, where we live now." -

"Yup," I said. "And I was ridin' in town to a pizza place that's not there anymore..."

This time Livie broke in. "The Pizza Box. Right, Paw?"

"Yup," I added again. "So I was at the crosswalk and misjudged the signal light, and it changed on me from yellow to red. I was peddlin' when I spotted your dad in a red sports car. He made me lose everything else in my mind, your dad filled all the spaces inside me. My eyes locked on his as I rolled past, then the next thing I remembered was the sidewalk curb came out of nowhere and sent me over the handlebars. I knew how to take a tackle, I tucked and rolled and was okay in the end. Only shook up about your dad."

"Paw played football," Ava said proudly. "He got to crash into people."

"I remember that day," my mom added, probably to take Ava's mind off banging into people. "It was your paw's birthday. He turned fifteen. Your daddy was close to sixteen years old. I was driving into the Pizza Box to meet your paw for dinner to celebrate, and I saw him climbing out of the bushes, all scratched up. Your daddy explains it the same way—he watched your paw take the tumble. They've loved each other since that day. They've never had other boyfriends either, just each other. I'm proud of your paw and daddy."

I nodded, liking the touches she added.

"Dash called me and told me he met you. I'd never seen him content like that. When you'd spend the night, I felt the love between them," Amelia said, grinning.

"You spent the night with Dash after?" my mom asked. I watched her doing the math in her head. She didn't need me to answer and gave a hearty huff. This couldn't be the first time she figured it out.

"Beau. That was entirely too young," she murmured.

"Too young for what?" Kailey asked. My smile grew as my mom's face came into the screen. I laughed when she pointed a finger at me. I needed that moment to ease the tension.

"What was he too young for, Gigi?" Ava asked. My mom turned and kissed Ava's forehead. She said nothing more to Amelia's laughter. The sound was music to my ears.

"I enjoyed listening to Beau tell Dash no when he tried to talk him into anything. Dasham was always too smart and too charming. He got his way more than he ever should have. Beau never let him win one single time. I'd work around the house, loving the way Dash tried to talk Beau into his will," Amelia said, smiling brightly now.

"Don't give Beau a big head," my mom said, still disgruntled. "He and I are going to talk about this when they come home."

"She looks serious, Beau," Amelia said, drawing her feet up on the sofa. "Do you remember packing Dash's shoes to move to Chicago. We had to wrap each shoe individually."

"I remember," I said. "Then you were the only one allowed to pack them in the truck. Dash told me about when he was younger, and he was afraid of lookin' pretentious."

Amelia smiled so big that a laugh followed from both of us.

"For a time, he only wore clothes that came from the GAP. He felt like everyday people shopped there." She shook her head at his silliness. "He was always so clueless in his attempts to appear normal."

"I agree with that," I said and reached over to take Dash's hand. "I'd say he's still like that. He can't shake his wealthy upbringin'."

"No, he can't," Amelia agreed. "I watch the girls grow and see so much of him inside them. Livie's a younger Dasham. She has his smarts and willingness to follow the rules. Ava's an older Dash, testing life's limits. Mia will have his charm, his need to be grounded to the world. He's always been so good to me. I hope I've given the same to him."

"You know you have," I said, immediately. "He loves you. You know that. We all do."

She swallowed deeply, a trickle of tears spilling over again.

"Why does Abuela call Daddy Dasham and no one else does?" Mia asked.

"Dasham's your dad's full name. When I met him, I thought he was dashin', so I shortened his name to Dash," I explained. "And it took."

"Like Prince Charming?" Livie said. "They said he was dashing when we were on the ship."

"Yup, just like that." I grinned at the comparison.

"Tell us more about what Dash was like when he was little," I said, happy to listen to anything Amelia had to say. I had nothing but time from now until they checked in. Mia popped up beside Amelia, giving the tablet to Ava, getting straight in her grandmother's face.

"Don't cry, Abuela," she said. "We love you."

"I love you too. Do you want to hear about when your daddy was your age?" she asked, running a tissue over her eyes. Ava came in beside Mia, holding the tablet. Livie crawled on the other side.

"Yes," they said in unison.

Amelia launched into her storytelling, gently tiptoeing around the secret bits of Dash's life. I leaned in, hoping Dash could soak up all the love swirling around him—the life he cherished above all else.

An hour sprang forward as I basked in Amelia's recounting of Dash's escapades. From his attempt to save the turtles, his efforts as a young boy to take on the stock market, to the happiness he experienced after meeting me. I'd never heard many of the stories before. Amelia focused on the good times and stayed away from any of our difficult periods. Duke and Dixie didn't even try to assert themselves into the conversation. They listened patiently too.

Suddenly, the night nurse pushed through the door, juggling fresh blankets in one arm, and a dinner plate in the other. "Everything about to happen is being performed around the new rules. Someone important cares for you two. The isolation protocols have been removed so your rule breaking self doesn't have to be escorted out. I wasn't sure if you'd eaten," she said, yanking me back to reality as she placed both items on top of the rolling cart.

"I have to go," I said. "Daddy's nurse is here. Can we continue this tomorrow evenin'?"

The girls turned instantly forlorn when I said I had to go, then gleeful when I mentioned another evening spent together in this way.

"That's a good idea. I feel better talking about our guy," Amelia said. "Thank everyone at the hospital for all they're doing for us."

"I think she just heard you."

The nurse smiled as she checked Dash's vitals and his equipment.

"I'm signin' off. I love, love you, and miss you." I waved and smiled then pushed the end button on the screen and got to my feet, moving the multi-purpose rolling cart out of the way.

"I brought you a dinner tray and new bedding. They've explained to you how to lower the chair, right?"

"I figured it out. I slept a couple of hours this afternoon," I said. "Thank you for bringin' food." My perfectly-timed stomach grumbled its appreciation too.

"The staff's been watching. They didn't remember you eating anything today. Your father-in-law's getting a bed sent up here for you. I thought it would be here by now. It's against hospital policy but we're in a new set of rules..." She let that hang there. I knew the pull Carter had and he wasn't afraid to flex his abilities either. "It's interesting to watch the top brass bend like they are. All of us are laughing behind their backs."

I nodded, understanding exactly what she meant. Extreme money made people act differently all of the time. How Carter stayed grounded was probably the place where he connected best with Dash. "He's my stepfather, but I guess my father in-law too. That's funny. I never considered the connection." My gaze darted to her kind face, trying to gauge the amount of dysfunction in my statement. She seemed to have no judgment about my words.

"I didn't know who he was, but others recognized him on the spot. Then they felt like they knew Dash. I guess they're photographed together regularly."

I remained quiet, knowing Dash would find that hilarious. Carter and Dash tried to stick it to his father any chance they got, but while doing so, they'd become incredibly close.

"How's our guy doing? I understand he's doing better."

"They keep tellin' me that, but he's not awake, or movin'," I said, going to the opposite side of the bed from where she worked.

"Did you do his hair?" she asked, adjusting the tubes on his face.

"I tried. He's particular about his hair. He'd be embarrassed by my efforts, but I tried," I said, eyeing the modest flip I had managed.

"He looks great," she said and began working on the iPad attached to his bed. "Do you two live around here?"

"No, we have a house in Sea Springs. We have children and dogs there." My stare remained fixed on Dash's face. "We have triplet girls who are three and a seven-month-old son."

"That's a big load. I have an eight-year-old daughter and I can barely keep up." My gaze lifted to her commiserating.

"I have a sister around that age. Carter and Mom had a daughter. The more I talk about us, the more I realize we might appear super dysfunctional, but it's not. We're all lucky to have each other."

"Mr. Carter claimed Dash as his son, and your mom's Kailey's mom, so Dash is your stepbrother and husband?" Her gaze twinkled and lifted to me, showing she was teasing. "Honestly, from what I see every day, you guys are the high point of functional. I promise." A couple of guys pushed through the door, guiding in another bed. I couldn't imagine lying there, awake, watching Dash breathe all night, but it had to be better than the hard, vinyl chair.

"Do you want me to turn the music back on?" the nurse asked about the speaker I placed on a stool by his head.

"I'll do it and make the bed," I said to the two guys shaking out a sheet. Luckily, the nurse backed me up when they ignored me.

"He likes to stay busy and do things for himself. Leave it. It's good." All three left the room together, leaving behind a deafening silence. My gaze traveled to Dash.

"Please wake up. I need you. Please."

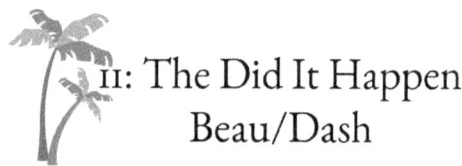

11: The Did It Happen
Beau/Dash

Beau

The Following Evening
Houston Methodist Hospital

As exhausted as I was when I crawled into this bed, was exactly how frustrated I was when I didn't fall asleep. For the past two hours, I watched Dash and the ticking clock above his head. My eyes were gritty as hell, and I was damned drained, but sleep eluded me. My stomach churned, prompting me to rise and take a seat on the edge of the bed, giving another crazy long yawn. I eyed the food tray, as my stomach gave a solid grumble.

With my foot, I caught the backside and drew the rolling tray toward me. I lifted the silver cover, spotting a couple of prepackaged items. Juice, crackers, Jello, and a small bottle of water. The juice appealed the most and poked a hole in the top with my thumb.

"Dash. Dash!" I yelled watching his face. Nothing changed, of course. Why were the doctors and nurses saying my guy was doing any better? He looked gaunt and malnourished, more so than before.

In a couple of gulps, I drained the juice container and brought the cracker's edge to my mouth to open. "The problem, Dash, is that you're the talker between us. I need you to wake up and prove to me that the staff's correct, and that you're in fact gettin' better, because I don't see it. Wake up right now."

I lowered down to my sock-covered feet and tossed the empty juice box on the tray. I'd pushed our beds close-ish together but still had feet between us to allow easy access to the staff. I sidled up to his bed, wishing I could be beside him, surrounding his presence. The one thing Dash and I did outstandingly well was cuddle. We did it so well that Duke and Daisy generally wanted up on the bed to join us, to get some of our love directed toward them.

"Duke's probably gonna have to up his anxiety medication. I intended to talk to you about it when I came home. He's duckin' and hidin' more than normal. Dixie stays close. She helps coax him out. I know we don't like to over-medicate him, but it's painful to watch him be scared. He's so smart and such a good guy. I think it was part of the reason I was on edge before I left." My gaze shifted back and forth over Dash's face, seeing Duke vividly inside my head. "Maybe there's somethin' I'm missin' in his trainin'. He's protective of us and our children. I wish I wouldn't have gotten 'em fixed so fast. I'd like to have their puppies. Silly, huh?"

No matter how he teased me about them always being underfoot, he loved those dogs and regularly took them quietly upstairs to be with him and West at night. I continued to stare at Dash's handsome face as I put the edge of the saltine in my mouth.

"Do you remember when we first got together again the second time, and how I refused to text you durin' the day?" I asked between chews. "I had all my excuses ready whenever you complained. The truth was, I felt mightily inferior to you. What did I have to say to someone like you? I was a hit-in-the-head jock my whole life to that point. I didn't think I was smart enough to hold that kind of conversation. Then the spellin' in the text messages... It freaked me out."

I popped another cracker in my mouth, chewing as I spoke. No sound came, the cracker absorbed all the saliva. I reached for the water bottle on the tray, unscrewing the cap with two free fingers while keeping the crackers in my fist. I took a quick swig, recapped the water bottle, and turned back to Dash.

"Do you think West will wanna play..."

Dash's eyes opened, locking on me.

"Dash."

His lids closed again. *No.* I dropped the water bottle and crackers to the ground, placing both of my hands on his chest, shaking him. "Wake up, Dash! Please."

He lifted his eyelids once more, this time with his brows slightly furrowing. He attempted to speak, but nothing coherent issued forth.

"You're sick. You've been out of it for a while. Keep restin'. I'll be here."

His expression remained defiant for a few long seconds before his eyelids surrendered and shut again. The tears were back as I leaned forward to kiss his cheek. "Rest. We need you well. I'll tell everyone the good news."

I kissed him again and reached for the nurse's call button and my cell phone. I didn't care about the time of night. My mom needed to know, because I needed to tell her.

I had to convince myself that I truly saw Dash open his eyes because we were fourteen hours into the day, and he hadn't done it again. What I had previously refrained from doing, and what I was currently doing right now, was googling how often medical personnel lied to patient's families.

I wasn't really doing that, but I was trying to figure this out.

It seemed to me what Dash was doing was normal after being intubated. The rest of the possibilities scared the shit out of me. The list of symptoms for Legionnaires' disease seriously hit everything Dash had gone through. Google also tagged it as a possible case of rabies.

What resonated the most was the rallying event that took place at the end of life. Could that be what was happening with Dash?

My heart ached, and once again, Dash and I were alone inside his room. Mom and Carter had stayed the day, and had currently gone for something to eat, and promised to bring me food back. What I needed was for Dash to open his eyes, if nothing more, to make sure I hadn't dreamed him awake.

From my spot on the built-in bench close to the window, I stood up, tucking my cell into my shorts pocket, a pair Dash had bought for me along with most of my other clothes.

"Wake up, Dash," I said. With one hand, I held onto the top of the bed. The other rested on his concave belly. I couldn't stand the weight he'd lost while lying in this bed.

I shook him like I'd done over and over today. This time though, while alone with him, I bent in and quietly whispered in his ear, "If you'll open your eyes for me, I'll blow you as soon as we're alone. You can fuck my throat like you like."

My gaze locked on his closed eyes and nothing changed. Hmm. Dash thrived on intimacy yet tended to become vulgar when trying to persuade me that sleep was bad, and sex was good.

"Dash, you know how much I like to lick your ass. I'll do it to you the second they remove the machines. I'll rub your prostate while I lick you like an ice cream cone. Hell, I'll add ice cream to our good time. It's been a long time since we added anything edible to our sex. Please open your eyes to tell me you agree."

He didn't.

I tried the only other thing that Dash wanted, and I'd said a hard no to. "You win. We can have more children. As many as we can afford. I only ever said no because I didn't want to take any experiences away from the ones we were lucky enough to have. I was wrong. Please open your eyes."

He did. For several long moments, we gazed at one another while his fingers tried to grasp mine. I smiled as my heart flip-flopped in my chest. I lifted my hand from his belly, avoiding the tubing to gently stroke his face. "I love you."

The hospital room door swung open. My mom hurried to Dash's bedside. Her eyes—so much like mine—filled with tears as she reached for Dash's hand. "Dash, darling, you're awake." She pushed the nurse's button as Carter came to her side.

Dash gave a valiant effort to speak. His words were soft and garbled under his oxygen mask.

"You've been sick, son," Carter began. My mom stepped out of the way, allowing Carter to step closer to Dash. "You've been intubated for several days. It's going to take time to get your voice back."

Carefully, without thought of the repercussions, for him or me, I leaned in to kiss his lips then did it again. "I love you." My face stayed inches from his. "You have to focus on getting well. We need you, Dashing."

He managed to croak out two words, "How...long?"

"A couple of weeks. Carter and Mom came because I was unreachable. Carter's the reason you've come this far. He stayed with you and had doctors all over the United States consultin'." I lost Dash's gaze as he searched out Carter. Their connection was palpable.

"Discount," Dash managed to say after several moments. I wasn't sure I heard him right, but Carter burst out in laughter.

"I'd believe free, but we can talk about that later."

Dash tried to smile, but it didn't reach his lips.

His gaze sought mine again. "Tired."

"Sleep, I'll be here."

Dash held my hand marginally tighter. His eyelids blinked a few times before shutting all the way. He was back asleep again as the nurse stepped inside the room.

Dash

Ten Days Later
Houston Methodist Hospital

"I really don't want the kids to see me like this," I confessed, understanding how ridiculous I sounded since I'd be home in about an hour, a place I'd fought to be for days now. They still had no clue what had hit me, but the outcome wasn't good. The frail weakness refused to release its grip. I felt like a limp noodle, unable to walk on my own. It exhausted me to have Beau dress me, and this relentless cough made my lungs feel like giving up by the time it ended.

"They miss you," Beau said, bending to prop my feet on the wheelchair's footrest. "They're excited to see you and be here at the hospital. The staff who took care of you want to meet the kids. They're getting balloons and teddy bears from the gift shop."

What had really happened? In what world had Beau become the reasonable one between us?

"How's my hair?"

"As well as I could manage. You look like a model. I like your hair longer."

I was fully aware of my appearance, and it was nowhere close to a model.

"Do you like my beard?"

"Of course." I always liked him with facial hair, no matter the amount. The noise at the room's door drew both our attention, Beau standing to his full height. "Remember the carnations."

I did forget my gifts and reached for the rolling tray to grasp the four stems that Beau had picked up from the gift store downstairs.

The door latch released. My heart softened as Mia, in her pigtails styled just how I loved, rushed for me. She wore blue jeans, a jersey T-shirt, pink sleeves and a white chest, the words *I love my daddy* imprinted on the front. Her runners flashed with color as she bounded forward. "Daddy, I missed you." Her upper body fell against my thighs, hugging me. "Are you still sick?"

"I am," I said, laying a palm on her back. "But I'm gettin' better every day."

Beau had Livie and Ava on each hip. Livie's head rested on his shoulder. Ava hugged Beau around the chest, staring at me. They each wore the same outfits, only Liv's was in blue, and Ava's in lavender. We'd assigned them colors at birth to tell them apart and they'd stuck.

"I don't like us being separated," Livie added. "You're skinny, Daddy. You don't have the fatness on your tummy anymore."

"Is that right?" I managed a grin before Beau had a chance to scold her for stating the truth.

"Mia, give your sisters a chance to see your dad," Beau said, putting Livie and Ava on their feet. Mia jumped up, Beau catching her to lift into a hug. I hugged both girls too, grinning sweetly up at me from my lap.

Kailey laughed and gave me a side hug. "What's that tube in your nose?"

"Oxygen," Carter answered beside her. His hand rested on my shoulder, giving a squeeze.

"And he's coming home to get better?" she asked him instead of me.

"Yes," Carter answered again.

"Where's Amelia and Linda? Did they bring West?" I asked, handing each girl a flower. They beamed as if I'd given them the rarest of jewels.

"Abuela and Gigi are waiting in the van for you. With West," Ava said. "Abuela's a big crybaby. She cries all the time now."

"She does, Daddy," Livie seconded, bringing the carnation to her nose. "It smells pretty. Bumble bees collect pollen from flowers to eat. Did you know that?" Her blue eyes landed on mine, waiting for my answer.

"I've heard something like that. Tell me more when we get in the car to go home."

"Tell your dad thank you for the flowers," Beau said, and in unison, they did. "Let's go. We're to walk the hall, ride the elevators down, and the nurses want to meet you four before we go outside. Be good and say thank you without me havin' to tell you, okay?" Again with the unison *yes, sir.* "You can walk beside your dad, but don't get in the way of his wheels. You'll fall and he might too."

"Maybe hold my hands as we go?" Carter asked, wiggling his finger for Liv and Ava's small hands.

"Your muscles are still big, Paw," Mia said, locking her legs around Beau's waist. "You can carry me." One less child to worry about losing their way.

"Let's go before I change my mind and stay here with people who don't talk about my belly size," I said as the silent medical team member began pushing toward the door.

"Daddy, your voice is scratchy. It sounds funny." Ava wrinkled her nose in distaste.

I couldn't even keep from chuckling at her perfectly-timed delivery.

Beau grabbed our last bag in the room and started out. I loved watching him both coming and going. Although arousal wasn't happening for me these days, I still appreciated his firm ass in a good pair of Wranglers.

Was I ever going to be the same again? It didn't seem likely without a hell of a fight.

12: The Old Man Beau

I was skeptical about this grand plan on the first evening Dash had come home from the hospital. Actually, I was sorely outnumbered in my rejection which didn't technically mean anything to me, but with the way everyone rallied behind Dash, and he enjoyed being with friends and family at home, I let it ride.

Our living room was bursting at the seams with Scott, Lauren and all their brigade, Mom, Carter, Kailey, and my own clan including the dogs, minus West asleep upstairs, all crammed inside the nice-sized space like sardines. I shook the third round of Jiffy Pop popcorn over a stove burner as the microwave warmed another cup of Amelia's chicken and rice soup for Dash.

Minced chicken pieces, brown rice, and finely-chopped assorted fresh vegetables. A nutritionally packed soup, designed to give Dash energy. Amelia had done her homework on Dash's dietary needs. She used the same care with Dash as she used with the children. This was his third bowl.

"Paw, hurry. We wanna start the movie," Ava said from her spot on the floor where the L-shaped sofa came together. Dash was stretched out there, covered with a thick blanket. Neither

Amelia nor the kids wanted to leave his side, and honestly, I felt the same way.

"What else do we need? Juice boxes, beer?" I asked, distributing the popcorn to the group.

Scott raised his can and nodded.

"Paw, Daddy looks old like Pop-Pop," Mia said. "But Gigi said we shouldn't tell him."

"Hey," Carter, the pop-pop Mia mentioned, said, faux hurt in his tone.

"Pop-Pop." Mia jumped up and launched herself at him, believing she'd hurt his feelings, giving Carter a tight hug. "You're not old. You just look old with the wrinkles on your forehead and the gray in your hair," she explained right in his face.

"Mia," I said, not at all sure what to say to make this right.

Scott burst out with a hearty laugh. Dash gave a low-level chuckle too.

"Mia, I said you shouldn't say things like that out loud to anyone, including Pop-Pop. Those things make people feel bad," Mom explained.

Mia's expression fell instantly, her entire focus shifted back to Carter. "I'm sorry." Her palms went to his face, caressing all over. "Uncle Scott's getting gray hair too. He's not that old either."

"My feelings aren't hurt, sweet girl. Don't worry. I understood what you meant," Carter said, accepting Mia's hug.

"Hey, my feelin's are hurt," Scott said boisterously. "I'm here for the movie and popcorn, not to get roasted by my goddaughter about bein' as old as her pop-pop." His funny outrage helped shift the spotlight off my girl. Carter put her on her feet, and she bolted the four or so steps to Dash, putting her crossed arms on his chest, staring at him.

"Daddy, I'm sorry. I was just telling the truth."

"Kiss my cheek," he said, smiling, and she did. "I'll work on looking younger. I don't want people to think I'm your paw's dad."

"Shoo, Mia, before you make it all worse," I said, taking the seat beside Dash. Mia happily laughed and carefully dropped down on Duke, her pillow for the evening. My guy's inner pride kept him from taking too much help, except from me, because I didn't care how he argued against me. My sole goal was to get him back on his feet.

"I'm ready, start the movie," I said. Carter was prepared, the lights dimmed and the film began to play. It was a family-friendly show, *Playing with Fire*, featuring John Cena. The guys appreciated the wrestling reference, probably Ava did too, and the rest enjoyed kid-mania.

My focus shifted to Dash. He did appear older, not only due to his condition, but from the epic battle he fought to be here with us. His weary gaze lifted to mine.

"They're a mess," he said wispy and out of breath. The hospital discharged him with an oxygen tank, and despite his grumbling about its annoying presence, I insisted he use it. I was going to win the oxygen battle if I had to duct tape the tubes to his face. "Can you help me lift up?"

"Sure, hang on," I rose, my feet between the kids, and angled Dash to a better position to eat. "I got you." The grunts and groans he gave came from the effort to help, ate at my soul. I stuffed the pillows behind his back to keep him upright. His appreciative blue eyes lifted to mine. I leaned in to plant a kiss on his forehead, but he gently shook his head.

"My lips," he whispered.

"If you keep the oxygen on. I don't care what the meter reads. Make sure it stays on."

He nodded in agreement, but I was skeptical. Still, I pressed my lips to his and placed a wad of paper towels under his chin. After retrieving the soup bowl Amelia held, I slowly fed him. I insisted on this responsibility until his care team arrived tomorrow. Two-thirds of the way through the bowl, Dash gave out. His eyes drooped. His head lulled to the side. I cleaned his mouth and moved the tank closer to him, tucking a blanket around him to better allow sleep.

I completely missed the movie's plot, had no idea what was going on. Anything with Dash took time, the timeliest was probably feeding him. The popcorn and drinks looked appealing. I reached between the girls for a handful of popcorn. I didn't get a chorus of *heys* which meant they were engrossed in the movie.

Minutes later, Livie's gaze never left the screen while she climbed into my lap. They'd been sticking nearby all day. Shortly after, the other two joined her, sitting between me and Dash, popcorn and juice boxes in hand. Their new pink sequined dress shoes—a purchase my mom made for them and Scott's youngest daughters—hitting all the wrong places.

"Be careful of your dad. Maybe y'all should sit back on the floor."

"No, let 'em stay. I missed them," Dash murmured. Mia was the closest to him and laid her head on Dash's arm. They were like little rays of sunshine, beaming joy most of the time.

Thankfully, we were all back home together. I might not ever let any of us leave again.

Two hours later, with Carter's assistance, we walked Dash to our bed and tucked him in tightly. I went back to the living room to find Scott standing by the front door. My mom and Amelia were past him inside the kitchen, tidying surfaces that were already clean. Scott gestured for me to join him on the front porch, meaning he wanted to talk and I needed to listen. We were business partners. I hadn't kept up my end of things, but dang it, I was tired and emotionally stretched thin. Tomorrow morning was only ten hours away.

He opened the door and stepped outside, leaving it ajar for me. I couldn't read his expression, not that I tried. "What's goin' on?" I asked.

Scott had already reached the north side of the wraparound porch, the bright moonlight illuminating him. He stuck his fingers into his front pockets, no doubt to ward off the chill in the air. His attention was focused in the direction of the dock we couldn't see from there.

"I don't know that I've ever told you what a good parent I think you are," Scott said distractedly. "You took to it like a natural. It's impressive. I didn't have your ability. Lauren bore the brunt of it all until she taught me how. I should've helped her more in the beginning."

"You're a good father. Y'all love each other. You've done right by them from the beginnin'," I said, walking toward him. I leaned my ass against the railing, and crossed my arms to ward off the chill. I should've grabbed a jacket.

"I have a confession about parenthood that I haven't shared with anyone, even Dash. I believe a nurturin' mother's role in successful parentin'. Dash plowed through the process, and our surrogate got pregnant so fast. That's when I really began watchin' Lauren a lot, Amelia too. The way they handle children doesn't come natural to me. I read books and books about raisin' children. I took so many online parentin' classes secretly. Dash reaches that special nurturin' way better than I do. We had a pretty big argument before I left about how strict I am with them and him. I'm too rigid. Maybe if I wasn't bein' me, I'd have noticed the sniffle was more than just allergies."

Scott turned to face me in a rare serious moment. "Couples argue. It's part of havin' a relationship. Life's tough. It's not about a single moment. But if it was, how could you have changed what happened? They don't know what made him sick." He angled his position to stand in front of me. "Nothin' would have changed except that maybe you'd have gotten sick too. Where would your family be then? Maybe the universe was in play by gettin' you away."

I let those words roll around in my head, my chin lowered hitting my chest. "I don't know what a good parent I am. If Dash died, I wanted to too." Extreme fatigue set in hard at my confession, slumping my shoulders. I loved my children. How had I ever let my thoughts slip to such a selfish place?

"You know how I feel about Lauren. I get it. And it's not exactly your choice to die when Dash does, but I get the sentiment." He mirrored my posture, crossing his arms over his chest. "So about work. I wanted to tell you that my old man came to help. We've had a crazy amount of last-minute charters for some reason. We're booked solid every day. I didn't want to bother you, but he's helped me keep it goin'. I adjusted the pricin' once we were full. I've been puttin' money in your account. Dad's gettin' paid five dollars an hour. But now he wants to invest in us. He wants to buy a Nautic Star to help get us to the next level. My parents wanna move here and help us. All of us."

"Okay," I said and paused. That was a crazy expensive boat designed for deeper sea fishing. We'd be able to charge double or triple our pricing for a standard charter. "Does your dad want to operate a boat? It's gonna be a minute before I'm back. Maybe if I get Dash set…"

"That's not what I'm suggestin'. We got this handled for however long you need to begone. He wanted to invest in us and help fill in for you. He appreciates what you've done for us and wants to give back. Maybe we can all sit down in January and work it out."

I nodded. I didn't have a grip on my family's financial situation. Dash took care of it all.

"Forget I mentioned it," Scott said and slapped my arm. "I'm headin' home. We'll talk later."

"No, actually the idea's pretty damned intriguin'. We gotta talk to your dad. What does he want for the boat, stuff like that? January's better for me to have that discussion. I feel like I'm twisted up in my family's finances. Dash isn't workin', and I don't know what that means for us. Maybe I need to pick upshifts at UPS or open some overnight charters. We could charge a lot more for those." My worried gaze riveted on Scott. "Dash takes care of our finances. I'm not sure what we have."

"I still have funds available if you need it," Scott offered. "You put all that money in college funds for my kids. Take it back, or we can borrow against it. It's my responsibility to put 'em through college, not yours."

I stared at him, the best friend a guy could have. I wanted to cry again. "I'm not takin' the kids college funds. It was right to secure all of our children's future, but who knew we'd have so many kids?" And I built this house too big. Dash made many expensive changes. What did we have saved for a rainy day?

"Let me figure out what's happenin' with us, and let's reconvene," I finally said, shaking my head free of the crazy, escalating, wild thoughts.

Scott nodded his agreement.

"I think buyin' another boat's the right thing to do," I added. "What does he want for it, again?"

"He doesn't want anything except to be here with his grandchildren and to fish. He's proud of us, and my mom won't be on his back about fishin' so much if he's helpin' us."

The chuckle I gave was genuine, because I knew all the players involved, and Scott was telling the absolute truth. His parents also treated my kids like they were their own. I pushed off the rail and scratched my hairline, knocking back the ball cap I hadn't realized I was still wearing.

Scott snapped his fingers and pointed at me, locking my attention on him. "We'll make him a silent investor that only gets paid if we can pull this all off."

"Sounds good," I said.

Scott was already trotting down the front steps. He lifted a hand, jogging toward his house. I went inside. The kitchen lights were off, the house silent. It was barely eight thirty. The girls had to be in the bath. Instead of going to my bedroom, where I really wanted to be, I took the stairs up to help with the children's nighttime chore duties. Amelia had carried this load for weeks. She deserved a night off.

13: The Recovery
Beau

I headed into our bedroom, where Dash was peacefully sleeping. He had rested more today than he had over the past couple of days. His care team must have tired him out. Duke and Dixie were quietly lying on their beds, staring out the large window to our backyard, until I came inside the room. I tossed my baseball cap on the dresser, and tore out of my T-shirt, throwing it closer to the bathroom. Then I went to the dogs, bending and taking the few minutes—maybe ten—to quietly pet, and love on each one. They were remarkable creatures. I'm not sure how I sensed it, maybe it was through Duke's heartbeat or the way his head fell between my crossed legs, but Duke felt calmer. Dixie scooted against the length of my thigh, content that we stay just like that through the night.

"How much longer until you join me in bed?" Dash murmured in the quiet of the dim room. Dixie lifted her head to the voice then stood. Not in her normal rambunctious way, but cautiously plodding to Dash's side of the bed.

"I didn't mean to wake you. They looked like they needed some attention," I said, getting to my feet.

"I think you were right," he replied. "I may have overdone on my first night home. I hope it doesn't set me back. I'm exhausted." He snaked a hand out of the heavy blanket to reach for Dixie's head. "I miss my old life."

"You've been through hell, Dash. It's important to give yourself a break, reevaluate in a couple of weeks," I said, dropping my shorts where I stood. I kicked those toward my T-shirt and pushed back my side of the blanket. I left our bedroom door open, allowing the dogs to roam free. My fingers went to Duke's head, scratching behind his ear. "Do you need anything before I lie down? A sip of water?"

"No, I'm fine. The catheter makes me uncomfortable. I hope they remove it tomorrow." Dash stared at the ceiling as I climbed into bed. It was always cold inside this room.

"Do you need more blankets?" I asked.

"More than the five covering me?" He chuckled. Apparently losing thirty pounds hadn't messed with the internal heat he always generated. "Come closer. It's been too long since we slept together. I don't like it. You make me believe everything's going to be all right, or that I'm safe, or whatever I feel."

I scooted closer, finding his hand. His sleeping position had been set up at a pretty decent incline to help with his lingering cough. I tucked my free hand under the pillow at my head. I needed to be closer, and lifted his hand to his lips, pressing against his scaly skin. Something else I needed to work on.

"I wanted to be home," Dash started, his face turning to mine. "But now, I'm not sure if it's good for the children to see me this way."

"I disagree," I said. "We're a team. A family. We need each other. They were beginnin' to act out. West, our mild-mannered little guy, was fussy most of the time. They needed you home. And now you'll have three little nurses tryin' to take care of you, and West scootin' on his belly to get to you."

"What if I don't get better?" Dash asked, his brows wrinkled, his handsome face turning to stare at the ceiling. I watched his Adam's apple bobble as he swallowed the worry he was having.

"You've come so far, Dash. I think they expected the worst but here you are. There's no reason to think you won't return to your old self. Have you met you? You're pretty stubborn," I said, trying for a laugh. I didn't get that, but he managed the faintest of smiles.

He swiveled his head back to me. "You shouldn't have to be a nursemaid to me. You have UPS, the charter company, this family." That was all his lungs could handle, and he took deep breaths and closed his eyes.

"I'm on leave at UPS. I have six weeks off and a gazillion hours of vacation and sick leave. Scott's got the business taken care of. He says we've been busier than ever. His old man wants to invest in us with a substantial deep-sea boat. We'll be able to offer expensive charters. Our company seems to be doing good."

"Listen to me, Beau," Dash started with labored breaths. "You, Amelia, and our children are taken care of if something happens to me."

"Dash, stop. You're on the other side of this health deal. Save your breath."

"Beau. I need you to promise me that when my time comes, you'll seek happiness. I don't need to ask you to watch our children and Amelia, I know you will." A tear slipped from the corner of his eye down his temple. I could hear the fear and weariness in his labored breaths. A second tear followed. "Since the first second I saw you, all I've wanted is your happiness, and I hoped that was with me..."

The words ignited a frenzy of hysteria that caused a scrambling chaos over every inch of my body. I rejected him discussing my greatest fear. Instinctively, I responded with a barely audible "*pfft*." Of course, I'd never find another. Dash was irreplaceable. As his tears continued to fall, I had to stop them before another round of coughing tortured his body.

"Yeah, right. Tell your lies to someone else. I doubt my happiness was ever on your agenda. What you truly wanted was to prove your soulmate theory was correct, and your resoluteness to make it happen. I never stood a chance against you. And if you think you'll look down at me with peace as I kiss another dude...hahaha."

The tears stopped. Dash grinned a big, toothy smile, continuing to stare at the ceiling. "Your bad memory messed with my manipulative, selfless speech where I ensured you only thought of me until we were together again. You hooking up with someone else is gonna piss me off in the afterworld. And whatever I can do to show my anger at you, I will. That's the truth."

I propped myself on my elbow to better see his face. It took a second or two for him to glance my way. "If you leave me, I'm hookin' up with Stone on your desk in your office. He's packin'. Don't think I didn't notice."

"How do you know he's gay? I've seen no evidence?" Dash said, not with accusation, only genuine curiosity. I leaned in further and gently kissed his lips. "He watches your ass too long. I can't blame him. It's a great ass." We shared that look of understanding that close couples did all the time. "I think I'm done sports climbin'. For the whole trip, I missed my family. And I like a real bed."

"Hmm," Dash murmured. "I missed you."

"Again, you're lyin'," I said and dropped back to my pillows. "From the second I left, you grew sicker and sicker. You were down almost immediately."

"Remember when you used to take everything I said at face value?"

"No, I don't remember that time," I answered honestly. "I believe I knew you were full of it from the start."

Dash's hand tightened around mine. "Hmm. You sure made me work for us from the beginning."

"Stop bein' chatty. Go to sleep, reserve your energy. I'll handle us until you're back solidly on your feet."

His fingers threaded through mine. "Thank you."

"You made me repeat in sickness and health twice during our vows. I think you had foresight that you'd needed double the care than me. As my attorney, doesn't that mean false pretenses?"

He softly chuckled, echoing me. "I remember you saying in the hospital that we could have more children. Maybe three more."

In my mind, I thought of *a* baby, meant one. I let it ride for now. Not too much longer, he fell asleep.

The following day

Of course, Dash didn't hesitate to overdo it, again. The sigh that left my body was a full-length deal that ended with an exhausted groan. That man might honestly be the most frustrating human being on this planet.

It was hard to assess whether he had regressed from all the activity yesterday, but he sure hadn't gotten any better. I began to draw lines with him, and since I had to help him move around the house, it actually worked.

I left Dash in bed as I followed my mom, Carter, and Kailey out the front door so we could talk. Those tasked with watching Dash, namely, all our children, and dogs, and Amelia were set straight on the importance of following my instructions and not Dash's. But getting outside with these three gave me a quiet chance to give my sincere appreciation to Carter without adding my emotionally overloaded husband to the mix.

I stood a couple of feet from my mom and Carter who were in a tight embrace. Kailey stood beside me, seemingly as uncomfortable as I was. "Do they do this a lot?" I asked.

"Yeah," she said, taking her cell phone from her back pocket. She lived an easy, sheltered life, but she was also getting old enough to become a real human being. Meaning, she played age-appropriate games on her phone. "But you and Dash do that stuff longer than they do. It's all kind of gross. I don't like the idea of exchanging spit. I'm not going to be that way."

I chuckled at the truth of her tone. We'd see what happened. "I felt that way too when I was young. I wanted to be a fisherman on TV. Scott and I planned to have our own show."

She smiled at me. "You're close. Dory told me that you and Uncle Scott had a YouTube channel that got lots of views. Maybe turn that channel into a fishing channel. Put cameras on the boat and make TikTok videos too." She shrugged like it was the simplest thought. And it was. Scott and I had done a few small videos for advertising on Facebook, but we were missing most of the social media that the world watched. Huh. Maybe the kid was onto something.

"Bye, Kailey," my mom said, coming to her, worry and fatigue on her face, as the private car turned into the circle driveway. "I'll see you here on Thanksgiving then we'll all travel home together. Be good for your dad." Her tears sounded in her tone. She should be going home with them, I'd tried to get her to go, but she'd insisted on staying until Dash truly began to be better.

He required a lot of work from all of us right now.

"But you get to be with Beau," Kailey said, her brows knitting together at her mom's tears. "You miss him all the time. I don't understand why we haven't moved closer to him. This is where you grew up, Mom. Dad goes everywhere to work. I could go to school at the one the girls go to."

"You're right, baby," she said, gathering Kailey into an awkward hug, squeezing her body tightly. Her one arm went one way, the other another way, and her upper body arched into mom's. None of those positions appeared natural. "Talk to your dad about all that, okay?"

"She still hugs me the same way so get used to it." I winked at Kailey, always aware of the connection she and I shared, the one our mother created and nurtured to remain sure and strong. My arms crossed over my chest, holding in the warm feelings these two always created inside me.

"Mommma, stop! You're pulling my hair. We're gonna be back next week." I didn't blame my sister, I'd have knocked out of that hold seconds ago. And our mom didn't care or release Kailey until the back door of the car opened. As a group, we meandered toward Carter.

"Thank you for everything you've done," I said, sticking out my hand to him. He took it, but shook his head no at my appreciation.

"This is what family does, Beau. Dash and I are incredibly close. And you'd be there for me in the same way." His words interrupted my genuine appreciation, winding us back a few years when Carter hadn't been my favorite person. My grin beamed my truth. "All right, Dash would take care of me in the same way, and he'd insist you be there with him."

"That I can agree with," I said, chuckling lowly. Carter drew me into a hug. "You've come in and saved the day several times for us. If not for you, Dash would be a used car salesman. Thank you for his life, mine too."

Wow. Where had that come from?

No lie that I'd never uttered such an oath aloud before.

Carter liked my joke, grinning. His head tilted, leaning forward to talk quietly. "I just received a call from the Harris County Public Health Department. Contact tracers have found others ill in the same way as Dash, in the family he represented. Two members have died. One's still in the hospital. Another only had cold-like symptoms. The rest of the family was unaffected. Whatever's happened, it's become a bigger deal. I've asked them to contact me until you or Dash are ready to take this on."

"Is it Ebola or somethin' like that?" I asked.

"I don't believe so, but I don't believe they know what it is either." He stopped speaking and reared back to allow Kailey inside the backseat of the car.

"Dad, tell Mom we'll see her in seven days, so she stops crying," Kailey said. "And we need to move here. It's better than Northern Virginia, and Mom won't miss Beau, and all the rest of them."

She dropped it like it was hot while playing her game on her phone.

"Pretend like you love me, Beau," she said dramatically, giving me a tight side hug. It was something she said and did regularly to lighten the mood, but the tears clogging her voice made it more pathetic than any other time.

"I'll call you tonight," Carter said, getting another quick kiss from his wife, before ducking inside the vehicle.

"I think we need to move New Year's Eve to New York City this year," my mom said, tugging tissues from her jeans pocket.

"Oh no. Not flyin' four small children to New York City to celebrate a fireworks show with the four small children previously mentioned. Especially when I can give them sparklers in the backyard and they're just as happy." The tease landed like I hoped, everyone chuckled.

"I never looked at it that way," my mom said, beaming up at me. "I wanted to make memories. You have memories with your grandparents."

"Huh." I winked down at her. "We never went anywhere except here. And Mia might have a chance at skippin' a stone properly, but if a frog hops by, she's gone, hoppin' away with it. But the roughly ten acres behind us has come up for sale." I pointed over my shoulder with my thumb.

"I hear you. I hear all of you," Carter said, reaching for the car door to shut in our faces. He lowered the window, adding, "Let's get Dash well then go from there."

On that note, the car drove away. Once it was out of sight, we finally turned toward the house. She held on to me tightly. "I never said it, but the way Dash kept declining so quickly, I was afraid this wasn't going to end well." She untangled from me, wiping the tears under her eyes. "I didn't let myself go deeper. I tried to be present in your place, but now that he's safe at home, on the mend, it's all emotionally overwhelming. I love that guy."

"I think he's overwhelmed too," I said, slowly climbing the steps as she trailed behind me.

"I'm not overwhelmed. You are," Dash called hoarsely with humor through the open living room window. My eyes narrowed, seeing him clearly. He was supposed to be in bed where I'd left him, and he'd outsmarted me again. Now I had to remember to push that wheelchair out of reach.

"I like the idea of them moving closer." I lifted my finger, shaking it at him.

His *I-got-you* laughter was music to my ears.

14: The Overdo
Beau/Dash

Beau

Three Days Later

"You're overdoin' it," I said with force, glaring at Dash in the bathroom mirror. I was seconds away from a big fucking fit right here inside our bathroom. "I'm not gonna say it again."

"I feel like that's untrue," Dash said, squirting a decent amount of toothpaste on his brush, ignoring me completely.

"You clearly don't love me enough to do the important parts of a fast recovery."

"I love you beyond reason. You know that," Dash said calmly, splashing water on his toothbrush.

"You had back-to-back therapy appointments today," I said to his profile, tossing out a hand because it needed to be thrown out, no other reason. Definitely not for Dash to try and understand reasonableness. That was never going to happen. "You should be asleep right now. Dammit, you're a frustratin' man. Why do I have to keep sayin' this? Did you lose brain cells while you were sick?"

"Maybe," he replied. "Makes sense. I like the beard, it frames your face perfectly. Makes your eyes pop."

I instantly turned to the mirror to assess the growth. Beards were weird. They itched. There was literally zero way to keep it clean when you ate. I felt gross, always bringing the napkin to my lips after every bite. But I didn't have to shave much. We'd see how it went. "You think? I think the light facial hair was complex enough to deal with. This takes it to a different level."

"Keep it. If I ever build an arousal again, I'm gonna like that between my ass cheeks. Well, I'll enjoy it in every way." Dash bent to rinse his mouth, then dried his lips before rising again to stare at his own frail, skinny body in the mirror. Eventually his gaze rose to his hair. "I'm thinking about keeping it longer. It needs a style. Lauren's coming over next Sunday to shape and dye it. What'd you think?"

Our gazes collided in the mirrored glass. "You always look good anytime you change it up. Try it. If you don't like it, change it again," I said. Fashion and design were always his go-to distractions. I only went along with whatever he wanted if it didn't cost a lot of money.

"Fake it 'til you make it," he muttered, which was his anthem these days.

That phrase bothered me. It didn't speak of allowing his energy to return in a healthy manner. To prove my point, Dash's entire body swayed to the left. My hands darted out, grabbing his chest to keep him upright.

"You'll have a setback if you don't make better choices, and I'm tired of sayin' it to you. If you want me to continue to help you, then you fuckin' need to rest, eat the small meals we bring to you, take warm showers sittin' on the chair, and take the medicine for your cough. You handle the therapists' programs like a pro, but you're pushin' yourself too hard durin' your downtime. We also have to do better at readin' the summary of your day, and what's comin' at you the next day."

"Fucking?" he quipped, at my use of the word. "That's my word. And what happened to you not talking about it with me anymore? You just said you weren't saying it again."

He knocked the faucet handle to turn off the water. Fatigue etched fine lines in the corners of his eyes. They were turning into deep ruts. The skin over his mouth stretched across his teeth. He was seriously skinny. I'd thrown away his array of pajama pants, and helped him into a pair of fitted boy shorts and a T-shirt that three weeks ago highlighted his small belly. Now, the fabric hung off him.

"Help me to bed," he asked sensually rather than mechanically, but I knew the truth, he'd never manage to get to the mattress on his own. He tossed an arm around my neck, his body angling against mine. We began the slow walk to the bed.

"If you'd let me carry you, we'd be faster. Your chill bumps wouldn't spring up," I said, focusing on his steps as we angled through the door into the bedroom.

"Changing your tactics?" he spit out. "Just say you want to turn on the heater."

I almost sighed as he dove into another regular disagreement. I liked the room's temperature to be warmer than ice cold.

"Beau, I need to push myself, otherwise I might not shake this." Dash grabbed for the edge of the furniture to help him stay upright as if I'd ever drop him. "I can't stand for my cock to be limp when you're around. It's never happened before. I at least plump when I see you. What happens if I don't get running properly again? You're a sexual guy—"

I covered his lips with my palm, stopping the insanity of his explanation and excuses.

"Can I just record a message to you?" I asked. "Because it's been days since you've been home, and you won't allow the truth to sink into your thick skull. Your body's healin', and you're overly-exhausted. Of course, you can't grow hard. Recovery requires time, rest, and effort with the therapy team, and you have to eat the food made for you."

"Apparently, I'm not into rice or soggy vegetables. I like more consistency to them. I enjoyed the spaghetti squash meal you made, but it needed salt and pepper. And there's something funky in that smoothie. It tastes like what soap smells like. Maybe it's too spinach-y. And it needs more honey or date sugar, something to sweeten it."

Slow and steady, we finally made it to his side of the bed. "Thank you for tellin' me. I'll amend the recipes. You liked the roasted vegetables, right?"

"I like them a lot," Dash said. "The carrots too. Those hit for me. At some point soon, I need to check in at the office," Dash murmured, stifling a yawn as he took a sitting position on the edge of the bed. My palm popped up to cover his mouth again. I didn't want to hear it, yet he still chatted through the stifle. "I've barely spoken to my staff in weeks. They're too inexperienced. They need me. I've only gotten this level of talent because I've recruited them when they're green. Others didn't see their potential." He shoved away my hand when I didn't move it voluntarily. "I'll have Stone come by..."

"Dash, get underneath the blankets." Shockingly, he minded this time, but I had to scoop his legs up and help him move better onto the mattress. "We both can talk on the phone with Stone."

Again, his defiant glare met mine. "Beau, I don't need a nurse. I need you to help me rehab back, not keep me in this bed. You know how to do all this. Feed me good tasting food, not hospital quality. You know all the proteins and macros and how they work together. Help my physical therapist. Learn what they're doing and exercise with me when they're gone. It's why I'm home now instead of the hospital. Please help me."

After I tucked him in, I caressed his cheek until he turned to stare at me eye to eye. "That's what I've been tryin' to tell you. Recovery from somethin' this debilitatin' is a balance. In the hospital, you weren't tryin' to be everywhere. You worked out, did all the therapies, then rested. Your meals were custom created. You'll grow exponentially better every single day like you did in the hospital. Augh."

Dash cocked a brow at me. At least something between us cocked.

"Dash, you have all the tools to do everything right," I said calmly. "Your errors are with tryin' to do too much too fast without downtime for recovery. You're not bein' lazy or unproductive when you're restin'. Read those law books you drag around all the time, that way when you're ready, you'll hit the ground runnin'."

His pretty blue eyes eased as understanding set in. "I miss our alone time. You want me in this bed then get in here with me. We've never gone this long without being together."

"We have been apart longer than this. When we were in Chicago, you were workin' with your best friend, Lon. I was kicked out of that role without a backward glance. So, I hired a sex worker to take care of me when you began all those late nights, because no matter how I tried, I didn't fit in."

I dropped that somewhat untrue statement while having to mash my lips together to keep from laughing at his outlandish expression, and went for my side of the bed.

"Humor doesn't suit you," Dash murmured.

"Alexa, turn off the overhead bedroom lights." The dogs lumbered inside the room to their doggie beds in the corner. I gathered the therapy notes from today and scooted close to Dash, tucking pillows behind my back to sit at Dash's same angle.

A ravaging cough came out of nowhere. It was brutal. My one hand went to his back, rubbing upward to help push the gunk up. With my other hand, I reached for the boxes of tissues, shoving several into the hand covering his mouth. Several moments later, he gathered himself, and croaked out. "Read."

I did, under the soft glow of the lamps on our nightstands. "It says you're improvin' on your therapies, but you need to rest more and your lungs need a break," I said, my knees rose to balance the papers on my thighs.

"No, it doesn't say that." Dash twisted his upper body until we were old-schooling it with his head laid on my chest, his arm circling around me, keeping him in place against me. I circled an arm around him, making sure we stayed connected. I'd sleep just like this to better help him get through the coughing spells.

"It also says there's a moderate risk that you aren't my soulmate. That my actual soulmate doesn't argue with me so much."

"See how stupid treatment plans are?" Dash murmured. Seconds later, he began to snore, deep puffs of breath tickling my chest hair.

I placed the folder on the nightstand and tucked my hand around his head, my thumb gently swiping over his hair. Sea Springs had several new and trendy plant-based restaurants and stores, and a meal prep company to order from. There was also one that fascinated me, because it sold different levels of mineral water. My kind of store.

Dixie came to the edge of the bed. It was funny how they still asked to go outside when the doggie door was feet away. I motioned her out, trying to envision what the next few months looked like for us.

"Alexa, turn off the bedroom lamps," I whispered, the room went dark. I stared at the ceiling, wishing for sleep to take my mind off what the future looked like.

Dash

Six days later
Thanksgiving parade

The silence inside my empty home always gave an eerie vibe. Before I broke all of Beau's overstated rules, I locked the dogs out of the house to keep them from getting underfoot, confining them to the backyard.

For the most part, I felt steady on my feet, managing to walk short distances on my own from my bed to the bathroom. But I regularly found myself out of breath, needing frequent rest periods before I started again. And stubbornly I refused to use this silly walker when anyone else was home.

Today, though, I conserved my energy. Dressed in their finest Thanksgiving costumes, the girls and the rest of the family had left for their school performance. They were beyond thrilled to celebrate a holiday they hadn't known existed until weeks ago. Though, they did wish the holiday had gift giving associated with it. And they weren't a hundred percent clear on why we give thanks, after all, according to everything they knew to this point, the Native Americans and pilgrims needed to thank each other for their friendship. Boy, learning that truth was going to hit hard.

But the turkey thawing in the refrigerator was officially given the name George by Amelia, and had regular eyes checking on its status of defrost. The girls loved the entire process.

I was on my sixth full lap around the kitchen table, weaving through the living room and making a turn through the bedroom. When fatigue overwhelmed me, I rested for no more than five minutes. I also relied on the breathing techniques I had learned to help my lungs to continue to expand properly, without giving out. Other than that, I gripped the walker as if it were an extension of my body.

As my feet changed gait to include a shuffle, I'd take a tumble if I didn't take another break. But thanks to my superior time management skills, I anticipated my clan arriving home soon with pizza in hand. Which meant I needed to get back to bed before Beau went berserk because he thought I was overdoing it.

Like clockwork, the headlights of the Tahoe circled the inside wall of the living room. They pulled into the front of the house. A bead of sweat trickled down my temple as I hurried to stash the walker and open the doggie door for the two greeters to meet the rest of the family.

With a brief glance in the bathroom mirror, I caught my reflection and quickly tucked the longer strands behind my ears. There wasn't much of a style, but the grown-out pieces didn't look bad. The dark roots weren't near as dark as I remembered. Maybe I had a new look.

As for the rest of me, I still appeared gaunt, too skinny, and looked old, but not as bad as before.

"Daddy! We're home. Paw got us pizza as a treat," Ava called from across the house, her flat-footed run clomping toward me. Duke and Dixie's claws clicked on the tile floor keeping stride with her.

"We got cheese pizza for us," Mia yelled louder. "And pepperoni for everyone else."

The level of excitement meant this pizza dinner, which Beau had contrived with no pushing from me, was really something special. Finally, he understood the excitement of breaking the rules now and then.

"And apple juice boxes," Livie shouted, probably with the most excited voice of all three. "Paw said you talked him into giving us treats every so often and I believe our parade is often."

West tossed out incoherent babble, not to be outdone by his sisters. Ava met me at the bedroom door, still in her brightly-colored costume, her face beaming at me. "Do you want to watch the performance in your room, or the living room? Paw said we can eat in here with you if we sit still and not spill," she explained. "Gigi's gonna give West a bath. He spilled down his shirt. Abuela's gonna watch her shows."

What was happening inside this home? Beau never allowed meals outside of the kitchen. Ava read me like a book, shrugging. "Paw's being different. At the end of the show, Paw gave us a bunch of flowers from you and him, and you weren't there to hear thank you."

Joy filled my heart with her reasoning. "That's nice. I'm glad we did that for y'all," I said, gripping onto the doorframe. My legs wobbled. "Y'all can come in here. That'll be fun."

She dashed away, squealing at the top of her lungs. "Paw! He said yes."

As I started for the bed, I heard the pounding of their tennis shoes, a flat-footed run from across the house. I climbed in, readying myself for the onslaught.

"Paw, bring the pizza."

Within seconds, Ava's shoes were flung to the side, and she sat crisscrossed in the middle of the bed.

"I have the plates and napkins!" Mia hollered as she burst into the bedroom like a whirlwind.

"Mia, get a big towel for the bed," I said, settling into my place on the mattress. Tonight, it felt good to be off my feet. She bounded onto the bed, left the plates and napkins in Ava's care, and rolled off the other side, disappearing inside the bathroom.

Everyone else entered the room at the same time. Beau held pizza boxes, napkins, and a six pack of apple juice boxes. We never had apple juice, because Beau worried about their teeth. Mia tossed the towel at me as she climbed on the bed, kicking her shoes off. They flew in different directions. Livie still wore her head gear, flowers, apples, and corn stalks popped out the top of the headband.

"They're eating on the bed?" I asked, tossing out the towel. They had their seats before the towel fully floated down.

"With lots of rules," Beau teased, not giving me the hundred percent win. He placed the pizza boxes on the dresser as he listed the conditions. One finger popped out to indicate the first. "They have to act like regular human bein's or we're done."

No argument from me. Joyful laughter erupted from the girls.

A second finger popped up. "No roughhousin'." That sounded reasonable.

A third finger followed. "Drinks stay on the nightstand. If you want a drink, ask quietly so your dad can hear everything you said."

Wow, three out of three. Beau and I were in sync again.

"We don't roughhouse," Livie said, her happiness laced with a tinge of her Paw being ridiculous. "We're girls."

"Really?" Beau asked, giving her a silly obvious look, and pointed to Ava. "I think y'all could show boys how to roughhouse properly."

"Paw's funny."

Beau went through the process of opening all the juice boxes, allowing everyone to take a sip before they went to his nightstand. I got to keep mine on my side. Plates and napkins were distributed, and small sliced pizza was passed around. He gave me two slices of pepperoni.

I realized Beau's plan of attack for my health was to parent me. How had I not figured that out before? And I acted like a child. Oh my god, we were dysfunctional. Thoughts of Daddy spanking me just turned yuck.

When everyone had what they needed, Beau plugged his cell phone into the television's input panel and navigated the touch screen until the still video of a crowded pre-school auditorium filled the screen.

"Daddy, we come in on the right," Ava said, staring at the screen.

Livie instantly corrected her. "The left."

"We look the same though," Mia interjected. "Nobody could tell us apart." Yeah, that was going to be a real problem someday too. Beau took his place in a side chair close to me. "I sometimes tell people I'm Mia and they don't know I'm not. Livie won't do it, but me and Mia change bows too. Nobody knows."

And there we go. They were officially naughty and figured out a major life hack that was going to make Beau and I crazy.

"Only me and Mia. Livie's not fun. She's smart and bossy," Ava popped out with hints of insult. "She can't be a little bad ever."

"So you know that what you and Mia did was wrong?" I asked, all three heads turned my way, no remorse on their pretty faces and nodded. They were so dang confident.

"We only do it at school," Mia added, as if that made it better.

"Remember, you never pretend to be each other to adults or in important situations," Beau explained and pointed us toward the television.

How about they never pretend to be each other?

The volume elevated then instantly lowered, the screen paused when Linda came to the open doorframe, holding West on her hip. "We came to say goodnight."

"Come join us," Beau said, lifting out of the chair, motioning for his mom to take the seat. "Pizza's on the dresser, extra juice boxes are there too." As he took West from her, the little guy was growing so fast, he headed for his side of the bed. The space between us became West's play space. When Linda took her seat near me, Beau started the performance again. Tears developed in my eyes with pride for my girls. There were perfect performers. I wondered if everyone envied their greatness.

# 15: The December Dash/Beau/Dash

Dash

Twelve Days Later

"You're killing me, babe," I said, breaking the oppressive silence in the vehicle. "Your obstinance isn't going to change anything. I'm going back to work."

Bossy Beau was chauffeuring me at a snail's pace, at least five miles per hour below the speed limit, to protect me from... Well, I didn't know what. The weight of his displeasure hung heavily in the air. And the regular fifteen-to-twenty-minute journey from our garage to my parking space in front of my office had stretched into a torturous thirty-minute ordeal.

I bet everyone who had ever known my husband understood what a pain in the ass he was when the micromanaging surfaced.

The stone-faced giant had ultimately given in and was driving me to the office, only because the other option I'd offered was to drive myself. Apparently, there was no universe that would allow such a thing, making him more frustrated with me.

"Without the doctor's approval," Beau muttered through gritted teeth. He kept his gaze fixed stubbornly on the road ahead.

I gave an exaggerated eye roll and dropped my head on the seat's headrest. "Beau, I did what you said. You were right. There's a process of healing. You're a miracle worker. I'm getting myself back more and more every day. Going to the office to sit behind my desk... It takes nothing out of me and does everything to help my perspective."

"*Pfft*," Beau said. The single syllable was loaded with tons of contempt.

"Did you just *pfft* me?" I asked, irritation bubbling up as we circled back to the argument we'd had all morning. "What's that even mean? And I *pfft* you right back."

"*Pfft*," Beau said louder, dismissively. "You lied to me."

"No, I didn't." At least he shouldn't know any of the half-truths I'd told him since we first met. "When did I lie?"

Beau finally looked at me when he turned into my designated parking spot in front of the law firm's front doors. His expression was one of betrayal and resignation. "Go on to the place that matters the most to you," he said, his grip tightening on the steering wheel. His other hand tossed out in a silent *pfft* this time.

"You know that's not true, Beau. I haven't been here in six weeks."

"I know that you were always overdoin' your rehab, walkin' the house with your walker until exhaustion. So much for my miracle healin' abilities," Beau said bitterly, turning his head forward, refusing to look at me.

So much for being sly. My heart sank. "I only did what the therapist suggested."

"Lie," Beau repeated, his voice final and unwavering.

"Please don't have me going in there like this. It's already overwhelming to consider the sheer volume of work waiting for me. It'll be a challenge to get caught up. This office pays our bills. I need to get a rundown on what's happened while I was away," I explained, staring at the etched glass of the entry door. My law firm. I was proud of my accomplishments. The journey wasn't easy, but he and I did it together.

Physically, I was still a shell of the man I once was. The suit I chose to wear today was one I wore ten years ago when I was much younger and way hotter. At a time when my hair was mostly blond, but I was regaining weight and muscle. My lungs were still struggling, but I knew the signs to watch for. I didn't plan to overdo it. There was literally no reason to keep me from the office.

"Since we're suddenly ready to get back to normal," he started, his tone clipped, "I spoke to our banker. Any account I'm on has minimal funds. Why don't I know that we don't have money? And I'm reimbursing Carter because I get that he's been takin' care of us. That's my job, and I'll borrow from my 401K."

Wow. How had I not realized how thick Beau's calves had to be from all the jumping to conclusions he was doing. When I took over our finances, I vowed to take care of our family. How could he think otherwise? Every dollar I made went to the betterment of us.

I didn't try to justify a thing. Walking a few laps around the interior of our house shouldn't make anyone angry. I reached for the door handle, pushing it open. My increased heart rate messed with my breathing which wasn't good. I hopped out and managed a slight slam as I sent the door flying shut behind me.

Beau

I didn't know how long I planned to sit in front of Dash's office, but I was three hours in, and my face was fatigued from holding an angry glare. My arms were tired from being crossed, fist tucked under my forearm to help hold the flex.

The sudden ring startled me. My mom's name appeared on the screen, allowing me to relax the tense hold, and I reached for the accept option.

"Hi, Mom," I said kindly because I wasn't the militant monster Dash accused me of being. I was head over heels for my guy. But he wasn't the only one navigating the healing phase of his random, unexplainable, and nearly deadly illness. It was tough watching him banging on death's door.

"Hey, babe, I have some news I want to discuss with you before we proceed," she said.

"Okay, what's up?" I asked cautiously.

"The land behind your house, extending from the back of the grove of trees to the property behind the Lee's house is for sale. We're considering purchasing it to build our primary home. We'd like to be closer to the kids, you know that. What're your thoughts? If it doesn't sound like a good idea, tell me."

"I'm completely fine with it. I'd like to see Kailey more. The kids are crazy about you and Carter. Amelia refuses to slow down and take some time off. Maybe she'll trust you with the kids. She has this weird belief about how Dash being in the hospital means something dark was surrounding us. I don't know. I didn't understand her explanation. She needs downtime to sort through all her feelings. Can you build it now?"

"I had my worries we'd be a little too much for you. It's funny how we're back to the same place I started my life. You went off and crafted this fabulous life for us all. I'm excited..."

I glanced back at the office. Five or six of Dash's employees surrounded him, standing in front of the lobby window. Dash lifted his hand in a patronizing wave, or maybe not. Perspective rapidly evolved for me. He did look better; his playful spark was back. My guy might be tough with everyone else but tried to be kind and present for me.

Dash moved from the group, heading toward the main entrance like a man on a mission. In a flash, he was rushing to the truck.

"Mom, I'll call you back." My finger pressed the end call button before I finished the sentence.

He flung open the passenger door, his intense stare locked on mine as he hopped inside. "Get us somewhere private," he murmured, working quickly to latch the seat belt in place.

"What for?" I stammered, but the sense of urgency automatically had me starting the SUV and dropping the gearshift in reverse.

"Let's make a baby," he blurted out.

I stomped on the brake, halting us halfway between the parking space and the road. My guy flung forward, the seat belt catching him due to the sudden stop. "Dash, that can wait."

Both his hands sliced through the air, V-ing together to draw my attention to the massive hard-on inside his tight slacks. "We were teasing you as I realized my stunning guy's so devoted to me that he spent his day in wait, ready to help if needed. My balls began to tingle and my dick went stiff. I'll come fast, but not here. Go to the back of the building."

Funny how all the squabbling stopped the moment we finally got on the same page. My cock built in record speed, my mouth began to water. The dedicated focus I had on taking care of my sick husband shifted in an instant. I was going to make love to him so hard.

Dash

"How do you know about this spot," I asked, eyes wide as Beau drove us off the beaten path into a jungle of tall grass and weeds.

"Did you forget I'm basically a local road map?" Beau shot back, lifting the gearshift into park. "I know every inch of this side of town."

Instead of coming at me to solve the problem in my pants, he left the SUV. The engine was running, and I was left alone inside the vehicle. Just when I was about to explain my situation—that maybe he misunderstood my arousal—the back door swung open, and he started unbuckling the car seats and placing them on top of the truck.

"I'll help," I said and reached for the door handle.

"Let me do it, Dash. Conserve your energy. We'll go slow. It won't take long." The middle seat dropped to make a flat surface. He shut that door and went to the back of the truck and removed that row of car seats. He was brilliantly efficient, and I unfastened my belt buckle. My heart pumped excitedly, my breath slightly labored. Fuck it, I'd figure it out.

My door swung open, Beau standing there. His big chest heaved while pulling his T-shirt over his head. "If it gets too wild, we hit the brakes. Agreed?" The T-shirt landed on the floorboard at my feet. "I'll do all the work. Less effort on you."

"Oh yeah." I had believed he and I would make out then rub one off, but Beau was a man with far better ideas. He carefully took his blue jeans off, standing on top of his shoes.

"Undress in the car, then crawl over the console. There are stickers out here, the little fuckers hurt like hell." He stood before me, nude. His cock hard and proud. I fisted his shaft, giving a solid tug. "I got the lube from the hidey spot."

"I never had any idea you moved so fast," I said.

He knocked my hand away.

"Less talkin', more action." The door closed in my face. I hustled to remove my clothes like a Tasmania devil on six Red Bulls. The car rocked as Beau climbed in, positioning his big body. I heard the snick of the lube's cap, the tropical scent filled the small space, urging me to crawl into the back where our picnic blanket was spread out.

My guy built a paradise in the backseat. My hard-as-stone cock quivered as I watched Beau sticking his slick fingers into his ass, loosening his hole, normally my job. The sight of his perfect ass, flexing as he scissored his fingers, working himself open, caused my arm to slip out from underneath me. I toppled halfway over the console like a horny teenage boy chasing after this same guy.

"You good?" he asked, pausing his fingers in his ass. The other hand circled his thick cock, rubbing up and down.

"So good. Only lost in the view of my gorgeous husband. But I enjoy being the one to get you ready for me," I murmured and licked my bottom lip before pushing the flesh between my teeth. My dick swelled, my balls drew up with need. Beau's breath puffed like a dragon, filling the silence inside the truck, sending delightful goose bumps dancing up my spine. It might be my favorite sound on earth. My skin heated and flushed, transforming me into the steely predator I used to be. I crawled between Beau's spread thighs. The palm on his cock slowed on the upstroke.

"I started without you." Beau delivered the truth then winked at me. I loved a well-placed wink. "Because you're so slow."

My grin grew broader. I missed my playful tease of a husband.

"You set the pace," Beau said, lying on his back, spreading his thighs wide. His hands reached for my forearms, bringing me over his body. Nineteen years of making love to Beau and he was still entirely too tempting. The excitement grew, my mouth needed to be on his, with his strong arms draped over me, keeping me close, gently caressing my skin with his calloused palms and fingertips.

When I made it close to Beau's lips, I soaked in every detail of my man.

His stunning face, strong bearded jaw, and twinkling amber eyes, did it for me every time. "I love you."

"I love you." Beau's lips quirked into a soft grin. "You always slow us down when we're supposed to be quick."

That was no lie but look at my playground. "You touch a place inside me that I crave and can't get there without you."

I trailed my fingers across the velvet steel of his torso until I reached Beau's tight nipple where I rolled the small bead between my thumb and forefinger, twisting and tugging at the nub. Beau loved good nipple play, and his hips curled against my thigh. His big body tucked into mine. His strong hand cupped my head, pulling me to kiss his lips. With my other hand, I found his second nipple. He trembled. His tongue licked out, tasting me in a sweet sampling of lips, melding his mouth against mine.

Within seconds, the kiss turned passion-filled, instantly racing to needy. His rumbled groan tripped up my heart, as he ate my mouth like a delicious meal to a starving man.

We had a lot of making up to do. Beau's body had always been my wonderland. I pushed back, breaking the kiss to stare at the two steel rods between our bodies. Fast was important, being caught by the local police wouldn't be good for either one of us, but I had to taste his cock before much more happened. My mouth watered as I reached for his shaft and pressed a kiss against the salty drop of pre-come at his tip. I licked my lips, then took a swipe up his length, preparing to take him into my mouth.

I'd missed Beau's cock. The feel and weight of him inside my mouth teased every single one of my senses.

Whatever issues I had with my body, all the aches and pains I had dealt with for almost two months, all eased as peace filled the cracks keeping me from healing. On my second pass over his cock, a possessive growl sounded from above. He experienced the same connection; we were again one.

In direct contrast to everything I was feeling, Beau's hands came to my chin, lifting my mouth off of him.

"Later," he murmured huskily. Hot flashes of searing amber held me in place. "Spend more time, later."

My palms caressed and tickled over his muscular belly. "I feel better. Much better. Let's do this properly," I said, pressing my lips against his oblique.

"Stay focused," Beau said. "We can go to bed early tonight, spend the night makin' up for lost time, but right now, we have to speed this along." A squirt of lube poured over my cock, his hand spreading the slick down. "Lie down, Dash."

I tucked my lip between my teeth, needing the soft flesh. I could've put up a fight, but my guy was a brick wall in every way, and he was doing this all for me. Beau rolled to the side, reaching for me to join him in the way he wanted. I did what my caveman asked and took my place, my back against the blanket. Beau lifted to straddle me, knees against my torso. He gripped my cock, giving another tug, as he moved on top of me.

"I'm gonna fuck you good later," Beau murmured, teasing my tip against his hole. "Everything you want, all the things I've missed, but not right now. Let me love you. Then let's go home."

Anticipation churned in my balls. My guy eased down on top of me, going slow as he adjusted to the size of my cock. The muscles and cords around his neck and shoulders tensed and flexed. His eyelids slid closed. He sat on me, breathing in short, crisp bursts, taking most of me on the first descent. Blinding pleasure arched my back. I fisted my hands in the air as I screwed my eyes shut. Beau surrounded me with scorching heat, burning me from the outside in. He rose to my tip, then came down again, seating fully on top of me.

"Breathe through it, baby."

Yeah, as soon as I could. "You're a god," I whispered, all mouthy and breathless.

He moved his hips with controlled purpose. His strong stomach muscles rolled in fluid ripples, matching the cadence he created. Slow and sensual. I lifted my hips, moving together as one, our bodies perfectly in sync. The pleasure built swiftly when Beau rolled his hips against me.

My body quivered. I tried to follow his rhythm, desperately wanting to meet him push for push. Beau reverently caressed my hips and stomach before grasping and squeezing his hard cock.

"You're so fucking tight," I whispered, my hooded gaze barely stayed focused on the beautiful sight before me. I was already barely holding on by a thread. "How do you do it?"

"Let me, Dash," he groaned when my hips began to piston with his. My breath turned ragged. Beau's moves became desperate and jerky as he fought for control of his body. Of course I didn't want this to end. I gripped his cock with both hands, desperately wanting his release to spill inside my hands and over my body. He needed to mark me, stake his claim. Beau clutched my forearms, helping me stay upright.

"Oh yeah." All of the feelings coasted over me. The deep binding connection kept us together. The oneness had me moving my hips faster against his. My world was a thing of unbridled beauty.

"Right fuckin' there," Beau hissed, panting under the exertion. "That's it. Come with me, baby," Beau managed through gritted teeth. His head reared back, giving into his own blinding pleasure.

"You..." I managed. The way his ass gripped my cock, milked my orgasm free.

He tumbled forward, landing me on my back. He caught himself on his elbows before crushing my body. Every single movement and sound played in technicolor. The second he slipped from me, I wrapped my arms and legs around his body. A bead of sweat ran the length of Beau's temple, landing on my cheek with a splash. I wanted our physical connection to last forever.

Our hearts beat in unison. This was where Beau and I excelled. His forehead rested against mine. "You're still breathin' heavy."

"It'll be fine," I whispered. "Listen to me. Our money's making money. You have access to it all. The joint account information is in the safe with our wills and other important documents. I've always been an *us* guy, even when it didn't seem like it." I tightened my arms around Beau when he tried to move off me. His familiar gaze set on me.

"I'm sorry about..." I covered his mouth from saying anything more.

"Carter didn't pay for anything, but I like how you wanted to be the one caring for me. We have UPS health insurance, which is still pretty good, but I also pay for a secondary insurance policy for all of us. That information is in the safe too. We'll probably have to pay for the therapy done at home, at least part of it."

Beau managed to break my hold, bringing me to my side, facing him. He propped his head on one hand and rested the other in the dip leading to my hip.

"I have my 401K. If we need to, we can take out a loan against it."

"You're a sweet guy..." I started, only to have Beau laugh in my face.

"Says no one ever," he scoffed.

"Yeah, you're probably right," I said honestly. "But I love the way you love me. Always looking out for me. I'm important to you."

Beau tried his best to hide a grin. It didn't work.

PART 2

16: The Huff
Dash/Beau

Dash

June 2023

"Chop, chop," I hollered from the bottom of the staircase. "We're in the final stretch."

"What does chop, chop mean?" Mia asked from the top of the stairs on the second floor, inhibited from her descent due to the professional-grade gates we had installed at the top and bottom of the staircase. "And final stretch? Does that mean the reporter person's almost here?"

"It means he wants us to get downstairs for a once-over to make changes before the *Huffington Post* reporter arrives," Livie explained, coming to stand beside her sister, seemingly distracted. Her concentration and fingers worked deftly at adjusting the midsection of her dress. "I can't get my belt to lay properly. I don't like wrinkles, Daddy. Trade me belts, Mia."

"Liv, I'll help you," Beau called from somewhere on the second floor.

With a sigh, I dropped my chin to my chest as Mia and Livie left the gate to make the wardrobe change. Seconds ago, I'd only needed four more children plus my husband at the gate to get my whole family downstairs. Now, we were back to seven missing members.

"Fisher, go stand by the gate and keep your hands tucked in your pockets. Hunter, stay by my side. West, get your boots on, man. I shouldn't have to ask you twice."

Hearing my love wrangle our children into order sent happiness shooting through my system.

"Like Fisher can ever do that," Ava said loudly.

"Maybe today he can," Mia, always the positive one, argued on his behalf.

I was compelled to trot up the stairs to save my little champ. Fisher was our overactive two-and-a-half-year-old. Being made to stand alone would be a fate worse than death for him.

Beau and I now had six vibrant children, all bursting with uniquely different personalities. West was like Beau's mini-me, mirroring him in looks and words—our pint-size cowboy in training. Since West was the first male in either the Richmond-Brooks or Lee families, Scott also had a pretty solid influence on my oldest son. Only time would tell how that might play out.

Behind Fisher in age came Hunter, who was biologically Beau's son. They had a year between them. Whatever trouble Fisher found himself in, Hunter was there with him too. One of Fisher's favorite pastimes was to tackle Hunter. Hunter was taller and bigger than Fisher who was my biological son. They'd happily roll around on the floor no matter where we were, wrestling until pieces of furniture and decorations lay in rubble.

They'd even knocked over a cereal-stocked endcap at the grocery store while in Amelia's care. She adored those little guys but had developed a strict policy against going out in public with them unless additional adult supervision came along for the ride.

Fisher and Hunter were a handful for Duke and Dixie too. By the dog's very nature, they couldn't resist the urge to join in on their fun. Other times, the dogs were vigilant watchdogs, barking to alert us whenever the boys took their fun times too far.

Who knew that having two boys so close in age could create such chaos?

I hoisted Fisher over the gate, placing him on his feet. "Hold my hand. We'll go down together."

Hunter came sprinting toward me, eager for a lift too. I left Fisher at the gate at the bottom step. "Stay here, hands in pockets. I'm going back for Hunter." West was now standing right beside Hunter. Good, three down, but the wrong three. Two minutes of waiting time and these three would make my super clean house a mess. I stared at Fisher, waiting for any sort of confirmation that he heard me.

He tucked his hands back into his pockets and nodded. On the pivot, I jogged back up the steps and lifted West over. He was handsome and dashing in his normal cowboy wear, but today, we were all color coordinated so his pearl button shirt was a fancy color.

I placed West on the step beside me. He could walk down without a problem, and hoisted Hunter up. I kept hold of him against my side as I started down. So maybe ten full seconds had passed since I pulled Fisher over, and my boy was already climbing over the bottom gate to get to the other side. "Hey! Fish, don't you do it."

He grinned proudly, clearly thrilled with his progress, and nodded his understanding while trying to move faster to get over the gate before I got to him. With Hunter still tucked under one arm, I made it to Fisher when his second leg rounded the top of the gate. I managed to grab the waistband of his khaki trousers to keep him from falling to the floor. "Fisher, you must behave today. This is not behaving."

"I think he should stay upstairs with Abuela. No chance, he's good on his own," West commented, clumping down the steps in his boots.

West wasn't wrong. I put Hunter on his feet and adjusted my grip on Fisher to bring him eye level. He looked less like me than the girls did, but he was still a cute little guy, with a good nature and free spirit. Even if I was quite possibly looking down the well of many different prison stays with all the trouble he was bound to get into. "Fisher, are you going to be good for me today?"

It was the same smile and nod as seconds ago. Such a charmer. "Yep."

"Good boy," I said. Either he didn't understand the meaning of "yep" or he just thought it was easier to agree with me and do what he wanted anyway, I wasn't sure. Either way, I didn't believe him. "And do you remember the code word we say whenever you need to settle down?" I asked.

"Fisher," he blurted and began kicking his feet in the air.

"Correct," I said, and put him down on the other side of the gate. "Please listen to us today. We have to be gentlemen while our company's here."

Shockingly, he stayed still as I opened the gate, and the other two boys went through. The rest of my pretty family followed into the space between the kitchen and living room.

The girls were in the same style dresses, adorned with flowers in the yellow and blue color palette the rest of us wore. Their sandals matched too. Fisher and Hunter wore the same outfits all the way down to their new runners.

I recognized the inequity for the girls. Each one had developed their own sense of style as well, but they were adorable when dressed alike. And today, how they appeared mattered more than their feelings on the matter. Yes, I was certain therapy was in their future.

"You look pretty," I said to Ava.

"Daddy, I look like a clown," she said, passing me.

"You can do this for me and Paw. It's for an hour tops. We'll take pictures first. You'll then talk to the reporters and say only nice things about our lives. After that, Gigi's waiting for you because I don't trust any of you not to be heathens." The children gravitated into a single file-line. "You look very nice," I said to Livie.

"You do too, Daddy," she said. I beamed at the compliment made from manners we instilled in them, not from any inspection she gave me. "I like the sandals because the flowers match the dress. I like when things match."

All three girls had skipped first grade, going straight into second grade, but Livie's intelligence was off the charts. She was so smart that it was becoming apparent that she was far more advanced than the courses she was being taught.

"Beautiful as ever, Mia."

"I'm meh about it." Mia passed, hopping off the last step then twirling her dress in a circle. "I like how flowy it is though."

Then, my guy brought up the rear. "Meh?" he teased Mia.

I swear time froze for me. He captured my attention and held it until he broke the spell, moving past me. "The color suits you."

I knew suits made him uncomfortable, so I opted for a snug, high-end athletic-style shirt and a pair of starched new blue jeans. Wranglers really highlighted both the front and the back of his body. New runners, the same style as the boys, brought the look together.

"Fisher, stay on the kitchen side of the house. Hunter, you stay on this end." Beau had hold of Hunter's shoulder and placed his back against the wall. "Troops, line up for inspection." Beau began to walk the line of our children, using a playful military tone. At the same moment, the doorbell rang. I left him to tuck in shirts and straighten pleats and bows. He also gave each one of them small words of encouragement.

As I went to the foyer, I heard Beau say, "Best behavior. Everyone helps Fisher be good without fightin' him."

"Why does Abuela not have to participate?" Ava murmured. "She handles Fisher the best."

"Because she's the matriarch of our family which means she does what she wants. She's the boss," Beau answered. I couldn't argue with the logic.

I opened the door and swung my hand out in invitation for our guests to enter. The subsequent greetings were efficient, if not louder than necessary on my end. My crew needed to be aware of the reporter was in the house. Her camera guy flanked nearby. Best behaviors began now.

"Come meet my family." As I rounded into the open-floor concept of the downstairs, pride swelled in my chest.

All the children circled Beau with Fisher on the outer edge, snapping his fingers together. His entire body wiggled while he mimicked me speaking. Our little guy was the fun cherry on top that made the scene perfect.

"Girls and boys, this is Ms. Pebbly, she's the reporter with *Huffington Post*, and this is Mr. Smith, the cameraman. They're here to talk to us about our lives for a segment for Pride month."

"Pride month's a time to celebrate our fathers' accomplishments, and the family they created," Livie explained to her brothers and sisters, giving a nod after her explanation.

"That's correct," Ms. Pebbly said. Livie beamed.

I began introductions from the top down and put on my best Vanna White display. "Let's start with Beau, my husband."

Ms. Pebbly shook Beau's hand, grasping him so tightly I wasn't sure she planned to let go.

"I'm Zoe. Thank you for allowing us inside your home."

"This is West," Beau continued for me. "Our triplets Liv, Mia, and Ava. Hunter's our youngest. Then Fisher, our middle son. He enjoys movement."

"Pleasure to meet you all."

"Nice to meet you too." They all chirped in unison. A practiced response we worked on over the years.

"Six children in seven years. That's ambitious," she said, pulling a portfolio from the bag hanging on her shoulder. People made those kinds of remarks as if we'd planned it that way, and I guess we had, but I never considered it a challenge to have back-to-back kids. Not that we'd had to carry them ourselves, but we'd been involved every step of the way. I'd have many more if I could get Beau to agree.

"Here's the itinerary for our afternoon together," she said, passing Beau, then me, a sheet of paper. Here was where problems originated. Exact schedules were hard to follow with six precocious children. Beau's pointed glare locked on mine.

They also wanted a tour of downtown Sea Springs where my office was located. They also wanted pictures of the family, but scheduled those at the end of the interview.

"We've set up a playdate with the kids to keep the chaos at bay. Can I tweak the schedule? We planned to take pictures on the patio. It's comfortable out there. You can chat with the girls while the boys play. We also have two German shepherds who are members of the family. Then Beau and I can sit with you as long as you'd like."

Again, I felt the intensity of Beau's laser-like glare boring into me. This time I chose to ignore it. Yes, I understood he and Scott had a full day of back-to-back charters. Beau had transitioned with UPS to a part-time position and had gone full-time with the charter company. Today, Scott and his father handled the load solo. Beau definitely held the weight of their burden.

"Let's check the lighting outside," the reporter chimed in, seemingly unfazed by my shift in scheduling.

Beau hurriedly stepped past Zoe to get to the door first, needing to give his command to keep the dogs from going nuts over new visitors. Duke and Dixie were waiting by the back door, already eager to participate. Beau stepped out, with instant control of the dogs. I wanted them in the family photo too.

"I know it's June, but we have a system that keeps the porch under climate control," I explained, encouraging the reporter outside ahead of me.

As I reached the back door, I heard Mia ask, "Do we come too, or do we stay here?"

Every one of the kids was standing where we'd left them, including Fisher who bounced like a jackhammer in place.

"Come, please." I waved them over to me.

"Fisher." The code word grabbed his attention. He instantly stopped moving and realized everyone but him was at the door. The little guy took off running toward us. I stopped him before he made it outside and bent close to his ear. "Remember to continue to be on your best behavior. We're snapping some family pictures first. Give me your picture smile." And he did, a brilliant grin he easily wore all of the time.

Ava and her smart mouth stuck her head back through the opening of the door.

"Yeah, then you play because no one wants to talk to you," Ava popped off. Fisher wasn't one to be bothered by his sister and pushed past her to find his brothers.

"Ava, only nice words and friendly voices," I disciplined like a broken record. People may think Fisher was the challenging one in the group with all his excess energy, but he was a breeze compared to Ava's bad attitude.

"I don't have any nice words or friendly voices, Daddy," she quipped, grinning. And yes, I did know that about her.

"Then try your best," I said, crossing my fingers for a good showing today.

Beau

How did Dash continually keep raising the bar? And how on earth did he magically turn our patio into a cool oasis during the scorching June Texas heat? I didn't even want to know how much all this cost, all the way down to the electricity we used.

Last year, he installed a drink station outside including an ice maker and a drawer-style refrigerator. Amelia had whipped up some pre-poured fresh lemonade with cherries inside. My only duty was to add ice in the adults' glasses and check the lids on the kids' squirt bottles. The more complicated feat was having to deliver these to the table without spilling anything.

"That's where my pop-pop and Gigi live," Livie said and pointed to the giant home behind ours.

"Their house is huge," Mia added the obvious. "Our uncle Scott lives next door. Daisy Mae's our cousin and she's seventeen years old." Mia's tone showed that she thought Daisy Mae's age was an amazing feat. "On the other side of Uncle Scott and Aunt Lauren's house, are our other grandparents, G-pa and Granny. We're all a close family, but not always with the same blood. Right, Paw?"

I grinned at her, loving how she included Scott's parents in her family circle. Outside of that freestyle, we'd practiced what to say, and she had done perfectly.

I balanced the tray and began passing out the glasses and kids' squirt bottles to the table. Once everything was delivered without spilling, I turned to the yard to call the boys over for their drinks. Whether Dash had seen them or not was questionable. Perhaps he hadn't wanted to call attention with the reporter there. But somehow, all three boys had reached new heights of naughty.

Duke came happily running past me with Fisher riding him bareback. His strong hands clung to Duke's fur, his body lying on the dog's back, bouncing as he passed by. West and Hunter ran beside them, urging Duke to go faster. Fisher wore a smile the size of Texas. I felt the joy of both dog and child.

All my boys, every last one of them, was in trouble over this one.

I took long strides toward them. "Guys, come get your drinks," I hollered. My tone relayed the message I really wanted to give: Get off my dog, and stop acting like delinquents.

Eight eyes landed on me. I saw the exact moment they realized they'd gone too far. Duke abruptly came to a halt. Fisher flew head over heels over Duke's head, who did his best to keep Fisher from getting hurt, circling his big body around to absorb the fall. The other two stared like deer in headlights. "Come get your drinks."

Again, not the invitation it seemed.

"Hey, Beau," my mom yelled, interrupting the intense whispered reprimand her grandsons were about to get. "Can they come over and play? When the girls are done, I made fresh peanut butter cookies."

By the time my mom finished, I'd made it to the boys who hadn't taken a step toward me. "Gigi saved you," I said sternly. "Don't ever ride Duke again. He's not made for that kind of play. You could have seriously hurt him. Do you hear me?"

"Yes, Paw," they said in unison. Their sad eyes stayed focused on me. I didn't fall for their sorrowful routine for even a second. They were worried because they got caught.

"Take your drink and go with Gigi," I whispered. "I'll come get you in a little bit. There's gotta be some sort of punishment for your bad behavior. You embarrassed your dad today. He does so much to make sure you have good lives, and he asked one thing of you. You couldn't give it to him. And now, I have to get Duke checked out..."

"No, Paw, Duke liked it," West interrupted.

My head might have exploded right then. "Go."

The three grabbed their drinks and took off running, Hunter doing his best to keep up. Duke and Dixie came from the other side of the yard, running toward the gate my mom opened. Those boys were a handful. For some reason, I wanted them to be smarter than I was at their age. I was almost to the table when I remembered the interview currently taking place.

"One last question before you go. How do you view your family?" The dumb question threw me off. I didn't like it one bit and planned to say that very thing when the three girls understood the inquiry in a different way and answered.

"We know that families are all different," Ava started. Mia nodded her support. "I think lots of our friends have a mom and dad, and that was weird to learn."

Mia nodded again. "It's weird."

"But we have a really great family. We love each other very much. Daddy and Paw are really good parents. They make our family whole," Livie said in a clearly thought-out explanation. "Paw's our schedule keeper and makes us follow the rules. He's worried about nutrition and the food we eat. He talks to us about the health of our bodies and sometimes makes us exercise with him in fun ways."

I'd made it to the back of their chairs. My palm squeezed Livie's shoulder. She glanced up and back, beaming at me.

"It's true, Paw." Livie's gaze landed on Dash. "Daddy's the one that laughs and plays with us and buys us things. He has to follow Paw's schedule too, but he's like our brothers. They break the rules as much as they follow them."

"I like when Daddy picks us up from school," Mia interjected. "He takes us for a treat. The other day he took me to the store to get new art supplies for my class, and I didn't even ask him."

"He also sneaks us candy," Ava said, telling on her dad. Dash's eyes darted to mine, and he lifted his thumb and forefinger to signal only a small bit of candy.

"Even though me and my sisters look the same, we're all different people," Livie said thoughtfully. "Paw and Daddy make sure we all get to be who we are. Ava likes the color black. She takes up for everyone who's hurting. Mia likes to go fishing with Paw. They like being outside together. I don't like dirt on anything. I'm really smart and like to read. I take ballet lessons. Paw and Daddy make sure we're able to do all the things we want. They do the same thing with my brothers. My parents are really good parents. Does that answer the question?"

Dash grinned and nodded.

"Wonderful perspective," Zoe said, taking notes as the film crew continued to film.

"Are we done?" Ava asked, taking a long slurping drink from her squirt bottle.

"We have to go to Gigi's before the boys eat all the cookies," Mia explained.

I was the one who decided the girls were finished. They had done Dash proud. We shouldn't jinx it. "Thank you, girls. Take your drinks and close the gate behind you."

I didn't have to tell them twice.

17: The Every Good Deed
Dash/Beau

Dash

"You've been together since you were teenagers. You met here in Sea Springs during summer vacation," she said, reading from her jotted notes. "Back in 2000. What was it like when you first met?"

"It was his fifteenth birthday," I said. "I was about a month shy of my sixteenth birthday. I was out but living in a bubble. He wasn't out yet. For me, I'd say awestruck might be the best way to describe the first time I saw him. How would you describe it?" I squeezed Beau's hand as I handed over the reins for an answer.

Beau smiled. "Head over heels, literally. The first time I saw him, I was ridin' a bike and crashed because I couldn't turn away from starin' at him. I went flyin' over the handlebars."

"Beau, you're from Alabama, a lifelong elite athlete until you left the university when your father died. Dash, you're from Dallas, skipping grades, attending private schools." She'd done her research; I'd give her that. "How were you able to stay in contact in a world of landlines and dial-up internet?"

I took the question again. Beau was only willing to discuss the here and now, or the lighter moments. "For a few years, all we were able to do was text. I didn't see him again until he'd had enough of the long-distance restrictions and came for me. The romance of it all was ridiculously sweet," I answered, lifting his hand to press a kiss on his knuckles. No question, if not on the outside, Beau was rolling his eyes at me on the inside.

"How did your families take the news of you being gay?"

When her gaze trained on Beau, wanting his answer first, he obliged. "My father wasn't happy, and it stayed a secret until his death," Beau said. I was proud of his response. She was pushing buttons on triggers she couldn't even know existed as if that trauma was ever going to be fully realized.

"I feel like we practically grew up together. We've been fully committed to each other since the night we met," I said, glancing over at Beau for confirmation. "You agree?"

"Yeah," Beau replied, causing my grin. My man of many words.

"What prompted the baby decision? How did Dash get his way six times?" she asked.

"Honestly," I started, but Beau surprisingly interrupted me.

"This guy," Beau said, nodding his head toward me. "Can be persuasive."

"So it was his idea?" Zoe asked, tickled by the exchange.

"I've always wanted a large family," I explained. "There are ten years difference between me and my next oldest sibling. I grew up as virtually an only child. Being gay never squashed my feelings of wanting a large family. Beau just needed a little convincing."

"My life's goal was far simpler. I wanted to be fishin' every day," Beau said with a slight laugh. "What neither of us planned on was three babies at the same time. No matter how we prepared, when Liv, Mia, and Ava came home, we were vastly outnumbered."

"Before the girls arrived, we'd been preparing for a baby by taking endless parenting classes and reading all the books. We were in the process of building this house when we found out about the triplets, and the entire home just expanded to make more room," Dash said.

"It was a lot durin' their first couple of years," I added. "But they were a breeze compared to the boys. Those little guys are a handful."

"What would be your best tip to anyone who found themselves in the same position?" she asked.

Beau took this question like a pro. "I feel like communication is the key. And we've never lost the deep sense of gratitude for what we've been given. Dash and I remain on the same page, always. And we have loads of help. We cherish our world. Agree?"

"Absolutely. Cherish is exactly the right word," I said. I loved my family endlessly. Having a partner who was exactly on the same page as me, living our lives together… It was everything.

"You own a local fishing charter company?" she asked.

"With a lifelong friend of mine," Beau nodded, cocking his head toward the Lee's home. "Scott Lee."

"And, Dash, you have a local legal practice in town?"

I nodded too. "Correct. Sea Springs has been good to us. We're happy here. It's a good community of people. Of course, we've run into some belligerence, but only on a small scale."

"And your father in-law is Wesley Carter." Zoe went into full-on fangirl mode with her giant size-of-Texas grin and breathlessness creeping into her tone. "Wow. I bet birthdays and holidays bring the best gifts."

"Carter's a good man. My mentor and parental figure. He's married to Beau's mom, and I take credit for their meeting."

Beau finally let the eye roll go, glaring pointedly at me.

"Here we go again," Beau said as if it was the most boring and inaccurate story ever told.

"I do take credit," I said, brushing him off. "He came to see us. Your mom was there. Seems a reasonable enough claim. We wouldn't have been in Chicago if it weren't for me. But more importantly, our children are crazy about them."

"I understand this is a delicate subject. How do your parents fit inside this world you've created," she asked, looking at me. I'd never spoken of those people with more than what I'd said earlier. Did I want to change that now?

It seemed like I did. "Early on, they didn't approve of Beau. He didn't fit the mold they lived within. At the same time, I learned that my sexual orientation came with a strong disapproval. We've severed ties."

I could see the questions on the tip of her tongue, but we had previously discussed not mentioning them. She didn't push for more. With a decisive nod, she shut her notebook in the same quick efficient way she had done everything so far and got to her feet. "We can follow you for the additional video of Dash's law firm. We'll leave from there to make the flight home."

The dawning of understanding that slid across Beau's brow as we got to our feet, didn't have to include that cocked brow of accusation pointed at me. All right, Beau. Yes, I had to shell out some advertising money to make this all happen for us. And yes, I'd kept that tidbit of information from my mister. This was a good source of passive marketing, yes. But another motivation was for my mother and father to see how well I was doing, and what a lovely, beautiful family they were missing out on.

I clutched Beau's fingers before he tried to talk his way out of the next few hours. "Come on, babe. The kids are occupied. We'll have a downtown date night when we're through."

I turned on the charm until the cameras stopped rolling. All said and done, I felt sure I was made for the screen.

After that endless, drag-on day, Beau was giving me the silent treatment, but not because he was angry. He was just completely wiped out from the long, boring interview experience we'd shared. The couple of hours of primary interview ended with a late lunch at a longtime favorite café a few doors down from my office with Ms. Pebbly and her cameraman. From there, it appeared every resident in the city had decided on an early dinner at the café. From the booth we sat in, several of my clients and work colleagues came over to be interviewed. Most had also worked with Beau, singing his praises about friendly community development.

But now, we were finally home. Amelia had the children down to sleep. Both Duke and Dixie had received the love they required and were now settled in their beds for the night. The house was beautifully quiet. I went to the control panel near the bathroom door leading to the swimming pool and searched through my extensive music playlists. With a smile, I picked something sexy. I had a lot of making up to do. My guy had been a real trooper all day.

Beau finished brushing his teeth and dropped his shorts and underwear to the floor, kicking them aside. They'd make their way to the laundry basket soon enough. His tight-fitting athletic shirt followed over his head, discarded on top of the shorts.

I loved watching Beau undress. It was my personal porn. Tonight, he removed the shirt with his back to me. The way his muscles rippled this way and that mesmerized me. His biceps bulged until both arms dropped back to his sides. The fatigue of the day melted away as Beau opened the shower stall door and flipped on the faucet. The instant heat had him stepping inside. The shower spray hit him in the chest. All that fur was getting wet, and I wasn't there to run my fingers through the mass.

My cock firmed right up, and I tore the clothing from my body. I continued to watch his normal shower stance, the one he did every day. He leaned forward with both hands against the back wall of the shower. He bent his head forward to let the hard spray hit the top of his shoulders and cascade the length of his gorgeous body.

Based on phases of cock building, he was at the starting gate, and I was a straight-up nine and a half out of ten. He wasn't near my level of arousal. Even better. It was now my job to get him caught up with me. The fatigue of the day vanished as I perked right up. I dropped my last garment on the floor and headed toward what I thought of as heaven.

The click of the shower door drew Beau's attention, but he barely moved his head to see me enter. The tight way he held himself eased as he gave me the sin-filled grin I loved so much. His amber eyes darkened, hunger entering his gaze as he moved to circle my waist. He brought me between him and the spray, the water pounding my back in all the right ways. Beau stared at me tenderly before his lips went to the area where my jaw and ear connected. My guy nibbled there, small bites, tender kisses, and sweet swipes of the tongue. My hands circled his head and neck. Beau still enjoyed marking me.

His lips pressed against my ear as he whispered, "Baby, go natural for me. You're spending too much time dyeing, shaving, and waxing. I like your hair darker and let me see some hair on your chest. You like it on me. I'd be into that too."

I reared back, looking doubtfully in his eyes. Lauren spent a lot of time and effort keeping me blond, but it was getting harder and harder to hide. Even my five o'clock shadow was darker than when I was younger.

"It'll make those pretty blue eyes pop."

"Do you think so?" I asked, skeptically.

"Absolutely," he growled seductively. His lips attached to the crook of my neck, and he sucked there on the sensitive skin. Oh hell yeah, he'd claimed his method of making love. I was the prey, and he was my predator. We were going at it rougher tonight. The way he enjoyed making love to me.

My body loosened while absorbing his love, tender nips and sweet caresses. My arms stretched around his shoulders, holding him to me. The perfect relaxation that left the day in the dust. I slid my palms over his back, paying homage to all the hard work that built this body into my favorite playground. My fingertips ran the ridges and grooves until I cupped his neck and close-cropped hair. I closed my eyes.

"You're leaving a mark in a hard place to hide," I whispered against his ear.

"Expect more. All these gay dudes about to watch you in the video, they need to remember their messing with a married man."

"You're ridiculous," I said, moving my hands to his cheek, bringing those sinful lips against mine. Beau swept his tongue inside my mouth doing a deep dive. The instant clash of tongue and teeth turned the kiss carnal. I wanted to give him the fight he enjoyed, but damn, it was hard. Beau dominated me in every way.

A guttural sound slipped past my lips as Beau roughly and possessively yanked my body against his, stepping us under the spray. As suddenly as he took my mouth, he left me there hanging. His nose trailing against my cheek and ear. "How do you want it?"

"For you to dirty suck me here in the shower. I want all the sounds and feelings as I shove down your throat," I said with no hesitation. "Then take me to bed and remind me who's my boss."

His line of vision met mine. "You're my prince, but you've been naughty with your half-truths. There must be punishment."

My grin was immediate. "Exactly like that. I've been very bad."

Beau took a knee and roughly took my stiff shaft into his fist. A powerful tug followed as he bent to lick the slit in my tip. I was transfixed by the sight, unable to look away as the warm water trailed off me onto him. Beau swallowed me whole, a practiced and perfected technique, effectively turning me from the inside out. Before reality slipped past the extraordinary pleasure, Beau began fucking my cock with his mouth. Gagging and gulping with the aggressive way he took me down his throat and pulled my cock free again. His free palm gripped my ass cheek, fingertips digging into the flesh there.

My hips instinctively moved into the same rhythm Beau sucked me. Beau pumped my cock in and out of his mouth, over and over. The way he loved me sent tingles racing along my skin. The neurons inside my brain misfired as I coasted on nothing more than sensations.

His finger slid between my butt cheeks, seeking the pucker of my hole. He used the same rough force to open me, his digit easily finding my gland where he rubbed and flicked over and over until my arousal shot to the stars. It took effort to stave off the orgasm ready to spill.

The pleasure was welcomed. I was now floating on a different plane. With my eyes screwed shut, I coasted there. A place I wished he and I lived together every single day. What a fucking turn-on.

Heat washed over me from the inside out. My spine turned to jelly, my back hit the shower wall, barely able to stay on my feet. He was so good at fucking me like he hated me. I loved each and every minute. "Damn."

"Mmm…" Beau's throat vibrated around my cock. His calloused fingers fondled my balls. The tip of my guy's nose pressed into the small hairs at the base of my cock. His tongue cradled my length, before he pushed my cock through his mouth and down his throat again. I loved, loved, loved that move. The sensual sensations ran rampant through me. When Beau swallowed, drawing me further down his throat, shooting stars sprinkled my vision in the headiest ways. The warm spray of the water, beating against my shoulders, intensified every unguarded wave of arousal rushing through me. Beau regularly filled my emotional cracks; he was magic right now.

I put my hand on Beau's head, petting the short strands there. Then traveled lower, my nails scratching against his skin until I cupped the back of his neck. With the pads of my thumbs, I caressed this way and that until I had my hands fisted into his beard. I was tired of fighting my orgasm. My need was taking over. I thrust my hips into Beau's mouth, rougher than usual. The way Beau changed into a heat-seeking missile at my suggestion of making love tonight turned me the fuck on.

I should be paying homage to him for the day he gave up for me. Yet, here we were. Beau loving my body with precision and care. An instrument he had taken time to learn to play, drawing melodies and the rhythms within seconds of his hands on the strings. I felt his love.

Moments later, Beau pulled his mouth off my cock. His amber stare lifted to mine. "Let me do this. You're close to the end, and the water's turnin' cool." His voice was hoarse and husky. Beau escalated the finger play in my ass and tugged at my balls with force. I was a goner.

"It feels so good," I murmured as I reached for the wall of the shower. I eased back, resting there. My eyes closed. Oh fuck, it felt good.

The urgent glide of his warm talented mouth lulled my senses once again, allowing him to take whatever he wanted. His palm gripped my sac and applied pressure. Yeah, I liked that move a lot, canting my hips, teetering between heaven and hell. Beau's eyes lifted to mine again. My hands fisted, one around his ear and the other into the air. He added a third finger to my hole, maybe a fourth.

Fuck, I loved ass play. Reality beats my fantasies by a mile. The battle was lost.

"Gonna come." My vision blurred as I shot my load down his throat. He took every last drop.

Beau

I reached over to turn off the faucet while wrapping a strong arm around Dash's legs, keeping him upright. I rose, holding his spasming body against mine. His one arm hooked around my shoulders, his head cradled into the crook of my neck. Dash felt like I was the one who liked it rougher. That wasn't true. Through pleasure, I helped relieve Dash's heavy burdens. Owning his body like I owned his mind, preparing him to start tomorrow anew.

"You do it for me every time," I whispered. The evidence of my arousal was sliding down the drain with the rest of the water. I reached for a terry cloth bath towel, awkwardly wrapping it around Dash as I continued to hold him flush against me. "Let's go to sleep. We'll find another time this week for me to fuck you."

If being smitten so far into a relationship was possible, the devotion, and sheer love I had for him welled inside me, day after day, week after week. Right then, I only wanted to put him to bed, wrapping myself around him, coasting on our beautiful life. My cheek rested against his forehead.

"I love you. I'm proud of what you've accomplished. The podcast's gonna be awesome."

His lips pressed against my neck. "You're always giving to me. I don't do my part."

"Not true. I came. Don't worry," I whispered. "Our sex turns me on, I can't hold it." Dash clutched tighter around my neck. My heart tripped in my chest. "Come on, let's go to bed."

"You'll have to hold me," Dash reared his head back. "All night, like we used to do."

Got it. Same page.

I lifted the towel to run over his hair and gently down his body. Then I did the same for myself. Curled up in our comfy bed, sleep came easy.

18: The Anniversary Beau

July 4, 2023
Sea Springs Texas

First off, I wouldn't have chosen a tuxedo. Then the white suit jacket against all black slacks, ties—his a bow tie, mine a standard knotted necktie—dress shirts and vests, was also weird to me. A Great Gatsby-themed party in a world of graphic arts and anime was a bold choice. I readily admitted the use of CliffsNotes when my class read the book in high school.

I had no idea what was really happening in our backyard for that matter, but Dash had again taken my year to plan our anniversary, and gone way overboard on the theme and the decorations. Well, maybe Stone, Dash's personal assistant, had done most of the work, but no doubt he'd only followed Dash's vision.

Round tables and chairs were sprinkled over large portions of the backyard, enough seats to have our hundred or so guests be comfortable. A large, multi-course buffet was set up on one side, both jazz and swing bands on the other, playing in intervals. The porch had a full bar and bartender. Dash and

I were swaying together on the portable dance floor between the bar and the swimming pool which was currently full of children.

Twinkling lights, sashes, and beautiful fresh flower arrangements decorated the yard. The same style flowers were made into centerpieces atop the white table drapes. Candles flickered, adding a softness to the party. Somehow the bugs stayed away, and Dash cooled the air from one side to the next, with equipment that made very little noise.

The beautiful part of tonight was the happy love that seeped off Dash into me. We danced together arm in arm, listening to an older multi-genre playlist while the last remaining band took a break. While we swayed in place, everyone else danced to the rhythm of the complicated jazzy tune. The fringe on period dresses bounced this way and that, and spiffy suits and tuxedos topped with straw hats moved all around us.

Amelia handmade the girls' flapper dresses, and the boys' wore three-piece suits. They looked adorable until they stripped down to their bathing suits. Fisher and Hunter were the first inside the swimming pool. It was all it took for the other children to follow.

"The next song's our song," Dash said, tilting his chin up to me, lips puckered.

I eyed him closely before bending down to accept the offer. "We apparently have lots of songs. Which one's this one?" I asked. Over twenty-three years of bimonthly new songs, we had to have amassed over a hundred and fifty by now.

My guy, with his love of music, knew exactly when the next song was slated to begin. He stepped fully into me. No space between us. "When I heard it again, it imprinted on me. This is our official song. Nothing can change it. It fits us."

The songs changed with a small pause.

He rested his cheek against my shoulder, our elbows tucked into our sides. Tingles raced across my body as I pressed my cheek against his forehead.

"Unforgettable…" The song hit emotionally right where Dash had wanted it to. My guy nailed it. I listened to the sultry tune, holding Dash closely. The lyrics were hypnotic and truthful. I squeezed Dash tighter to me. He held me in just the same way. My emotions laid bare as the words resonated.

On one side of my leg, Fisher circled his arms around my knee. He was still wet from the swimming pool, moving back and forth with us to the end of the song. Our tiny dancer had no shame in joining our special moment and was probably the only thing that might pry Dash and I apart. We glanced down between our bodies to see Fisher's giant smiling grin staring up at us.

"Dance," he stated proudly.

Another small hand tugged at the end of my jacket from the other side. I suspected it was Hunter, mirroring Fisher in every move.

"Abuela says we have five minutes before the fireworks. So you have to stop ignoring your guests and take a seat," Mia said, and hooked a thumb over her shoulder. "Abuela said that, not me."

"Hmm." Dash tilted his face to mine as if remembering where we were, then glanced beyond.

He and I were the only ones on the dance floor. No one remained in the swimming pool. He brought his hand to Mia's shoulder.

"Go get the blanket we brought outside and bring it over here. We'll watch the fireworks from the floor."

Where Stone had helped create Dash's vision, Amelia was the sergeant at arms, taking the role seriously.

"Okay, but she's gonna lift her eyebrow when I tell her," Mia said. I chuckled softly. My girl wasn't wrong. Ava, Fisher, and Hunter saw the look regularly.

"Guests," Amelia beckoned a moment later, her voice amplified by the microphone she'd purchased years ago in order to talk over the children. "Please take a glass of champagne and get comfortable. The fireworks begin in four minutes."

I lifted Fisher into my arms. He crawled high until he circled my neck. My fearless boy didn't like the dark.

A waiter came to us with two glasses of bubbling champagne. Our children were like adorable little magnets, wrapped in terry cloth towels, holding plastic glasses of sparkling juice. Mia graced me with the blanket. I fluffed it out, letting it float to the floor. The family, once you included my mom and Kailey, barely fit on the surface. Carter was stuck in an airport somewhere between here, and the other side of the world.

Scott and Lauren, his parents and their children were somewhere around there too. As if on cue, Scott cleared his throat into the microphone to gain everyone's attention. "I have a few words to say before the fireworks begin and while everyone can still hear me. Beau, we've been friends since birth. As you brought Dash then each of the children into our lives, you've given me, and Lauren, a larger family to love.

"The preparin' of this anniversary party has brought back some pretty amazin' memories for me. Beau, remember when we were children, and we raced across the football field, end zone to end zone, and I won?" Most everyone there knew about the constant competition Scott and I still lived under. The laughter was irritating, but I tried my best to hide it, not wanting to give him the win. Scott nodded happily at me. "Then the time we bet on who caught the most fish from Dog River in a day? I won that too."

He wasn't shy, I'd give him that. Luckily, Lauren swooped in, snatching the microphone from his hand. "Since Scott's told you about the two times he bested Beau, I'll add we couldn't have asked for better friends than Dash and Beau. Together we share an unbreakable bond, and Scott and I are better off in the world because of you two. Please raise your glasses to celebrate Dash and Beau's anniversary. Twenty-three years is a long time to be devoted to one another."

Cheers erupted, glasses clinked, including ours with our children, before we all took sips.

"Get comfortable," Amelia said. Fisher, who sat between my legs, stood and wrapped himself around my torso, until I was forced to hold him there. His face ducked into my suit coat. "We have a firework show to rival the City of Seas Springs' show last night. We'll begin in one minute."

Dash shrugged his suit coat off and began untying the bow tie. The property lights darkened. The candles were already blown out. Darkness enclosed us in her warm blanket. Hunter screeched and scrabbled for me. He trembled at the first boom. When the fireworks burst brightly in the sky, Fisher was torn between the color of the lit sky and the darkness that always followed. By the end, Hunter had crawled in the circle of my lap too, mimicking Fisher.

My little guys.

Late July 2023

"But I saw the invoice for the fireworks show," I hissed, making it around the hood of the Tahoe in record time, stepping on Dash's heels as he left the SUV parked in front of the house. "You spent more than I make in a year just on the fireworks. I get having a big deal for our twenty-five-year anniversary, but why twenty-three? And why so much money? We agreed to a budget."

Dash trotted up the front porch steps as if he didn't have a care in the world. "Beau, we're not hurting for money, and we celebrated an anniversary that means everything to me with these people we call children. After being on deaths door, I want to build lasting memories. The kids were delighted with the party. You were doe-eyed, and my heart was full of joy. Our friends and my staff haven't had any sort of formal celebration since the practice opened. On a normal day, the only people we hang with are Scott and Lauren. The entire evening was perfect for all of us." Dash clutched the front doorknob, and I slapped my hand against the wood to keep it closed..

"Did the party cost more than fifty thousand dollars?" I asked.

Dash pushed open the front door, causing me to topple past him into the house. Damn, he had me so flustered I got mixed up on what way the door opened.

"It cost about half that," he said, surprising me with his honesty.

"Why would you spend so much?" I asked, once I managed to keep my body upright.

"For you," he answered as if that was the obvious response and leaned in with puckered lips. I left him hanging and aimed for a critical brow raise and set jaw so he'd get a full sense of my displeasure.

"What did the school say?" Mia said from the kitchen table. She was the pixie-est looking one of the three with a new Tinker Bell hairstyle for the start of school. The cut fit her face perfectly, but I missed her long hair. They weren't little anymore, but sometimes, I was lulled back into those sweet toddler years, where we had to be careful of color placement between them, otherwise we wouldn't know which child was which.

What a serious mistake it had been to tell the girls that their school wanted to speak with us before the year began again. They'd been hounding us for days, wanting answers.

"Go get your sisters and Amelia," Dash said. "Meet at the kitchen table in five minutes. I want to change my clothes."

"I'll get the boys watchin' television on the porch while we talk to them," I added, heading for the backyard to bring the little guys and the dogs to the porch where they could be seen from the kitchen. I whistled and gained their attention like every other time. The dogs made it to me first for a good rubdown before the boys skidded to a halt in front of me. Hunter bent with his hands on his knees, dramatically puffing out breath like he'd run a mile in a matter of minutes.

"We need to talk to Livie inside the house. I'm gonna turn on the television out here. I need you to sit down properly, and be good until we're done," I said, using the remote to find the Nickelodeon channel. It usually held their interest.

"Livie's in trouble. Livie's in trouble," Fisher chanted, rocking his hips as he did his best to climb into the chair while keeping the dance going.

"Do you wanna watch another episode of Blaze?" I asked, ignoring Fisher.

"Yeah!!!!" That was all it took for them to scramble for their seats. I grabbed juice boxes from the outdoor fridge, and stuck the straw inside each one before handing it over.

"Put these headphones on," Dash instructed, coming toward the porch from our bathroom door. "They should be synced. Test 'em out while we're here." He offered each dog a treat, quickly gaining their favor.

I motioned for them to a seat near the boys. In addition to the huge windows separating the kitchen from the back porch, Duke and Dixie were the best sitters. We'd know before any of the boys' feet hit the ground, if they decided to leave the patio.

Who knew how long we had for serious talk time. It had to be fast.

"What's going on, Dasham?" Amelia asked, handing out juice boxes to the girls, sitting around the table that doubled as a kitchen and dining room table, as well as a laundry folding station, and desk for homework.

"It's funny when she calls Daddy Dasham," Ava said. She had gone with a shaved sides haircut, making her hair look normal when it was down, but cool and edgy when it was up. She was drawn to the darker side of life, and deftly opened her own juice box by ramming the straw through the small opening.

"Little Miss Ava," Amelia warned. "What have we talked about? You don't need to say everything you think aloud."

"Sorry," Ava said, of course without an inkling of remorse.

Dash had to help Mia with her juice box—she was our scatterbrained child, only because she read emotion and energies in people, while always giving a kind hand. She was also our most normal child in her jean shorts and a tee. If a bug dared to invade our property, Mia swooped in on a rescue mission, happily lifting the insect to safety. She applied the same techniques to snakes and spiders too, which was a win for me as well. Too bad her strengths didn't include inserting the plastic straw into the juice box without spilling it everywhere.

"What did they say, Paw?" Livie asked, exuding elegance in the same manner as a presidential first lady. Her hair was long, not a strand out of place. She sat naturally with her hands in her lap, her ankles crossed. "Do they want us to skip a grade again?"

"Sort of," I said, taking the seat beside her. We waited to explain once Amelia joined us.

"Those boys are gonna be the death of me," Amelia said, taking a seat next to Ava. "They have so much energy."

The trio of girls had already skipped the first grade together. They were all smart. I expected other years and classes to be jumped over, but Livie had a rare next-level intelligence. When the school nudged us to pinpoint her brilliance, we spoke with her pediatrician who agreed to work with their elementary school to perform a series of IQ tests. Today's meeting was the grand finale of everyone's efforts.

I threw out a hand when Dash stayed quiet. He needed to lead this charge. I felt like the village idiot surrounded by all these excessively smart people. "As we all know, this is really about Livie, and all the meetings she went through this summer. We've agreed to have Ava and Mia tested in the same way." Dash nodded. He did that a lot when trying to get the answer he wanted. "But today's results are all about Liv."

"We aren't smart like Livie's smart," Mia said, reasonably.

"She's not wrong," Ava interjected.

"We'll circle back to you two, but we have some big decisions to make before school begins in a couple of weeks," I said, motioning Dash to take the reins again.

"Before your paw and I sign any papers, we want to hear from you. Specifically Livie." Dash faced Livie. I put my arm on the back of her chair, sliding a reassuring hand up and down her back.

"Honey, you're in a league of your own. Your IQ's a whooping one hundred and sixty-nine. You're exceptionally gifted." Generally, Livie was selective in giving a smile, but that did it. She beamed at Dash, then turned the smile on me. Butterflies took flight inside my belly.

"I'm proud of you," I said, returning the grin.

Her happy face turned to Abuela, then her sisters. Mia was already grinning brightly. "I told you that you're smarter than everyone else," Mia said, reaching a hand across the table, encouraging Livie into the hold. Of course she didn't voluntarily take Mia's hand, germs and all, but they shared a silent stare while grinning at each other.

The doorbell rang, drawing everyone's attention in that direction. "That's your counselor, Mrs. Pinkney. She's here to answer the questions you have, Livie."

I let her in, skipping the greeting formalities since Dash and I were the ones asking her over tonight and started this meeting without her.

We probably should've waited... I'd have to apologize later for the misstep.

"So, how far have you gotten?" she asked, laying a pad and paper on the table before her.

"Just gettin' to the good stuff," I said. Dash and I had expected pushback from the girls. Livie, Mia, and Ava were a squad. They went most places together. How would they feel about being broken apart?

"We believe you should begin the new school year in junior high school," Mrs. Pinkney said. "With many reassessments as we go. This will be new territory for us all."

"Without Mia and Ava?" Livie asked. Her bright eyes turned worried. "What about my friends?"

"You don't have friends," Ava chirped, not mean-spirited, but as if only stating a fact. "Me and Mia have friends, and you tag along with us. You're smarter than the teachers, and you follow all the rules. Nobody else likes that."

"Ava," Mia said, her brows knitted together as she put her sister on notice.

My heart gave an ache for Livie. I had no idea this was happening. Tears instantly fell from Livie's eyes, her forehead hit her crossed arms on the table. Amelia was up, going to Livie's other side to comfort her. Dash looked as confused as me.

"I wanna... have friends. No one... likes me." Each word was said between pain, tears, and hiccups.

"Here, baby. Stop crying," Amelia said, pushing a napkin between her arms. "Take a drink from your juice box and find your calm. We can talk through it."

"What about your dance classmates? Aren't y'all all friends?" I asked, since that was why she had started dance lessons in the first place.

"They don't like her either," Ava blurted.

"Ava, are you talking badly about your sister?" Dash asked, using the serious tone reserved only for his work.

"No, Daddy, she doesn't," Mia the peacemaker jumped in. "Ava stomps on their crayons and breaks their scissors when they talk bad about Livie."

Whoa. Where had this solid left turn come from?

"Livie," Mrs. Pinkney said gently, but firmly. "Look at me, please."

Livie did. Her red face and swollen eyes broke my heart in two. I couldn't take the tears, but I knew they hit Dash harder. He looked ready to cry. The hiccups never stopped as she did her best to gain control.

"Mrs. Crabtree felt like you'd feel this way and has offered her office to become your classroom. We'll set you up remotely with the junior high. You know the office is only a hall away from your grade. You can learn at an accelerated pace while still being with your peers."

"So I'll attend class online at school with Ava and Mia?" she asked, the sniffles and quick breaths still making it hard to speak. Amelia handed her the juice box and encouraged her to drink, pressing additional napkins into her hand.

The counselor's warm, encouraging smile gave my heart a chance again as I scooped Liv into my lap, hugging her tightly.

"Yes. And you'll probably see them more each day than you did last year," Mrs. Pinkney said, then turned to explain that statement to the adults at the table. "As you know, they don't attend the same classrooms together, but Livie will have her sisters popping in and out throughout the day."

"And I'll get recess and lunch with my sisters?" Livie asked. "Because they're my best friends and make me stronger." Livie raised her chin as if she'd made her decision and wouldn't back down.

"Absolutely."

I felt the relief flood her small body. Her hand covered mine, wrapped around her. She glanced at me with her swollen, tear-streaked face.

"I think I'm okay now," she said and hiccupped again in my face. Her entire body shuddered.

"Livie," Ms. Pinkney started. "You're part of a small group of exceptionally-bright young minds. That's the way they reference you." She tore off a sheet of paper from her notebook and handed it to Dash. "This is the contact information for American Mensa. Mrs. Crabtree has taught Livie for the last two years and feels like she needs a support group. Once you give me the green light, I'll send her test scores over with the other information they'll need. They have appropriate age groups, and instruction lessons to keep their minds active. Most of the gatherings will be online, but there are in-person groups in Houston as well. They'll require parental involvement to create safe spaces for her to meet other children like herself. I believe that'll do her wonders in meeting friends."

Dash took the piece of paper, reading over it before passing it to me. "Livie, if you're in, we can do this on a trial basis. When you find your place, you'll sprout like a weed, nothing will hold you back."

She nodded and only gave a single hiccup while turning her body to better face me. "Paw, can we try the group in Houston? Daddy will say yes, but you have to too."

I glanced at Dash who smirked brilliantly at me.

"Livie-baby, I'll always do my best for you, but we didn't know this was a problem. You need to talk to us more."

She reached up, circling her arms around my neck, squeezing me. I accepted my hug and gave one in return while staring at Ava.

"What I want to know about now is this stepping on crayons. That seems excessive."

"Paw, you can't be mad. They're mean to Livie to her face, because she's better than they are in everything," Ava started, talking so fast I had to replay her words over. "It makes me mad. People are stupid."

"Ava," Dash's hands splayed across the table. "You aren't helping your case by calling other children names."

"Should we have been notified about her behavior?" I asked Mrs. Pinkney.

"I knew," Amelia confessed, her tone holding hints of possessiveness and anger. "I've never disciplined her for protecting her family."

Ava bubbled up with a laugh. "Abuela told me to squirt glue on their hair."

"Okay. Let's pretend I didn't hear that," Mrs. Pinkney said, getting to her feet again. "Can't blame her for family protectiveness, and Amelia always sends new supplies to school for the other children."

"That's right," Amelia said, her arms crossing defiantly over her chest. "Better than they deserve."

"Okay, again," Mrs. Pinkney said, taking her purse and notebook. I rose too, bringing Livie up and on my hip. I couldn't remember the last time she let me carry her this way, but I missed her as a baby and got a few moments to pretend we were still that family. "No, stay together, you don't have to show me out. Livie, I hope you like our idea. We'll be there to support you the whole way."

She nodded and extended her hand like an adult would do. I loved her so much. "Thank you, Mrs. Pinkney. My Paw's strong. He can carry all of us at the same time."

"I see," Mrs. Pinkney said, waggling a brow my direction. "I'll be in touch tomorrow. When I get a solid move forward, we'll begin getting her room together." She lifted a hand, waving goodbye to the group. Liv and I followed her out. When the front door closed tightly, Livie hugged me again.

"I feel better, Paw. You can put me down," she said, her legs going straight until I put her down.

"Ava, no more breaking other people's stuff," Dash started before I had a chance to say the same thing. Dash veered in a different direction. "Tell them your paw's stronger than their fathers, and he's going to beat them up."

I agreed with the sentiment completely, but I wasn't sure it was the right thing to say.

"Really, Paw, will you beat them up?" Ava asked, hopefully.

"Your fathers will do anything to protect their girls," Amelia explained, getting to her feet. She saved me from answering. I'd seen a lot of those dads, I could take them. Still might have to if their children don't get under control.

19: The Clients
Dash

August 2023

Fire and brimstone were the only words that could sum up the sauna-like experience of living in Sea Springs in August. No matter how I tried, I couldn't help the pit stains that appeared anytime I walked outside. I'd be more self-conscious if everyone around me weren't dealing with the same thing.

Thank goodness for remote start on cars. I cranked up the A/C for a good three minutes before taking the fifteen-ish steps from the office to my parking space. When I jumped behind the wheel, a chill ran down my spine. I'd take frostbite over walking in the bowels of hell, every single time.

My mind was still tangled up about Livie. If she wanted friends, she deserved them. She was a sweet girl, pretty as could be, with a laugh that brightened the gloomiest of days. She was also real, tough as nails, choosing not to live in a fairy tale world of rainbows and unicorns, or as Ava enjoyed, dragons and shadows.

I didn't think I could be prouder of Ava. How she came up with stomping on crayons for being mean to her sister might be the best moment of my life. We needed redirection for her frustrations, but I loved her standing up for Livie.

I was so lost in the thought it took a second ring for me to clue in to the incoming call. Stone's name appeared on the screen. I tapped accept out of obligation only. "This is considered after hours—it better be good."

"Dash, it's Stone. Have a minute?" he said, like his name didn't just cross the large screen in the Tahoe.

I liked the guy well enough, but wow, did he have the useless questions game on lock? After all, I did answer the phone, some things should be assumed by now. "Go ahead."

"I'm sorry to bother you, but I have two potential clients who I believe you'd like to meet."

"Have William—" I started, clicking through the faces I remembered seeing as I left the office.

"No, sir. They've driven from Oklahoma City and Dallas and will only meet with you. They didn't call due to the subject matter. It's worth the trip back. You'll want to meet with these ladies."

Dammit. Beau had taught me well. I had firm expectations regarding dedicated family time and leaving the office behind. Fresh minds brought the best ideas, and my children were only going to be little once. I glanced at the time, four forty-five. I ducked out a little early. Today was important—,Beau's mom had taken the girls back-to-school clothes shopping at a mall in Houston. Tonight, they'd use our living room as a runway to show off their new purchases. Amelia had even agreed to record her telenovelas for later so that she could be present for the modeling show tonight.

"Can I meet with them first thing in the morning?" I asked.

"They have to drive home tonight. It took them longer to get here than expected," Stone replied. "Now flip that SUV around and come back. I'll call Beau and tell him you'll be fashionably late. Trust me, you don't want to miss this."

The call disconnected. Another way to say it was that my well-paid assistant hung up on me. My jaw set and brows shot up in utter disbelief. I found the closest U-turn and whipped the ride around a bit aggressively.

My foot stepped on the gas. If I made it back to the office in five minutes, listened to the women state their case for five minutes, then gave Stone a forceful talking to, I'd be back on the road in twenty-five minutes. I planned a significant rant.

Beau's name popped up on my screen, I pushed accept.

"What's goin' on?" Beau asked. It was hard to hear him with all the splashing and laughing in the water in the background. My anger amped up a notch at what I was missing out on. I wanted to be there playing in the swimming pool, sliding down the waterslide Beau had surprised me with for our anniversary. We saved a ton of money by having him install it, and Beau loved saving money more than he loved me.

"Stone asked me to turn around. There's someone at the office I need to meet," I explained.

"He said it could be a couple of hours before you're home," Beau said, unhappily. His tone took me back to years ago when I worked all the time, drawing my brows together. "The girls are excited to model their new clothes. If we need to put it off, tell me now."

"Babe, I'm not sticking around for longer than a few minutes. I'll put the women in a hotel tonight," I said. "And Stone will be fired tonight, so I might have to make the reservations myself."

Beau chuckled, which made the entire situation worse. We both knew Stone was the glue holding my business together. He was never allowed to leave. Contractually bound to stay by my side until the practice closed without asking for a raise. And he signed it, showing his level of dedication.

"I'll call you when I'm on my way home," I said, taking the turn into my reserved parking spot. Again.

"Everybody, say bye to Dad," Beau called. A chorus of Daddies and Dashes rang in the background, which meant they were having a great time without me.

"Tell them bye for me," I said, putting the gearshift in park. "Quick question—why are you home?"

"Charter canceled last minute. They paid in full, so we came home. Scott's got West with him," Beau said. "They're at the public school's FFA barn."

Today had crawled by, and honestly, the last few weeks had been slow. Most people in the area were dealing with wrapping up the final tourism dollars of the season, or going on vacation themselves. This would last a week or two longer. Had I known they'd all been home, I could have joined in the good times earlier.

"No wild parties without me."

"Too late. We're waitin' on you. The kids voted on veggie nuggets and steamed summer squash," Beau added.

"Daddy, come home. It's gonna be so good," Mia shouted close to the phone.

Any good mood I had maintained instantly evaporated when I opened the front door to my office and the attached bells rang. I'd left the damned things there to give the office a personal, hometown law firm feel. Even if sixty percent of our business had come from other parts of the United States.

Stone sat at his desk, fingers typing on the keyboard, his head nodding me to the waiting area. Two women sat waiting. My office had remained in the same place as when we first started. We'd added Stone's office space, a reception desk, and a conference room downstairs. Most of the actual legal work was done on the second floor. As we needed additional space, the lease next door had thankfully come up for rent. Private offices were added, and we included an elevator in the renovations. Even with a hybrid schedule, I was still going to need more room soon.

When I glanced at the women, they stared big-eyed at me. A quick read of the situation was fear and uncertainty. Also determination.

"This is Teresa Rodrigues and Lucia Valentina. Ladies, this is Mr. Richmond-Brooks," Stone said. I nodded, as they continued to stare at me and remain seated. My gut reaction was that Stone brought me back for a pro bono case. I usually kept them private, and this could definitely wait until morning. Stone left his desk and led the way. I trailed behind the women. Teresa carried a large flexible file box. "It'll be best to take them to the conference room."

"Take a seat. Can I get you anything? Water, coffee, or soda?" Stone asked.

"Water would be great," Teresa said, her voice held hints of professionalism. Huh. I didn't see that when I first spotted them. My curiosity was begrudgingly piqued.

"Get us three bottles, Stone," I said before the other spoke. "Shut the door behind you."

"Yes, sir." Another thing Stone did that I had no use for was continually calling me "sir," and he refused to stop doing so. The term made me feel ancient. The insult needed to be stricken from all languages across the world.

"What brings you to the office today?" I took a seat opposite the duo as Teresa began digging into her treasure trove of files.

Stone quietly delivered the water and shut the door as he left.

"We saw your interview with the *Huffington Post*," Lucia said.

I nodded. Several new clients had come from our family interview.

"We'd lost hope," Teresa added. "We've been to quite a few attorneys who had varying reasons why we didn't have a case, but I don't believe that's true. It's just a lot to deal with."

She slid a document across the table, and I left it between us as I responded, "Give me the nuts and bolts. If I believe there's a chance of pursuing, we'll delve deeper into your files." I tilted back in my chair, a normal position for me, and waited to hear the rundown on the case they thought they had.

"We made this folder for you," Lucia said.

"We'd like to initiate a lawsuit against Jack Richmond, Richmond Holding, and several members of the Richmond executive team," Teresa explained, maintaining eye contact while my brow raised in surprise. A silent sigh escaped. I felt sure my poker face was solid, but they'd caught me by surprise. Stone was spot-on for reaching out to me. Regardless of how this played out, I wanted to hear it. "I understand it'll be a class action lawsuit."

And the plot gets better.

"I don't specialize in class action litigation, but I know legal experts who do. Class action suits can be tricky. Why not a lawsuit?"

"We've found seventeen women who've experienced the same situation," Lucia clarified.

"And what was that experience?" I asked. As soon as I said the words, my gut gave a hard twist.

"The senior Richmond and two of his sons have sexually tormented, preyed upon, harassed, and in some cases, many cases, raped women in their employment. In every case, we've been fired within weeks after things went '*too far*.'" Heedless of my request to keep the files for later, Teresa pulled photos—each showing different Latina women of varying ages, yet all with the same look.

My stomach did a full twisting layout this time.

Everything inside me said they were telling the truth.

What had my father done?

Questions rained down on me like confetti, but the biggest one was: If this was happening, how on earth had the rumors not leaked before now? As if reading my thoughts, she pulled out a signed non-disclosure agreement. "We were all required to sign this in order to receive severance. In every case, we were terminated for in-office misconduct."

My brows knitted closer together as I reached for the NDA, which was attached to a corporate case file for termination.

"Most of us have children or family who depend on us. We feared repercussions. If we signed it, they gave us a five-thousand-dollar severance package, didn't fight unemployment payouts, and gave a good reference while looking for another position," Teresa explained.

She sat back, elbows on the armrests, hands clasped tighter. "As far as we know, I was the last victim. Your brother, Jonathon Richmond, who's the chief operating officer had been making lude comments and occasionally put me in a position where he was touchy-feely with me. I knew it was wrong, but I needed the job and a good reference on my resume. I'm a managerial accountant who was promoted to the executive floor shortly after being hired. It was a real big deal for me."

Teresa shook her head, as if trying to clear some rogue thought. "I'm rambling, and I'm sorry. I began keeping the video recording on my phone because of how creepy he was. One evening, I was required to stay to finish a project, so I had my phone recording. Two of your brothers sexually assaulted me, but I don't remember it." Her cheeks reddened as she glanced away. "The next day I called in sick, because I was. I'm not even sure how I got home the night before, so I went to the ER. Because of my symptoms, they tested and found Rohypnol in my system. That's how those awful men got to me. I didn't tell anyone. I was scared and didn't know what to do. They fired me by the end of the day."

All the unsaid fear and emotion wafting off her made my lips mash together, and I cut my gaze to Lucia who picked up the thread and continued with her own horror story.

"I was assigned to the executive floor and had the same experience. I don't know everyone involved who attacked me. Your father brought me a vodka tonic, thanking me for working late. I woke up the next morning in his office, on his sofa, alone." Tears filled her eyes as she continued to speak. "I was so embarrassed. I thought I was going to work for a kind, Christian family man. He's a monster." The ire and hurt in her voice gave credence to her story.

"And you've gone to the authorities?" I asked. It was unimaginable to believe the hospital system that cared for Teresa hadn't called the local police department.

"Teresa did," Lucia answered. "I was afraid of the NDA they made us sign. I can't afford to pay back the severance and then some. They also didn't fight unemployment payments even though I was technically fired."

"I filed a report with the Dallas Police myself. The hospital didn't call them. I also filed a complaint with the Texas Workforce Commission, and the EEOC, and nothing's happened except I was notified by Richmond Holdings that I'd broken my NDA. They now say I owe them money." Teresa unscrewed the cap on the bottle of water and took a quick drink before continuing. "I was twenty-three years old when it happened. I'm also first-generation American. The fear stemming from my parents being immigrants in the United States frightened me to stay quiet, but I couldn't shake the feeling of being preyed upon. I have a colleague in human resources who connected me to Lucia."

Lucia's hand went to her chest, laying on her heart. These women were frightened, but brave. It was remarkable.

"I'm DACA. I never told anyone about what happened, not even my husband. I was ashamed of allowing myself to be in such a vulnerable position. I knew better than to even sip the drink he gave me."

"How old are you?" I asked Lucia.

"I'm twenty-six. It happened to me two years ago."

"And Teresa?" I asked.

"Last year, not even a year ago," she answered.

My outward calm didn't convey the inner chaos running laps around my head, but these women didn't need to see that. They needed my professionalism and my help.

"And you've made me this file that substantiates everything?" I asked. My chair popped forward, gathering the photos in front of me. I sifted through them, glancing at each one closely.

"Yes, sir," Lucia affirmed. "We've found seventeen women documented over the past ten years. We were told the women prior to ten years ago can't be a part of the case. But we have a list of those names as well."

"That's criminal. This is civil. We can look back further," I stated, distractedly. Every single woman looked the same. Long dark hair parted in the middle. Almond-shaped dark eyes. That was the obvious pattern I saw among them, which was a far cry from the blond-haired, blue-eyed clan I came from.

I let the silence in the room linger as I lost myself to the facts as stated. Seventeen women in ten years. My father and two brothers. I had never noticed any signs of this when I was a part of their lives. What involvement did my other siblings have? Did they know what was happening? Were they complicit? Damn, what kind of family did I come from?

My body tingled as I fully absorbed the egregious behavior.

"We fully expect you to tell us no," Teresa said, drawing my eye to her. "But after watching your videos with your family on TikTok, I felt like you were worth the try. You feel different than them. All other doors have been shut in our faces. You're our last hope."

I covered my mouth, elbow resting on the table as I placed the photos in front of me. I didn't know about TikTok, but Lucia had read me well.

"What do you hope to achieve with this suit?" I asked.

"I want to protect others from their pattern of abuse. We..." she gestured between herself and Lucia. "Would also like out of the NDAs so we can be honest, and for them to be stripped of their positions."

"Richmond Holdings is a public entity, and the Richmond family own the majority shares," Lucia said. Of course I understood the make-up of my father's company. "They're powerful, but they can't continue to abuse women. I'd like a bigger payment than what they gave us. Maybe twenty-five thousand dollars or fifty thousand dollars more."

"So do we have a case? Would you consider taking the case?" Teresa asked, I could almost feel her fingers crossing due to the hope in her tone.

I was left battling an existential crisis of what was real, and the best way to proceed forward.

"I'm open to reviewing what you've provided. These cases can be costly and the final results vary. A case like this can drag on for years. I know my father. He won't roll over easily, if at all. These allegations are appalling. It sickens me to think that any of my family is involved in these claims..." My jaw tightened as I reached for the pad and paper Stone left for me. I barely glanced over at Teresa who wore a smile on her face.

"Why're you smiling?" I asked.

"Because everyone else we spoke to barely listened to our claims, saying the damages weren't sufficient enough to take on Richmond Holdings. Some wanted us to put up a retainer. At least you're willing to look at the information we've put together."

"No one seemed to believe us," Lucia added.

"I believe you," I said as I jotted down bullet-pointed notes for Stone to begin researching. "But the rest is complicated. I may not be your best representation," I explained. "How do I get a hold of you two?"

Teresa pulled another piece of paper from the expandable folder. She slid it across the table toward me. It contained their complete contact information.

"Your assistant, I guess," she said as she cocked her thumb over her shoulder in Stone's direction, "made a copy of it already."

Mechanically, I gathered everything together and stood. I rounded the table toward the door and took the files they'd brought. "I need your permission to discuss this with my husband and a select few others. I wouldn't ordinarily mention anything a client tells me, but you brought this to me because it *is* my family. If I take this on in any way, it's going to impact my husband."

"Yes, of course," Teresa said, Lucia nodding.

"Are you staying the night in Sea Springs? Does Stone need to help you find accommodations?"

With all certainty, I'd be up most of the night reviewing their evidence and evaluating the emotional toll this would take on me and Beau. If I took the case, did it scream vindication? My father's law department would use me and my life against these women, but could they sell it to the federal court system to sway a class action suit of this nature?

"I think we've lost him," Lucia said, beyond the now open conference room door.

"That's rare indeed," Stone said. "I'll show you out."

Stone received another good job check mark, along with all the others he'd earned tonight.

When the front door rattled its closure, I stared at Stone who grinned like a Cheshire cat. I never discussed my birth family with anyone, but as my personal assistant and paralegal, he was privy to all of my phone calls, except with Beau. He listened to everything to help keep me on track.

"Get the smile off your face. I don't know if we can handle this. Employment law isn't my strong suit, and this'll cost us a fortune."

Stone kept grinning as he said, "But one way or another, in this climate, your father has to take a hit." Stone gave a loud clap of the hands and pivoted to his desk. "I believe this should be a class action lawsuit. Brianne should be reassigned solely to this case. She has an employment law background and thinks outside of the box. Of course, I'll handle the leg work. I might need to hire someone to help." He snapped his fingers then pointed at me. "Go home now. I suggest you tell Beau the truth tonight before they become clients. He needs to understand. He's a good guy. He'll support us."

Us? This was an entirely new side to Stone I'd never seen before. I let him keep talking until I made it to the front door. "They're probably already our clients. I'll handle Beau. He'll worry and be hard to get along with. Be patient with him." The giant decorative clock above Stone's desk read almost five forty-five. The kids went to sleep at nine o'clock during the summer. As I left, my mind didn't allow me to put work behind me this time. A first in many years.

20: The Boots
Beau/Dash

Beau

Most of the evening turned into a fashion show extravaganza as the girls flaunted their new clothes, strutting across the living room's make-shift runway in their best impressions of high-fashion models. They wiggled their hips and walked by kicking their legs out in front of them with their hands on their hips. They were hilarious and adorable and ours. The two youngest boys got in on the action until their teasing became too much. Now they sat at my feet, playing on my and Dash's cell phones. Duke and Dixie played peacemakers and were strategically placed between the two boys to keep them from roughhousing.

"I like that outfit the best on you," Dash said about Ava's dark jeans and vintage Cage the Elephant tee. She commandeered Dash's music system, and a Cage the Elephant song played quietly all around the house. With a pair of black military-style boots, her ensemble came together nicely.

"It's my favorite too," she said, excitedly.

Each girl struck a pose in front of Amelia, spinning this way and that for her approval."

"It looks good, Ava. But I liked it when the three of you wore the same sundresses. I made lots of them. Do it for me again?"

"Augh, Abuela, no. Sundresses are the worst," Ava said and twisted, strutting all the way back to the stairs.

Mia sashayed out the elevator, channeling Ava, but her step-out kick could have put an eye out.

"I'm wearing skinny jeans." She did a twirl, luckily staying on her feet in the end. I was impressed. She also wore a seafoam green T-shirt with sea turtles on the front. She stopped in front of me, one hip cocked to one side, her head tilted to the other, and her fist landed on the wrong hip. "I bought most of my clothes from Save the Oceans." She pivoted to Amelia for the final say. "Abuela, my shoes are made from recycled ocean plastic." The show paused when her gaze lifted to the ceiling in thought. "It's maybe from Save the Manatees." Her stare lowered back to Amelia. "It's something like that."

She shrugged and grinned happily.

"It's very nice," Amelia said. "But know what I'd like?"

"For us to dress the same again."

Dash chuckled at the way Mia rolled her eyes. Her good nature returned instantly, and she kissed Amelia's cheek before darting up the stairs. Livie came next. She wore a bright yellow, sunflower inspired dress. Her sandals and pretty hair clasp matched. She walked straight to Amelia.

Since the big schooling discussion and learning she had no real friends, which was difficult for us to absorb as parents, we'd all given her more attention and love. "Little girl, you look lovely. Put together effortlessly. I want your sisters to wear your clothes."

Livie beamed even as Ava came halfway down the steps, sticking a finger in her mouth and giving a gagging sound.

"Ava," my mom said, trotting down the steps, taking Ava's hand as they came to the bottom stair. "Livie concludes tonight's fashion show. Please give a round of applause to Livie, Mia, and Ava. Without them, there'd be no show."

Mia hopped down the stairs to land next to her sisters, already giving bows. We all clapped at their performances. Dash was the first to his feet. "Hunter, Fisher, tell your sisters they look nice."

That was one thing my kids did well. They parroted the compliment we required them to say, never looking up from the devices in their hands.

"Need help hanging everything up?" Dash asked just as the front door swung open. West, our little cowboy in training due to Scott's influence, was starting pre-K this year and couldn't be less interested in going to school. His new school clothes lay in sealed packages on his bed, namely, five pairs of blue jeans, five western shirts, underwear, and socks. My mom ordered them from Amazon.

A few months back, Scott bought West a cowboy hat to match his. My boy wore it now, along with a matching gray hoodie, starched blue jeans, and matching boots. Both wore aviator sunglasses with mirrored lenses. We were still in the long summer season, but no one needed sunglasses at this hour of the evening.

"Watch this." Scott put West on his feet in the living room, where his thumbs went instantly to his front pockets. Dash was on his A-game, already filming as Scott turned Spotify on with his phone. A twangy Brooks & Dunn country song began playing. Both man and boy began boot scooting, shuffling their feet in a dance, around the living room floor. West held the rhythm and movements like a pro until everyone began to cheer for him. He lacked no confidence as he raised his fists high with pride, the other children got involved, mimicking West's dancing style.

The song changed and Scott handed West a toothpick. They put them in their mouths at the same time. They'd added props to their show. West's thumb hitched back into his pocket, and he continued to dance, scooting without missing a beat.

West was an absolute cutie. Tall for his age, he stood out in a crowd, exuding my fearless vibe. West was naturally gifted with safety, meaning every time he hurled his body from the boat into the ocean, he popped up again. Thank goodness for a well-equipped life jacket. None of the children went without one.

"Well done," I clapped. The rest were cheering for themselves and West, offering a congratulatory high five to each other. The little guy's grin landed on Dash who was still recording, and he tilted his hat. I couldn't help laughing as I hoisted him up in my arms, giving him a tight hug. "You gonna be a dancer?"

West tilted his hat back on his head and swiped off his sunglasses. "I'm gonna be a cowboy and have a horse, and it's gonna be black as night. And me and my horse are gonna do cowboy things. Then I'm gonna get a cowgirl to ride on the back with me." The declaration was swift and sure. I glanced at Dash to make sure he'd caught that moment too.

"Those are mighty big goals, little man," Dash said. "Where are you gonna keep that horse?"

That question took a second to answer. "In the backyard."

What a great life goal. I hugged him tighter before Dash came and took him out of my arms. School started soon and these unexpected joyful nights would lose their frequency. They were all growing up too fast.

Dash

I tried to lay down a foundation where Beau and I would sleep well tonight.

We drank a glass of wine, talked together outside, and swam in our secret alcove of the swimming pool. When we came to bed, I made sweet, gentle love to him. I came on his ass to alleviate the need of a thorough cleaning then held my love in silence while I tried to sleep. From there, I tossed and turned, before finally giving up altogether. I quietly made my way to the living room and read the files I'd brought home by lamplight. The scattered pages went in different stacks in an attempt to utilize the organizational system my brain operated best with.

They'd gathered quite a bit of information already, and I agreed there were more than these women to add to the mix. Predators didn't stop preying, especially when they got away with it. The gaps were sometimes years apart, then bam, three times in a single year. It stood to reason that there was so much we didn't know.

The thought of the creepy sport between father and sons made me want to vomit. When had their sick games started? Who else knew?

I couldn't help wondering what life would have been like if Beau and I had stayed with that family. What if he hadn't rescued me? The emotional roller coaster of the whole saga was going to be a tough ride.

Given the extensive number of cases filed against my father with the Texas Workforce Commission, it became evident how deep my father's pockets and influence ran. I also had significant doubt in my ability to financially survive a multi-year battle against Richmond Holdings.

I questioned if it was even possible to find an impartial judge, free from my father's potential influence or interference.

Any investigation needed to be comprehensive and meticulous. There was a high probability that the incidents in question were not solely confined to the Dallas home office. I needed Lon—my old mentor from my Chicago days— to be involved. He was extensively connected. If we could file a case in Illinois where Lon resided, or even in Washington DC, where he also maintained a presence, that may solve the personal vendetta issue.

Would Lon agree to partner with me?

"Why're you out here?" Beau asked huskily, standing nearby. He startled me so hard that the notebook I'd been making notes in tumbled from my lap.

"Shit, Beau, you scared me." My hand flew to my heart. The number two pencil I held poked me in the chest. It hurt. Of course I couldn't say that to Beau. He was sliced, hooked, or bitten every day. But I suffered in pain in my own way too.

"What's goin' on?" he asked again, staring pointedly at the piles of paper on the sofa beside me. "You were distracted all night. What's happenin'?"

I stacked the documents I'd laid on the sofa and moved those piles with care to the coffee table in front of me. When I had the seat cleared off, I patted the sofa beside me for Beau to take a seat in a way that he angled his face toward me.

"When I was called back to the office this afternoon," I said and waited for him to nod that he was with me. "I had a significant case dropped in my lap."

"Who're you plannin' to pass it off to?" he asked. Although I always kept the sanctity of attorney/client privilege, Beau understood the inner workings of my firm. These days, I was a big-picture owner. I didn't keep many cases for myself.

"I'll handle this one," I said on a deep sigh.

"What am I missin'?" Beau asked. "Is it pro bono?"

"It'll be substantial and costly. I'll have to collaborate with a larger firm that has access to more resources, assuming everything works out." I felt the weight of the case pressing me down. It was incredibly difficult for me to wrap my head around my father being a sexual predator... An asshole, sure. Demanding and in control, always. A god complex where he thought he could crush anyone who got in his way, you bet. Maybe it wasn't such a hard leap to violating the rights of a person to their own body. It was overwhelming. Beau gently cupped my neck, offering comfort.

"Lon would partner with you, right?"

"He's the person I'd reach out to." A deep sigh escaped, knowing Lon's presence in our lives could reignite some uncertainties in Beau. He had insecurity there that I wasn't sure we fully resolved. "What I can say to you is that it'll demand a lot of time from me. The pre-suit phase will be challenging. I'll be away from home quite a bit, which I don't appreciate, but that's not the worst of it. The emotional toll will be toughest. It'll be difficult to compartmentalize the facts of this case."

"Then don't take it. No harm done. We need you here with us. Those were the agreements we made before havin' our children."

I gave him a closer look, trying to read his sincerity. I cherished my family, but they were safe. Beau and I built a life to keep them secure. If I left for days at a time, Beau would be here with them. I'd return home as often as possible, but the idea that any member of my family would continue to assault women, most likely growing even bolder because they persistently escaped punishment...

"So you've decided to do it without my input," Beau said flatly, allowing his hand to drop away. "This life we're livin' is because of you, and you can't give us fifteen years to allow them all to grow up before you disappear again? Tough cases consume you. You'll be trapped in that life until a judgement is reached. You'll win the case, and others will be waitin' in the wings for your help. I'll lose you again, and you promised me it wouldn't happen."

"Beau, I won't ever emotionally leave my family..."

My guy rose, drawing the throw he wore closer around him like a shield as he started for the bedroom. I closed my eyes, knowing in my heart that if he understood the details, he'd insist I take the case.

With quick, efficient movements, I cleared the table, securing the paperwork then followed Beau. I kept the overhead lights off, relying on the moonlight filtering through the windows to guide me to his side of the bed, taking a seat on the edge. He didn't scoot over, only allowing me minimal space. I clasped my hands, tucking them between my thighs.

"I firmly believe in attorney-client privilege, but I've also broken your trust in me. I do get consumed and have a hard time navigating my way out of my head. As much as I've wanted to share details of my different cases with my best friend, I never have. But I garnered permission to talk this case through with you. And you're right, I've made promises to you that I intend to keep."

Silence between us ensued, broken only by the heavy puff of breath.

"The reason for my delay this evening was due to two women who potentially have a case against my father and two brothers for sexual assault."

I waited, staring out at the swimming pool's rippling water.

Beau didn't say a word, but he scooted his legs to the middle of the bed to give me more room.

"The information they shared included seventeen possible victims."

"And you believe it to be true?" Beau said into the silence.

"I'd have to begin the investigation to see the truth for myself. My preliminary thoughts are Stone, Brianne, and I will handle the investigation. I'll know more as I speak to the different women myself."

"How bad is it?" Beau whispered.

"As bad as it gets."

A dramatic pause hung in the air for what felt like an eternity. "Here are my rules: You video call me and the kids every day. You stay present in their day-to-day lives. Livie needs us right now. If you stay gone for more than three days, I need a reason. When you're home, you're mentally here with us. We might have to hire another Belle full-time to help Amelia, I guess. They're a lot to handle. I always feel like I'm slippin' when you're not around."

"So you think I should take it?" I asked, glancing over as Beau began moving fully into the center of the bed.

"'Course. We make love two times a week, even if it has to be by video," Beau said, saying what was important to both of us. "And if it turns out to be true, go kick your old man's ass. I hate that motherfucker anyway."

The edge of the duvet lifted.

"Come on, go to sleep. Better decisions will come to you on a rested mind."

My love wasn't wrong, and I crawled in next to him. My mind eased.

"Sleep, Dash," Beau murmured against my ear. It was all it took.

21: The Backyard Dash

Usually, a closed-door meeting inside my office implied direct attention to a certain subject matter. Interruptions, both in person and by phone were expressly prohibited. Especially while I spoke to Stone about anything. He took care of me, always focused. He was a dog with a bone, but a lot of the times, his vision became singular. We had to talk it out to help him understand the bigger picture.

When Stone and I scheduled time together, mostly during the day, I alerted my family by text, asking for the quiet time.

So when my cell phone rattled on my desk, Stone lifted an eyebrow. Carter's name appeared.

"Hey," I said, after swiping my thumb across the screen and lifting it to my ear. I stared directly at Stone unbothered by his annoyance. "Are you around this afternoon for a meeting at the fence line?"

Since he was now my backyard neighbor, he and I regularly talked privately by stepping outside, leaving all recording devices inside. He and I had the best conversations, usually ending up at one of our houses, drinking a cocktail.

"In about an hour, I have a few minutes. Is that correct, Lisa?"

"Yes, then fifteen minutes at about three."

The first time I heard Lisa answer a question over a phone call between Carter and I, it startled me. Now, Stone was my Lisa, but he never made his listening presence known.

"I'll meet you there in an hour," I said, glancing at the wall clock. I was close enough to quitting time, meaning mid-afternoon, that I could wrap up the day. Maybe grab the boys from school and be home for the rest of the night. It'd show Beau I was serious about jumping in when I was able.

If it were possible, Stone appeared more frustrated with me.

"We don't allow distraction," Stone disciplined, frown in place. His back ramrod straight, suit pristine, and polished shoes. How had I not known he was gay when I hired him? "What if I have questions?"

"I don't believe you do. We've been thorough in your assigned tasks." With my fingers I started to enumerate what I had requested of him. "Draw up an engagement letter with the terms we discussed. Schedule a conference call with Lucia and Teresa. You'll, of course, need to be present on the call. I'll have you outline the terms. If it goes well, we'll send them the engagement letter to sign. Then gather all relevant data regarding court cases filed against Richmond Holdings and all of its subsidiaries. Identify and report every terminated employee on record from Richmond Holdings who filed a complaint with the TWC or EEOC. Work your magic. Be crafty, though. Try to get the info through public channels so we don't alert any employees directly at any agency that might send info back to our potential defendant. Fill in the blanks as they arise. Make an effort to locate Teresa's complaint with the DPD. I'd like to review it."

It seemed easy enough. I tilted my head at Stone as if asking what more I could say.

"What about traveling?" Stone asked, pen in hand.

"Where I go, you'll go, and you'll schedule it. Schedule time with Brianne. Again, you'll be present for that meeting," I said, rising to my feet.

"I guess that's enough for now. Be available by phone for questions." Stone finally rose from his seat. "Time frames?" he asked, his notebook still open as he jotted notes and went for the door.

"As soon as possible. Forward any findings to me in real time." I opened the door, allowing Stone through first. I don't know how he walked through the office, lost in thought, and never tripped over anything, including his own feet. Those were Jedi powers I'd never fully mastered.

"Hey," I hollered over to Carter, waiting on the other side of the fence line. I took a quick pit stop to swap out of my professional wear into something more comfortable, athletic shorts and a T-shirt. I charged across the manicured lawn in a pair of slide-on sandals. The sun beat down relentlessly, but I convinced myself the warm ocean breeze made a difference.

"What's happening?" Carter asked. Beau and I had an aluminum fence surrounding our property. It came to about five feet tall. A sliding gate was a new addition since Carter and Linda built their home behind us.

"So what's the scoop on my father and brothers being sexual deviants?" I threw the question out, watching his face morph through a series of expressions as the gears in his mind churned.

"He's had long-term mistresses. Those old-school guys tend to keep that tradition alive. Is that what you're asking?" he asked, raising a single brow.

"No, I've had a couple of women who worked in the executive offices of Richmond Holdings approach me with accusations of some truly awful acts. There's enough evidence that I believe I'll begin to take a deeper look," I explained, my arm coming to the top of the fence, helping to support me there. "How does this look for me to handle a case against my family? Am I coming off as vindictive or vengeful?"

Carter stayed silent for several long moments. "I can't say. Can you keep your cool with all the baggage between you and them? The next question: do you have the resources to cover such an investigation? I envision he'll bury you—"

I rarely cut him off, but did this time, lifting a hand between us. "When I dive in, I'll handle the pre-suit. If we do have a class action, Lon's agreed to partner. I spoke with him this morning.

I've beat my father before over my Dallas home. He fought me for years. With him, I'll have to cut through the emotional bullshit, and stay focused on the task. It'll be hard."

"I can ask around," Carter offered. "Someone has to know something."

I shook my head. "I don't want this on anyone's radar until I get through the investigation and build the case. I can't imagine pulling it off, but I'd really enjoy throwing Richmond Holdings for a loop."

"It'd be something if you surprised them. Keep your cool and remember you have a family who loves you," Carter said, my support system through all of my adult life. "Have you told Beau?"

"We tossed it around last night. At first, Beau was a hard no, then I released more information than I normally would, and he changed his mind. I'll have some rules to follow, but he's good."

"I'll talk to Linda. She loves feeling useful to you all. Kailey was shocked and happy to have Livie doing her same homework," Carter said. "That's quite an achievement in a school known for their academic success."

"Livie's struggling with the friendship side of being so smart. We heard of a Mensa support group in Houston. It'll be a lot for Beau to handle while I'm traveling. I need to hire someone to help him and Amelia. I wish Belle hadn't gone on to bigger and better," I said.

"Ask Linda for what you need. She's already picking them up from school. I've never seen her so happy as being here with the grandbabies. She's patient with West, Fisher and Hunter, and handles them very much like Beau does, kind yet firm. It's remarkable to watch. I can see the teacher inside her. I'm certain she'll make herself available for anything you need. Beau's become chopped liver to her since the grandkids arrived."

I couldn't help but beam. I understood the sentiment. These bursts of joy that we called children taught me love was not singular—centered only on Beau, but infinite.

"I believe Lon's your best choice. He has a whole department dedicated to employment law. They're go-getters," Carter said, giving my shoulder a friendly squeeze over the fence. "Keep me updated with whatever can be shared. I'll pay closer attention in my circles."

I watched him walk away, feeling more confident after our talk. Carter wouldn't steer me wrong. He never had.

"No, I'll get the boys," I said to Beau, hearing the distinct sounds of the churning ocean lapping in the background. Beau's voice jostled in and out. I swore I heard the zip of a fishing line being cast. My guy never tired of being on the water.

"Then go inside and find out why the school wants to talk to us about Fisher."

My brows knitted together. That was news to me.

"They want to talk to us?" I asked, watching the rear camera as I backed out of a garage.

"Yeah. They asked me to come inside this afternoon when we were in the drop-off line this morning. I didn't ask if it was negative or positive. I can only assume..." I waited for him to finish his sentence, but he didn't.

"What's the assumption?" I asked, again feeling left out of the loop. And my family was a circle I tried my best to stay within.

"Amelia had to sign a couple of notes about Fisher bein' disruptive in class. When I found out, I upped the way I work with him to learn to contain his urges. He's such a sweet guy, full of energy. He can't help his outbursts right now. He knows he's annoyin', but he's tryin', and that's all we can do until he learns to control himself."

Again, all of this was news to me. I was at a loss for words.

"I think they believe it's ADHD. I feel like they'll want our approval to have him evaluated for their special ed program," Beau said, as if we were in a typical Tuesday where life happened and I didn't know about it. Oh wait, we were. Fisher was barely more than a baby. Sure, he could have ADHD but that was an awfully young age to pin him down like that.

Instead of going in that direction, I stuck with my thought on why this was the first time I'd heard about this. Amelia was getting a talking-to too. A simple updating text message wasn't too much to ask for.

"Well, if you know the problems, and it's news to me, why do I need to go in?" I said with hostility. Except, I recognized that was the exact opposite of what I wanted to happen.

"Slow your roll," Beau said in a mix of compassion and authority. "We all know Fisher has some energy and focus problems. I was the one who happened to be droppin' them off this mornin'. You've got a lot goin' on..."

"Oh come on, being late one night..." I shot out, ready for one of our rare arguments. If he and I were a team, I needed to be informed no matter the situation.

"No, that's not what I'm sayin'. I just forgot. That's it. You were preoccupied. I gave you space then forgot to say anything. We had a nice night. I don't know anything except he's gonna be fine because we'll take care of him. Now my head's occupied with everything you got goin' on. The idea of bringin' your shitty family back into our lives is a worry. Not for me but for you." Beau stopped and took a breath as I pulled the SUV to the side of the road. He wasn't appeasing me, only causing me to worry more. "And I fuckin' hooked myself this mornin'. It hurts like a bitch."

I let go of a heavy sigh. Beau was always doing things that caused him physical pain, and I freaked out every time.

"Sorry about that. I don't know how you deal with that kind of pain every day."

Stone's contact number appeared on the screen interrupting the call. Thank goodness that Stone called to save us from any further discussion over Fisher.

"I'll let you know what they say once you're home. Stone's calling," I mumbled.

Or I'd let Beau know whenever I remembered to tell him.

"Tell them we're workin' with him and we want him to have the tools he needs to be successful in the classroom. He's gonna be fine," Beau said. Damn right he was going to be fine. "Bye, good luck."

"Bye." The phone automatically connected to Stone's call. "Stone," I said and gave an inward chuckle. It always threw him off when I answered the phone using his name.

"Not today," he said, after several seconds. "You're working me entirely too hard to deal with your shenanigans. I'm connecting Teresa and Lucia with you."

"Hang on. I haven't read the document you sent to me. I will once I pick the boys up. I'll make the pitch then pivot questions to you."

"Sure. I've created a list of independent counsel, a few we've worked with before, who can help them understand what they're signing," Stone said. A common practice we regularly used. I tried to have integrity in the way I handled my legal practice. In today's world, it was hard, but still incredibly important.

"Good. Let them through."

The call fell silent for several moments as I drove into the preschool Fisher and West attended. The call connected as I backed into a parking spot facing the school.

Until this moment, I had clung to the hope that I could back out if anything indicated a scam. I wouldn't know either way by the end of the call, but the more steps I took made the potential backlash more difficult to deal with.

"Teresa?" Stone asked. "Are you present?"

"I am," she said.

"Lucia, are you present?"

"I'm here," she said, her voice shaky with apprehension. That needed to end right now. We had a long way to go and shaky confidence wouldn't help anyone.

In that same vein, I had to remove the emotion from this case. My only focus needed to be on finding the truth. Getting on the road to learn the facts was in my future. I absolutely had to get off Beau's back. He'd be carrying my load for the foreseeable future.

"Good afternoon," I said, pausing as they echoed my sentiment. "I spent much of the last twenty hours reviewing your evidence. If you agree to our terms, I'd like to proceed with representing both of you. While I'm optimistic, it's important that you understand the potential challenges and uncertainties that come with any litigation, especially in a case of this magnitude. This won't be easy on either of you. If we're able to incorporate the additional women, it will significantly strengthen your class suit. We'll begin there."

I grinned when the school doors burst open. Eventually, I saw my boys standing with their teacher holding her hands. I waved to let them know I was there. A little Dash and a little Beau were excited to see me, even while being reined in for the meeting today. "Stone has an engagement letter, a beginning contract that outlines everything. Stone will overnight the letter to each of you to receive tomorrow, I believe. Correct, Stone?"

"Yes, sir," Stone said.

"I'm cautiously optimistic. We'd like to begin assessing the scope of services and responsibilities involved. We'll keep you updated as we go. The letter we'll send overnight to each of you needs to be read thoroughly and considered carefully. It will also clearly break down the fees and payments associated with the case, and how we'll be paid for representing you. If you have a legal professional in your life, I urge you to have them read it and answer any questions. Stone or I can do that as well. Once you decide to proceed, we'll begin the investigative phase. Please take as much time as you need to feel comfortable with the services we'll offer you."

"At this point, I don't trust anyone," Teresa said. "Lucia, how about you? Do you know an attorney you trust?"

"No, I don't either."

"Then after you receive the engagement letter and have read it over, Stone's always available to answer questions until you're comfortable enough to sign. I also have a law professor at SMU. Dr. Harris is one of the finest men I know. He'll be candid with you. I promise that we'll always be honest with you. You've been through more than enough."

I'd probably label her tone as one of hesitant excitement. "Thank you, Mr.—"

"Please call me, Dash. I'm embarrassed by my last name," I said truthfully. "I'm going to leave the call. I have a pre-scheduled meeting to attend. Stone can answer any additional questions. From this point forward, every communication is recorded to protect both of us."

"Yes, sir," Stone said. "I'll remove you from the call now."

"Thank you," Teresa managed before the call disconnected.

I climbed out of the driver's seat with Fisher bounding forward, running across the yard to me. The problem was the parking lot between us. In theory, he'd stop before hitting the pavement, but I questioned whether that would actually happen and jogged toward him.

Hunter weirdly stayed with the teacher.

Fifteen minutes later, we were headed back to the SUV, hand and hand. Five of those minutes were spent waiting for the office to meet with us. The administration team wasn't happy with the disruption Fisher caused throughout the school. I reluctantly agreed to have him minimally evaluated, always reminding them of the cost Beau and I paid the private school for six children. My boy needed to be treated with care and compassion while we worked him through his struggles. The frowns the admin team greeted me with needed to turn upside down if we were going to continue attending this school.

Honestly, I felt like the annual income they received from us could fund the new annex in Sea Springs. I clutched Fisher's hand a bit tighter. He was always happy, a joy to the world, never a hindrance. At least now, this school was on my page.

22: The Out of Town Beau

March 2024

"I can't anymore," I called. "I'm gettin' old and y'all are bigger. You tired me out."

"No, you aren't, Paw," Fisher said, swimming like a bullet toward me, outpacing West and Hunter. The current trick I was performing—like a trained circus animal—was hurling each one sky-high with their professional-grade life jackets on. They added arm floaties for additional security. Each one landed in the ocean, barely breaking the surface, instantly popping out of the water.

I swear, it felt like I was juggling them for hours, not the twenty minutes max that we'd been out there. It had been a while since we'd visited the beach together. Now, I remembered why.

Fisher reached me, crawling up my body with monkey-like determination. "One more time, Paw. Throw me the highest!" The same words he'd said every time he made it into my arms. "Throw me so high I reach the birds so I can fly away too." His palms came to my cheeks, turning my eyes to see him. "But I'll come back and find you."

"Good." I held him by his torso, feeling the adrenaline pumping through his body. His grin was bigger than his mouth could support.

I launched him in the air like a human cannonball. With no fear, he sailed through the sky before making a splashdown into the water. Hunter got to me next.

"Last time," I said and hurled him up. He weighed more than Fisher and didn't go quite as high before falling into the water. West followed, the biggest of the three, he barely made it above my head this time.

Before any of them could catch me again, I waded to shore where the girls sat in the surf, hanging out together.

My cell phone issued its highest volume shrill ringtone, everyone in Sea Springs had to have heard it. Mia darted up, running toward the umbrella to answer.

"Paw! It's Daddy," she screamed into the receiver. She had to have blown his eardrums. Her face crinkled, probably being lightly scolded by Dash. "I'm sorry for yelling in your ear, Daddy. I got excited because we miss you, and Paw was racing for the phone," she said, running the phone to me. "I told him I was sorry for yelling in his ear." Again, Mia shouted directly into the microphone. "He says he misses everybody, and he'll be home tomorrow..."

I took the phone from her.

"Hello, did she yell in your ear twice?" I asked.

"I learned my lesson and moved the phone away until you said hello." Dash was always learning and adjusting.

Me, not so much. I made it to the umbrella, glancing back to make sure the boys had made it to the girls.

Maybe not the best plan. Ava knocked Fisher to the ground who was laughing uproariously. "Paw," Ava called, "he kicked the castle Livie was making! It had a third floor."

"I didn't kick it," Fisher said in a way that made me believe he might be telling the truth. The laughter said something else altogether.

"Hold your ears," I said and gave Dash about a second to do so. Duke and Dixie, asleep close to my chair, lifted their ears in the spot they'd claimed on the beach once the fun day wore them out. "Give me a minute to talk to your dad, and leave the girls alone, Fisher."

"What're you doing?" Dash asked, his tone dripping with sarcasm.

"We came to the beach when everyone got through with their Saturday activities. The girls are workin' on Girls Scout badges that they didn't want me around for, and the guys are actively breakin' their spirit, so nothin's new here," I answered, taking a seat in my beach chair. The instant shade cooled me down.

"You went to the beach without me? I'm coming home tomorrow," Dash said, dejectedly.

Since my guy had become a weekly traveler, my life had turned into a chore. Not awful, but I now better understand why people were shocked about us having six children in six years. Exhaustion was a daily part of my life. I was ready for a nap.

"You promised to discuss bein' gone for more than three days at a time," I answered matter of fact, digging around in the side pocket of my chair for my sunglasses. "You're slidin' into a consistent four days gone. This is five. I haven't had sex in six days, which means you're busy all mornin' and night tomorrow. What if the next time you decide not to come home for seven days? You need to store me up. Can you handle three times tomorrow?"

"Ha ha," Dash said, instantly defensive of his sexual prowess. "You're not funny."

"Ha, ha. It's funny because it's true," I tossed back.

"It's not true. Far from funny, and we'll see how long it takes you to sit comfortably when I'm done with you," he boasted. "I'll be home more after this trip. So are you picking me up in the morning?" Dash asked.

"From Southwest?" I asked.

"Gate five at seven twenty-five. I miss you," he said, much more quietly.

Of course, I never gave him a break. The rest of Dash's life came easy. Someone had to keep him on his toes. "If you missed me, you'd have come home on time."

"Baby, I know you're giving me a hard time, and it's deserved, but I'm exhausted and the wind and ocean and you and the kids sound wonderful."

"So you've been productive?" I asked. We were months into the investigative stage of the pre-suit. This phase had taken longer than he believed it would, I wanted him home badly. I loved being a parent, and I loved my life, but all of that included Dash. With him no longer around, all the activity felt like a chore.

"Very. We added five additional complainants. Brianna and Stone have done an exceptional job. Stone's an incredible young man, the way he sniffs out information and digs into research is better than anyone I've worked with. He's a pro. I'm probably going to have to put him through law school."

"When do you file the complaint?" I asked.

"Next week," Dash said. "I'll fly back to Chicago, and that'll put an end to weekly travel. I miss you, Beau-beau. It's unbearable to be away."

"Are you with Lon now?" I asked, which I didn't normally do.

I took it as my job to never let him forget what he almost threw away, not in a destructive way, but to keep us both on our toes. But I rarely brought up Lon. They were too much alike. He still bothered me.

Silence held us both, answering my question. "So you're in Chicago right now?"

"I am," Dash said quietly.

"Has anything changed there?" I asked. The question was a far bigger one than it seemed.

My heart picked up its beat. Dash needed to come home. I needed him here.

"The city's still too busy and too fast. I landed here this morning. Lon and I talked about timing and other things. We're having dinner with Penny tonight for them to meet Stone and Brianne in person. Brianne's staying in Chicago for the time being. I'll fly back for an overnight trip next week. I want you to come with me."

"Do you miss that life?" I asked quietly. Dash had worn his success well there. It was busier, at a much faster pace, in a far different way than our slice of the world. "You're stuck here with me forever now, but that was a pretty glitzy life."

"I don't miss a single second. I do miss the complexity of the caseload..."

A scream pierced the confession, and I glanced over at the kids. Ava was chasing Fisher who darted away so fast, she couldn't keep up.

"Paw! Make him stop." Ava darted this way and that, until she abruptly halted and screamed to the heavens. Her fists and body shook under the force. "He makes me crazy. Now we have to start over again. We were almost done."

"I've gotta go," I said, my silly jealousy evaporating into nothing. "Remember when you wanted more children after West?" I said teasingly. "We should've included the girls in that decision. We have a solid divide now. I'm not sure this will end well for us."

Dash laughed but didn't disagree. "Go deal with them. Check for the correct gate in the morning. I love you."

Those three words ended every one of our conversations. "I love you too."

I tossed the phone on a towel, while getting to my feet. "Let's load up. I'll bring y'all back to finish the badge if we can't do it at home."

The dogs stood too, shaking the sand from their coats. The sheer volume of beach necessities had turned me into a pack mule. I sighed as I looked at all the stuff we had to get back home. I called over our two youngest. We had a new addition to our family fun in the form of child leashes for Fisher and Hunter. The only reason we used them was to keep them from running into traffic without realizing what they had done. It enabled me to focus on everything else while doing my best to keep them all safe out here on my own.

Seven twenty-five in the morning turned to eight forty-five as I waited in the garage facing Southwest Airlines arrival section for Dash to land. I arrived early enough to park with a clear view of the terminal's baggage claim carousels, waiting for Dash's text message that he was on his way out.

Every time he traveled, it was the same routine. His checked bag included the necessities: suits, shoes, and valuable grooming products. His carry-on was strictly reserved for his tech equipment. The airplane hadn't landed yet, the baggage handlers still had to unload the luggage, and my bright idea of renting a cheap motel to fuck my guy was looking less and less likely as the minutes ticked by. My anticipation for Dash's return was slipping into frustration. My body had its own grievances, and they weren't subtle.

The sharp buzz of my phone jolted me out of my thoughts. I glanced at the phone's screen. The name "Lauren Lee" popped up, and I hesitated before answering. She represented today's responsibility, something I wanted to avoid if only Dash could parachute out of the plane to make my sex dreams a reality in that moment.

"We're adding a second balloon arch leading into your side of the property, guiding people to the reception area in your backyard."

"That's fine," I replied, though my thoughts were far from decorations.

They circled back to Daisy Mae, the bride-to-be, and my unresolved feelings about her impending marriage. She was too young, far too young, to be tying the knot with her service member boyfriend and moving halfway across the world. I had always imagined a different path for her—college classes, a degree, a life of her own before settling down. But she was in love, deeply so, and they had been inseparable for the last four years. Who was I to stand in the way?

"The chairs are here being set up with the round tables for the reception. They have the table drapes. The bands each have a portable floor. I think the buffet is set up. The food arrives about twenty minutes before we start. The flowers are here now. The cake..."

"What's Scott doin'?"

"He's bouncing between trying to convince Daisy Mae to change her mind and helping the valet company rope off the parking area. He's not taking this well."

"I know. I wanted somethin' different for her, but I honestly don't know what that is," I said, staring at the sliding glass doors, opening and closing randomly with no one coming anywhere around. "I've been dedicated to Dash since I was fifteen. It's not easy, but I suspect no one's life is great all the time. A different road might only mean bullshit comin' at her in other ways. And livin' in Italy is gonna be badass," I said, understanding my sexual quest in a seedy motel was no longer possible.

My imagination really enjoyed the mental imagery of fucking Dash so hard, for so long, that he needed medical care.

We needed to be home, helping everyone get ready for Daisy Mae's big afternoon today. The wedding was planned to start at about two in the afternoon, in Scott's backyard. The reception followed, ending at about nine o'clock. Daisy Mae was taking an early flight to Italy with her guy tomorrow morning.

"Here comes pouty Scott. I'll see you two when you get here. I need Dash to take over the organizational part of the planning. I have to do everyone's hair before the wedding and do all my children's hair. It's going to take hours."

"Dash will probably sneak off and leave me in charge while he slides in line to get his hair done."

"I took care of him last weekend. He won't need a refresh until next weekend."

"We'll see," I said as a text message came through. "Go. We'll be home as soon as he lands."

"Bye, Beau. Thank you for everything. I don't know where we'd be without you in our lives," she said, tears in her voice. The feelings of appreciation and love were what the four of us all did really well. It was honestly the foundation that built everything we stood on today.

"Lauren..." The sweet sentiment welled within me, not easily meshing with the sexual demands my mind was still lost within, but I did smile, even if she didn't see it. "Bye."

I navigated to my notifications. Dash had texted me.

"*We're still in the air circling. I'm sorry to keep you waiting.*"

I wasn't sure I'd ever replied to a text faster.

"*You bought an internet package?*" I replied. That had to cost as much as the hotel I'd found. "*You know that's expensive.*"

"*Something's happened down there.*"

Then came another. "*It's going to be at least twenty more minutes before we land.*"

The third. "*Meet me in baggage claim.*"

Well, hell.

"*I found a motel two blocks from here. I thought we could get it on.*" I replied, knowing I was the only person who ever typed paragraphs in text format. "*Because you said you were arriving at seven twenty-five. Lauren's already wanting us to get home for the wedding. You have to land right now to make it happen. I need adult interaction.*"

I pushed *send*, never feeling more unreasonable in my life.

"*Oh, I'd really like a quickie in a motel alone.*"

Then another. "*I've missed you bad this time.*"

Another text arrived seconds later. "*I should be landed with baggage by nine thirty.*"

Then came. "*I wanna fuck your mouth.*"

And. "*Delete that text so the kids don't see it.*"

Fuck. Nine thirty. I sat back, dejected, staring at baggage claim. We had an hour drive home. If we stopped, even making it fast, we wouldn't be home before eleven thirty. We had to get the kids ready, dress ourselves, make final adjustments to the house, the yard, and help in whatever Scott had going on. We didn't have time.

My frustration turned to disappointment.

"*What do you say?*" Dash asked.

I chewed over my reply. The guilt of reality made my fingers type disappointing words. "*I don't think we can. I promised to help and Scott's already pissed off at the day. Had the flight arrived...*"

Dash didn't say another word. Not even to get me to break my promise to Scott. I waited until nine thirty before my boredom got the best of me, and I went inside to wait for him in baggage claim. It still took another half hour.

Later that evening, amidst the humming and laughter of activity in our backyard, I couldn't help but think we might as well turn the place into a wedding venue with all the events we hosted. Maybe then Dash wouldn't have to take another grueling case that left its mark—a semi-permanent frown etching itself across his face most of the time.

My phone buzzed, and the candid video made me pause. Dash real-time video called, showing himself in the center of a packed dance floor, our children clinging to his legs like monkeys. They were relentless, challenging him to move with their weight hanging on to him. They sent him toppling onto his ass in a heap of laughter and shrieks, and the joy in their faces was something I wanted to bottle up and save forever.

I found them on the dance floor. Dash, with his seemingly limitless energy, wore a grin that lit him up in a way I hadn't seen in a while. I snapped a few pictures, capturing the moment while the ache of his absence in my chest softened into something warmer. I wanted to be with them, in the innocence of it all, piling on and laughing like the world beyond our backyard didn't exist.

"Everyone, gather to the front porch and driveway," Lauren's voice crackled through Amelia's prized microphone, pulling me from my overthinking. "Scott's outside, guiding people where to stand."

The kids shot to their feet. Their wedding energy was boundless. They started to bolt toward Scott's house like it was their second home, which honestly, it was.

"Hold up," Dash called. His hands landed on the back of Fisher's shirt and Mia's arm. "We'll go together. It's dark and I don't want you getting hurt because people can't see you." His protective tone was both gentle and firm, the kind of authority that made me admire him all over again.

I went toward the gate, closer there than they were, and began to wrangle my six together, knowing they'd get distracted with a half-dozen other fun things along the way.

"Stay close," I told them, grabbing their attention with a new objective. "We need to take our birdseed pouches. Remember what I showed you—throw the birdseed high in the air when Daisy Mae walks past. Aim for height and distance, not each other."

Lauren had a small table strategically placed at the fence gate which was neatly arranged with ribboned pouches. Mia's face lit up at the sight—tonight's romance was something she was soaking in wholeheartedly. She shot me a grin, one that warmed my heart, and grabbed a sack. Her other hand wiggled into mine.

We searched for an empty place along the driveway. "You're a great paw for teaching them how to throw the birdseed properly." Dash's chin brushed against my shoulder as his arm circled my waist, drawing us to a spot a few feet from the festively decorated getaway car.

I leaned into his simple touch, savoring his warmth and unwavering inner strength. "I didn't want them blinding someone by chucking the stuff like a baseball. West, by the way, is determined to play T-ball. Starts in a few weeks."

Dash chuckled. His breath was soft against my ear. "What about the other two?"

"I'm steerin' Fisher toward basketball. He's got too much energy not to burn it off on the court." Before he could answer, cheers erupted around us. Daisy Mae and her groom emerged from the house, quickening their steps as they descended the porch stairs, their heads ducking as birdseed showered over them in a messy, joyful fall.

"Throw now!" I reminded my crew, lifting my arm to demonstrate the motion again. Of course, their aim was chaotic, most of the birdseed ending up on themselves. I couldn't help but smile, hoping at least one photographer captured the moment.

"Daisy Mae," Mia's voice rang out, cutting through the noise. Daisy Mae turned back, breaking protocol and beamed as she rushed toward the girls for one last hug. "You look so beautiful in your wedding dress," Mia said, her awe shining through.

Their hugs were a tangle of arms and love. "I'm gonna miss you three," Daisy admitted, her voice cracking as a tear slipped free.

"You don't have to miss us," Livie chimed in. "We have you on WhatsApp. We can talk every day."

Daisy nodded, her smile bittersweet. "Then we'll talk every day. Maybe you can even visit us."

Ava's eyes darted to Dash and me, her expression an unspoken question. I felt Dash nod subtly behind me, but deep down, we both knew the visit wouldn't happen anytime soon.

23: The Investigation Dash

Stone's fingers were a blur while moving over the keyboard. His gaze stayed glued to one of the three monitors on his desk, displaying a page of line by line blacked out text. He turned the monitor my way. "They released the complaint, but most of it's redacted. Why release it then?"

"My father's trying to play the victim," I explained, barely glancing up as I thumbed through the physical mail left for me on Stone's desk. "It's the reason for every extra moment we took to get this right. Why's the sound system off?"

"It's not off in your office," Stone replied, still typing. "Upstairs complained the music you were selecting was too distracting."

Distracting? A soft instrumental?

Heat crept over me. I began to feel my own sense of harassment from my team. Every last one of them needed to be placed on disciplinary action for having no refinement or taste for a better life. Music equaled the path to great things.

"Maybe you should," Stone said, his eyes finally lifting to give me a knowing look.

"Did I say that out loud?" I asked, though I knew the answer.

"No." His gaze moved back to the screen. "I know you too well. You want to begin the process of firing everyone who works for you." Yeah. He proved he'd read my thoughts accurately. "I say we should move them to a new building where they can't mess with this vibe. It's a great office."

Luckily, before I inked that decision in place, my cell phone vibrated in my front pants pocket. I was surprised to see Lon's name on a text. We rarely texted or emailed for that matter, strictly staying professional. All other communication was done privately, through untraceable measures.

"Richmond Holdings has responded."

"Stone's reading it now. They're ridiculous. We're gonna have a madhouse on our hands. I'll call you back."

Before the words were fully out of my mouth, the telephone's control panel lit up like a Christmas tree in the darkness of night. Instantly, every line flashed with an incoming call. Even though we'd kept a very low profile, and the last few days since filing the complaint had been quiet, I'd sent a directive for my staff to consider working from home. Those few here were the diehards. The ones who didn't like life outside of work, or music, or happiness, for that matter.

I had also approved private protection for Brianne, Stone, Beau, Amelia, and the children. I'd expanded it to include the women listed in the complaint. The expenses in this case were through the roof and we'd barely begun.

I left Stone at his desk and headed for my office to see what was being said online.

"Beau's barreling up in his old fishing pickup, tires screeching and so on," Stone said through the intercom system he used even though I was feet away. "Seems dramatic."

"Hmm." I stood behind my desk. When my husband was riled up, he rarely kept quiet. His voice carried, loud and unapologetic. I waited, knowing he'd storm through the door, straight for my office. Once here, Stone generally shut the door behind Beau, and stopped actively listening to give Beau privacy, certainly not me.

I heard the bells clang against the door as it was slammed open.

"Where is he?" Beau announced angrily. "Stone, you need to pack this up and go home. If you need help, I'll take you," he said with authority, as if he had the right to dismiss my staff.

The clomp of his booted feet came through my office door, and he scanned the room. His cell phone was at his ear.

"The sorry bastards made all this public like it hadn't been hangin' over their heads for a few days. They're attackin' you and said the allegations are a malicious attempt to ruin their family's bullshit values. They're talkin' about you like you're a piece of shit they were forced to do away with. They're givin' a further public statement at four o'clock. Come on, you gotta go home. I need to get the kids. Everyone needs to stay home and be safe."

His frustration ended with his hands flying through the air then dropping to his sides. Whoever was on the phone was forgotten.

"They're stirrin' people up against the way we live. Scott says it has to be bots, but it hit social media hard, instantly everywhere. You're immediately trendin'. It had to be a planned attack. It's not gonna be safe for you or Stone. Not in today's world. We gotta get you home." His thumb tossed over his shoulder. "I was buyin' bait and Scott called. That's why I was here so fast."

Stone came to the middle of the doorway, arms crossing worriedly over his chest, concentrating on Beau. I understood where Beau's anxiety came from, but as I stared at my guy in his best fishing attire, his smell wafted toward me. It wasn't great. There was zero chance I was getting into the cab of his truck. I felt sure Stone agreed.

My phone began a rapid-fire succession of texts from my colleagues and friends.

"*Game time.*"

"*Keep your head up.*"

"*The mudslinging has started. It appears you're the target.*"

"*I'll respond with a public statement. Stay low.*" That one came from Lon and was a rare statement of concern, which validated Beau's unease.

"I forwarded the phones to Lon's office," Stone said, his fingers hovering over his nose as if to fend off Beau's odors. "And told the people in the office to go home."

"Lon's handling the communication," I explained to Beau. "I miscalculated the depth of finger pointing. I didn't expect what you're saying to happen so swiftly. They must have hired a marketing firm to bombard social media. Let's get everyone home and reconvene from there." Stone didn't need to be told twice. He was gone, closing down his station. My inner chaos was working overtime which made my outward calm close to comatose. I reached for my suit coat, shrugging it on.

"Babe, I love how you're here to put yourself between me and harm's way, but everyone just needs to take a calming breath, which is hard to do with the way you smell," I explained.

"I've been cleanin' fish. Why's that even a concern?" Beau asked, aggravated, coming at me as I started out of my office.

"Is Beau taking me home?" Stone asked. "I have Febreze."

"Of course, he's not taking you home. I'm paying an exorbitant amount of money for your safety. You're fine," I said, locking my office door behind Beau. "Are you following me?"

"Yeah," Beau said, shaking his head at the obvious absurd question as he started out of the building. Once outside, the sun was shining brightly, the birds chirping. If the chaos was in fact true, it wasn't reaching us yet, which had to be a good sign.

"I love you," I added, splitting from him to head to my parking spot.

"What does that matter right now?" he asked, following me. "The kids don't even know about the security people. That school's front office can be dense. Have you told them..."

Beau was apparently the other thing I didn't plan for properly. He loved me by pushing my head down and inside the vehicle as I lifted into the Tahoe.

I locked him out as soon as I could and started the engine.

Hours later, Beau and I sat on the edge of the mattress in our bedroom with the door shut and locked, the television on. The media frenzy outside Richmond Holdings' Dallas headquarters had reached a fever pitch, blocking traffic for miles. Every local and national media outlet was present, based on the sheer volume of cameras waiting for my father's arrival. Their calculated response included both old- and new-school tactics, mainstream media, as well as all social sites covering this breaking news story.

My leg bounced, the tension was unbearable.

Beau's steely palm landed on my thigh. "It doesn't matter what they say. You've proved your case. You're in the right. We'll get through it."

I wished I believed him. If Richmond Holdings effectively turned the court of public opinion into believing this was a personal vendetta, the claimants would be branded liars and receive hell. It was coming for them anyway, but I hoped it would come after a substantial plea offer. They were behaving as if we were headed to court the next day.

"Maybe I should have just handed this off to another firm," I said, allowing my other leg to bounce since Beau stopped the first.

"Shh, it's startin'," Beau said, his focus only on the screen.

I watched the show my father and brothers put on, their wives standing dutifully by their side. They were dressed in their finest. Their council led the charge. I hadn't seen them this united since maybe when we were here in Sea Springs, opening the resort, when I was sixteen years old. My father had gained weight and appeared older than I remembered him.

He'd also won against this town, burying the livelihood of everyone here without a backward glance. He was ruthless to his core.

My thoughts shifted, realizing how I didn't fit with them any longer, not in appearance or values. My hair was darker, my frame was taller, leaner, and overall in better shape. I was happy… At least until the last few months. Their stern features were set in place. The combative attitude was natural, not a performance, making it easier to play the lying victims.

"Stupid motherfucker," Beau growled quietly. "I hate your old man. Try to come for us."

Beau caused me to tune into the words being spoken. I'd have to double back to listen more closely when I had time. All I managed to hear was Collin, the brother closest to my age, coming to the microphone, introducing himself.

"We're certain these false claims are nothing more than a shakedown. To prove to the world that Richmond Holdings has nothing to hide, I'm personally authorizing Stuart Intelligence, an independent investigation company, to conduct a thorough internal review of every allegation alleged against us. We will prevail."

Stuart? Until right that moment, I believed Stuart Intelligence was an integrity-driven international investigation company. I didn't believe they could be bought. Perhaps, I was wrong.

"Fuck, these people. Thank God, I never had to know them," Beau barked at the screen. At the same time, the doorbell rang. We both glanced in that direction. Seconds later, Amelia was banging on our bedroom door.

"Dasham, the authorities are at our front door. They can see me right now through the windows. Do I answer?" she called, fearfully.

"You know, they've been fuckin' waitin' to show up," Beau barked, pushing off the mattress and heading toward the door. "I assume they've been called by the man who still owns the biggest hotel in the area to question the safety of my children, due to my sexuality, and our livin' conditions. Not any real harm happenin' to them."

Thanks to Beau's insistence, all our ducks were in a row. We were a legal family, but my father was connected in Texas, boundaries could easily be blurred.

"I sent the children to your mom's house," Amelia said when Beau popped open the door. "They're through the fence line." Her voice was shaky, her face paling. I followed Beau out, seeing a police cruiser and sedan parked in front of the house.

"This is only for show, Amelia," I said. "They're trying to make me out to be the bad guy, so I'll drop the case."

"I want to drop your father," Beau murmured, harshly.

"Go to Linda's house," I said to Amelia. "Take the dogs with you. Beau, let me handle it. Stay quiet. They don't need to see your anger."

Two armed police officers stood behind a lady in a suit. I recognized her from court, a child protection service agent.

"What could you possibly want?" Beau asked angrily, swinging the door open wide.

"Beau, let me handle it," I said sternly, stepping in front of him, speaking to the woman. "I expected you. Perhaps not this soon, but I knew I'd be hearing from you. Would you like to come inside to talk?"

"Come in?" Beau hissed behind me. "Of course, they're not comin' in."

"Beau," I said, my chin tilting over my shoulder, talking firmly to him. "This is nothing more than a formality. I did make them aware of the class suit, and a possible retaliation call. Go calm down. No one is questioning our parenting. When you're yourself, come back. Until then, I'll handle this."

I used my body to cut him off from the others, swinging an arm out to invite the three inside.

"Since we were first together, his father has done everything to destroy Dash..."

Omigod, he had to stop. I swung around, my palms landing on his chest, and pushed. My gaze pleaded with him. "Seriously, go to Scott's. I'll handle this. Keep your phone on."

Beau glanced down at me, then past me to the agent before rolling his eyes and heading toward the back door. "I'll be on the porch if you need me."

"Perfect," I murmured, exhaling slowly. As much as I hated to admit it, I could already see a full CPS investigation looming on the horizon. We had nothing to hide, but even the process could be damaging if spun the wrong way.

Turning back to the trio, I forced a polite smile. Inside, I was fighting an internal battle, every nerve ending in my body screaming to stay sharp.

This wasn't about me or my family. We were in a battle of right versus wrong, good versus evil.

I led the three into the living room, my mind already mapping the conversation. Calm, measured, and cooperative. Every word, every gesture, had to serve the bigger picture. We couldn't let my father's theatrics derail the truth. Yes, I misjudged how fast things would deteriorate, but I was caught up now.

I squared my shoulders, ready for the fight of my life.

"Can I get you something to drink?"

24: The Shred
Beau/Dash

Beau

"Paw, this must be serious. Everyone's at the table at once, and there's no food, or drinks," Ava quipped from her usual spot at the kitchen table. Her legs swung back and forth beneath her chair, the rhythmic motion a sign of her restless energy. "Lay it on us."

I hesitated but met her gaze. My firebrand of a daughter who, of all the children, needed to absorb this warning the most. She had to learn to control her outbursts starting right now.

"This is serious, Ava. Out of everyone here, you need to heed this message the most."

"What happened today is likely to occur again. I want you prepared," Dash started from his seat beside me.

"What happened today?" Livie asked, her natural curiosity shining through.

"Hold your questions to the end, sweetheart," I said. "Otherwise, we'll never get through what your dad needs to say." Another tough request, Livie questioned everything in an effort to get to that higher plane of knowledge. "Remember, your dad's case has been tough, but he's standin' up for people who've been harassed badly and can't stand up for themselves. It's important that he follows through to the end."

West's hand shot in the air. A small smile tugged at my lips despite the seriousness of the moment. "Can it wait, West?"

"I don't know. What's harass mean?" he asked innocently. West was a good guy. Not sweet like Fisher or tough like Hunter. He'd wanted to get it right and needed to know more.

Dash's hands quietly slapped on the table, drawing attention to him. "In this case, harass means treating women badly." The ripple effect was immediate. Four additional hands shot in the air, followed by Hunter's hand, who looked more like he was mimicking the others than truly needing any clarification.

"My girls and boys, hold the questions to the end," Amelia said. The hands slowly lowered.

"I feel strongly that you're going to hear bad, crazy, untrue things about your paw and me. They'll be mean and hurtful words that will upset you because you know it's not true. I want you to ignore the bad words. If you can't ignore it, then absolutely don't show any emotion. Make your face look blank and never respond. Come home and talk to me or Paw. They're saying these things to discredit me."

West's hand shot up in the air again.

"Discredit is a complicated word. In this case it means, the bad side is trying to make me look bad instead of them. If you act out, or respond, they will make you look like the bad one too, not them. Do you understand?"

West's face looked uncertain.

"Daddy, I'm not going to do well with anyone talking bad about my family," Ava said, her shoulders slumping, seeing the task as insurmountable.

"Ava, sweetheart, I need you to let your dad handle this. I'm like you. I don't like seein' your dad made to look bad. It's incredibly hard on me, because I see him in the opposite way. He's a great man. He's my best friend, but in this case, we have to do what he asks of us. If we have an outburst, it makes his job harder," I explained.

Dash took the pivot, never breaking in our explanation. "If you hear anything about your paw and me, or about the way our family lives, keep your head down and your mouth closed and absolutely no more stomping on crayons, got it?"

"For forever?" Ava blurted in outrage. "Because it's not fair that they can say whatever they want and we can't."

"It's called taking the high road," Livie said reasonably. "We've been taught to do that for our whole lives."

"It's gonna be hard," Mia said and reached for Fisher's shoulder to give an encouraging squeeze, just like Dash and I did. Somehow, we'd gotten a lot of his outbursts down to fidget spinners and leg bouncing. He was trying his best, beautifully. I'd say he was the most sensitive of all with his newfound love of flamingos and sweet nature.

"Paw can beat 'em up," Fisher said. His expression lifted from the gadget in his hand, morphing from concentration to lightbulb moments of brilliance.

"Yeah, that's what I think," West added.

"He's stronger than all the dads," Fisher continued. "And those people who keep following us."

"Yeah. Paw got a hook caught in his hand and pushed it all the way through," Hunter added, his jaw clenching, maybe making my pained expression.

"Daddy," Livie said. "Do we only go silent if they say it in person to us?" Her big blue eyes were a telltale sign of something that might already have happened.

"What did you do?" Dash asked gently, but perceptively.

"The story about you was on the news station I follow, and they said it was you against your father, and then they talked about our lives, and the facts were all wrong," she said and paused, looking worried as she added, "I sent an email to them correcting the wrong parts."

"Livie," I started, my heart sinking, but Dash raised a hand to stop me.

"Those are the things we can't do, sweetheart," he explained. "If they reach out to you, forward their message to me. Do not reply. I know you all want to stand up for each other, that makes me incredibly proud." Dash placed a hand on his heart, tapping there. "But the people causing grief are trying to distract from the truth."

Dash leaned back, crossing his arms over his chest. "I took this case because of you three girls. No one should ever be bullied just because someone else holds power over them. What's happened is grossly wrong, and I couldn't let it pass. But it means we're in for a tough fight. The people behind the harm have a lot to lose. They don't want us to win."

I reached for Dash's hand and held it.

"Your paw agrees with me, and he's not going to do well if you are given a hard time. We want the best kind of world for you to live in."

"Okay, Daddy," Mia said. Fisher followed, chirping her response. Dash looked pointedly at each of them. Probably the sternest look he'd ever given them, until he received a nod from each one down the line.

"All right, go get ready for bed. I'll be up there in a few minutes to brush your hair, and teeth, and deal with your stinky feet," I said and received a cacophony of groans and nos.

"Abuela, you do it. Paw hurts when he brushes. You don't," Ava explained rapidly.

"Okay, come on," Amelia said, her warmth and caring nature filled the room. "I'll do nighttime duties tonight." She pushed away from the table, getting to her feet. The kids scattered. My grip landed on Fisher's forearm to keep him here with Dash and me.

"I can tell you're trying really hard and we're proud of you. Be proud of yourself too," Dash said, rising to go to the other side of Fisher's chair. Our boy didn't lack confidence. He jumped up, shoes on the seat, obviously knowing Dash was going to give him a hug. Fisher launched up before Dash was ready to catch him, but luckily managed it, squeezing Fisher tightly.

"I'm proud of you too, Daddy. Can you help me protect people the way you do," Fisher sing-songed, bouncing his head back and forth. What an interesting interpretation of what he saw his dad doing. Then his legs locked around Dash's waist. "Take me upstairs!" The grip he had on Dash's fine dress shirt tightened.

"I will but show me how you plan to ignore anything ugly said about any of us."

Fisher gave an instant angry look.

Dash shook his head no.

It took a moment of thought before his face went passive.

"Good boy. This house and your family are a safe place for you to react."

"Yes, sir!" His fist charged into the air.

Fisher tried to whistle to gain Duke and Dixie's attention. This time it worked, Dixie lifted her head. Duke followed. They lumbered to their feet.

"Perhaps it's time to remove the gates," Dash said to me, though Fisher, of course took the lead.

"Hunter's tall enough now. He only falls when I push him."

Dixie came between my legs for a rub down. The weight of the world seemed to hover over us like a dark cloud, but not inside these walls. I hoped it stayed out, giving Dash the safe place he tried to give to everyone else.

Dash

October 2024

Lately, deafening silence was my constant companion. The drive from my office to home was once filled with tunes from my lifelong love of music. Last summer, I'd begun a deep dive into revisiting the styles of music from the twenties. The 1920s. An era that fascinated me. I believed it was the foundation of the music we knew today. But was it really?

I hadn't cared about finding the answer since August of last year.

Huh.

The court of public opinion was relentless. A beast that fed on the scraps of truth and spun them into grotesque narratives. My immediate family had become the metaphorical toilet paper stuck to the bottom of a dirty shoe—dragged through the muck, yet still hanging on. Surviving each step of this lawsuit was one thing; watching Richmond Holdings hire the trash, mega-elite promotional company and equally as egregious law firm—known as the bastards of the industry—was quite another.

Of course, my father wouldn't admit fault. He wouldn't say, "You caught me. My bad."

But he also hadn't made any attempt to quietly negotiate a settlement. Not that we'd accept, but they hadn't even tried to keep this mess hidden. Instead, their entire battle strategy was to make me into the ultimate villain.

My family, my sweet children, his grandchildren were collateral damage, branded as the unclean filth of my supposed selfishness.

The viral clips were the worst of it. The savagely trolled plaintiffs, their entire lives were turned upside down. And my beautiful husband, Beau. Somehow, he escaped persecution. The public had latched onto his image as the all-American college football-playing, mountain-loving fisherman. His charters were booked solid, even during the off-season. It was as if they'd forgotten he was my husband.

What was I thinking, letting this get to me? Why did my heart hurt every single day? I was a damned good lawyer, how they had wormed their way past my carefully placed walls was a testament of how much I wished things were different. But this wasn't about me. The abused women deserved better from the system.

Stone had become a family confidant with as much time as he spent consoling and listening to all our clients' fears. He kept them on track. I felt a big bonus coming his way.

Maybe I was tired. Light dimmed the more exhausted a person was.

As I turned onto our street, I tried to summon my joy. My children were like hound dogs, sniffing out anything that was off. They'd pounce, peppering me with questions until I either lied or left the day behind. Might as well shed the melancholy before I saw them.

The cell phone's ring startled the shit out of me. Stone's name appeared on the screen.

A strong urge to ignore the call gripped me, but I answered anyway. "Guy, you're making a habit of calling after work hours. Put it in an email. I'll answer as I can. It's not a hard rule to follow."

Silence. The kind that stretched so long I checked the screen to see if we were still connected. If I spoke first, he'd win the silence battle. Keyboard clicks clattered in the background.

"The last time I called you after hours was last year. When I called you about this case."

"Wow," I said, trying to show my tease. "Correcting your employer? Bold move."

"It's not bold. We operate on a platform of open communication to evolve performance and productivity," he said. "I know because I created the employee handbook."

"Then not having the company's best interest is actionable..." I couldn't say it without laughter. Stone cared more about my company, honestly, our company, than anyone. Oh lord, was I thinking about law school and eventual partnership with Stone? My shoulders tensed.

"Sir, I'm calling for a reason," Stone said sternly, clearly not seeing my humor. "We received five bags of shredded documents. They arrived a few minutes after you left."

"Are you saying you received bags of shredded paper?"

"Yes. From an old school shredding machine. Example: let's shred our documents because we had to print them on paper—because we're old—kind of shred," he explained.

My brain zipped through a million thoughts, but Stone's words still made no sense. Piecing shredded paper together was a 1970's police-style movie kind of detective work. In the real world, we used flash drives, wiped histories, and VPNs to hide the trail.

I couldn't wrap my head around it. "Tell me again."

"We received five bags of shredded paper, maybe five minutes after you left," Stone repeated. "The shipment came from Richmond Holdings in downtown Dallas. When I asked who within Richmond sent this to us, they didn't know."

Fascinating. "Is there a way to piece the information together?" Seemed a legit next question.

"Not without putting it together strand by strand. It's not out of the question that this could be an attempt to spin our wheels. I could see their joy in making us put together a graphic message after a weekend's worth of work," Stone said.

"And it's Friday," I murmured. Beau was going to be angry.

"So where am I going to sleep?" Stone asked.

"Carter built a new guesthouse between us." Of course Stone knew, but I said it anyway. "We can spread out in there if it's vacant. I need to see if it's free. Come on over now. I'll figure a space for you," I said, my finger poised to end the call.

"It'll be more efficient if I can go home and pack a bag on the way to your house."

"Maybe I should send Beau to ride with you. How do these things play out? I've never had a paper shred case before," I said, my mind tumbling over Stone's safety and the security of what was dropped in our laps. "Are these old records?"

"Don't know," he said calmly. "The paper seems fresh. You've made me nervous. Am I safe with the shred? Do we need to have it securely transported?"

"Let me hang up. I'll call Carter then find Beau. You know what? Have the security guard load your car then you two ride over here together," I said, now worried how Beau was going to view this interruption to our routine. "See if Brianne's in town. Get her over here too."

Somehow, I'd made it to the driveway and parked in front of the house. Beau wasn't home yet. And a weird case just turned weirder. I certainly didn't want my father to make any more of an ass of me than he had.

Forty-eight hours later, Beau wasn't the only one growing a beard. While I worked through the days and nights with Stone, my mister slept, worked his charters, and played with our children. He also ate some of my tamale dinner while bringing it to the guesthouse.

Where Beau shined was in sending Livie out to help us. She thrived in the chaos, her sharp mind piecing together the fragments like a pro. If I could make this her daily life, I'd be her favorite parent forever.

But then we hit something, changing the entire energy in the small space.

We found text message threads from my father's cell phone, or so it appeared.

The realization hit like a punch in the gut. I instructed Livie to stop reading, but I couldn't stop myself. The messages were damning. Each page held a back-and-forth exchange that contained condemning behavior. Once we put the pages in order, the heinous acts were all laid bare.

I handed the latest page to Stone, who read it and paled.

"How do we prove it to be true?"

"We have to find the people who own these different phone numbers," I said. "The most consistent number has to be my father's or brothers."

"I can do that," Stone said with a yawn. He had his laptop on top of his lap, clicking away. "I'll probably need some real sleep. That was an obvious answer that I missed completely."

"Livie, baby, only follow the patterns. Don't read anything or I'll have to stop you and send you back to the house," I said, coming to stand behind her. She sat at the table inside the open kitchen and living room, a lamp was on nearby. Her fingers moved deftly as she brought piece after piece together.

Her gaze darted up to me. Her hands stilled. The disappointment was clear. "Don't stop me. I like it. I haven't read any of it since we saw the first bad word. But, Daddy, I'm helping the people too, so let me keep going."

My hand coasted down her hair. She'd been at it with us for almost the entire time. This might be the only occasion that she hadn't bathed in a twenty-four-hour period in her life. My heart tripped at her happiness at helping others.

Maybe she'll take over my practice someday.

Maybe I could shred a bunch of paperwork and put it in front of her, perhaps the dictionary. She'd have the best time. I grinned broadly, even through my exhaustion.

25: The Lon Beau

"Homework goes directly in the backpack," Amelia called from her spot in front of the stove. Her voice wove through all the tendrils of chaos happening in the hub of the house: the kitchen.

"I'm not finished," West said, pencil in hand, concentrating on the math assignment in front of him. "I don't really get the shapes being math."

"Put it in your backpack. We'll go over it after dinner," I said, working Fisher's folder into the small pack he wore.

"Paw, they don't give us enough time to play anymore. We go to school and home and homework and dinner and baths and reading then bed." West's hands splayed out as if trying to solve the complicated problem. "So we only get to play on the weekend?"

"On Saturday, you gotta go to practice and do chores, goofball," Ava said, shuffling her feet to the small area in the kitchen where a desk was supposed to be. Instead, we had hooks for backpacks and lunch bags to hang on, ready to be picked up on the way out in the morning. That station was critical to the success of the morning.

The girls' designated hook spaces were neat and organized. Even their shoes were nicely placed underneath. The boys clearly didn't get the value of order, or properly fastened zippers, or the strap on the end of the backpack that actually hung on the hooks. Chaos ensued within their three spaces.

To my mom's constant irritation, I knew I was the same way at their age. Maybe I was still that way, but I loved them. That love regularly drove me to return back to school with different assignments left at home. Sometime soon, I was going to have to show them tough love , which would be so much harder on me than them. It wasn't going to be fun.

"Paw, do you think it's ready for a badge?" Livie asked.

What she really meant was she wanted me to sign the bottom of the intricately thought through, and way overprepared form to earn a Girl Scout merit badge for both her and Mia. Ava had given up a long time ago. Mia loved the scouting program, being all earthy and devoted to keeping every single bug alive. For Livie, it was a competition that resulted in a small, triangle-shaped iron-on badge as an award. She had to have all of them by now.

She handed me a pen, and I scribbled my name at the bottom.

"I need six dollars before I turn it in." Livie beamed.

"Remind me in the mornin'."

"I need six dollars too," Fisher growled. He jumped into a fighter stance, pulling out two hip-holstered finger laser guns and began shooting me. He was excellent with the sounds, hands and mouth coordinated perfectly. Less than an instant later, all the boys began laser shooting each other.

"Abuela made the salad with peaches and blueberries," Mia's words tumbled out excitedly, dropping the table napkins in front of me. I was still sitting in the same seat I started in an hour ago. "It has the lemon poppy dressing. It's so good."

"Yum. Go wash your hands before dinner," I said, waggling my eyebrows at her excitement as a set of headlights beamed across the living room.

"Can you see who it is?" I asked Amelia, craning my head until I was standing, to see better out the front windows.

"Looks like Dash's Tahoe, but he's taking Lon to the airport."

Lon had flown in for the afternoon, the first time ever coming to Sea Springs, but Amelia was right, Dash was driving him to a private airport in South Houston. I knew that with certainty because I checked the schedule and planned accordingly. Which meant, when the kids went down for bed, so did I.

The world required too much work to continue at this pace for much longer. A yawn broke my mouth open as if to drive the point home.

"Daddy's home," West hollered, vaulting over a kitchen chair with the grace of a reckless rhinoceros. He bolted for the door, the other kids stampeding after him. Their laughter echoed and footsteps clomped as they went. Dixie and Duke came crashing through the doggie door at a full run to greet Dash too.

My breath caught as West opened the front door and revealed Lon's unmistakable figure. For a moment, the world stilled, going quiet. Tunnel vision showed two men standing in the doorframe—Dash, with his familiar energy, and Lon, whose presence seemed to absorb the room like a gravitational force. They were an eye-popping, heart-slamming duo, physically speaking.

How was Lon better looking today, than ten years ago?

"Daddy's with a friend," Hunter exclaimed, his voice piercing the quiet. My world slingshotted back into place as Lon stepped over the threshold into *every* room because of this ridiculously open concept home. My stomach flip-flopped, an exhale finally released, allowing additional breath into my lungs.

I hadn't expected to ever see him again.

Definitely, not see him here in my house.

Especially not tonight.

Dash knew my feelings.

The overwhelming green-eyed monster took over the reasonable side of my headspace. Except it didn't. Lon was the kind of guy who mesmerized you. I wanted to know him. I wanted to be him, and I wanted my own mesmerizing guy to stay away from him.

The life Lon represented was a polar opposite to ours.

"Paw didn't think you'd be home tonight," Livie murmured, her steps faltering as Dash ushered Lon further inside. Lon's sharp, discerning gaze swiftly scanned the large space, stopping briefly on each child.

In better lighting, I saw the age, but time had treated him unusually kind. The silver streaks in his groomed beard and dark hair added to his air of refinement. Somehow, he seemed more striking—his presence commanding and effortless.

"Good God," Lon said with a low whistle, his lips curving into a wry grin. "The girls are identical and beautiful. You'll be fending off the boys with a baseball bat, Dash."

The room hummed with unspoken questions, and the dogs bouncing for attention.

I was stuck under the weight of what Lon's return might mean. Fisher gave his quiet whistle, commanding the dogs.

My boy had my back in calming the two down.

Lon's discerning gaze settled on me. Sharp and warm, I felt instantly exposed, but okay with that. "You've got your hands full." He strode across the room like he owned the place, his hand extending to me. I clasped it. "Dash was driving me to the airport when I realized I hadn't seen your bunch in person."

His charming gaze caught Amelia coming around the table, and he smiled.

"Are you staying for dinner?" she asked.

Answer *no*, answer *no*, answer *no*, my inner voice chanted. I hadn't dealt with Lon since I left Chicago. No, I never directly blamed him for Dash's choices, but he'd certainly done his share to keep Dash tethered to a world that made no room for me. He was the only man to come between us. The memories hovered, unbidden.

"The plane's waiting, but you have a beautiful family. How are you all people pretty?"

"You're daddy's old boss," Livie said when the lightbulb moment connected. "You taught him how to use the law to help people."

"Correct. I'm Uncle Lon," he said, extending his hand for a proper handshake. He tucked her hand in his. She loved every second of the mature approach of life.

"You've met Livie, beside her is Ava, then Mia," Dash said, coming into the living room. "West, raise your hand. Fisher, then Hunter."

Lon's gaze swept the room, taking in each child, then the surroundings. "So who's gonna show me around this monstrosity. Do you ever get lost in this house?" Lon asked, stepping further into the kitchen.

"What the hell?" I mouthed to Dash.

My guy gave me a shrug, a movement designed to ask forgiveness, not permission. My self-esteem was going to take a solid hit after this encounter. Great.

"Stay for dinner, Lon. You can even stay the night," Amelia said. "You can stay in my room. I'll stay with the girls."

"What?" Lon said. "This big house doesn't have a guest room?"

"Too many kids," West said, mimicking my words that answered everything.

The six stood close to Lon.

Man, even my kids gravitated to the guy.

"I'll schedule another trip to spend some time. I've listened to story after story about you all. I feel like I could fit in here." Lon's index finger flipped toward Mia. "Mia, you're the easygoing one, very loving. Livie, you're super smart and neat. Then Ava..." His brow playfully dropped, indicating her normal expression, bringing them all to laughter.

"How do you feel about sticking around for dinner?" Lon asked Dash.

"We eat light and healthy," Dash warned. "Usually on the patio when it's nice outside. Can we eat out there? It's my favorite place."

"Sure," Amelia said, "redirect, my little loves. Set the patio table." One of the two salad bowls was between her hands as she headed outside. Everyone grabbed something and followed her out.

Dash walked straight up to me and stole a kiss from my lips. "I was driving—"

"My kids like him better than me," I hissed, begging my inner self to calm down and smile. Thankfully, I did.

"No they don't," Dash said.

"Did y'all get everything ready for next week?" I asked, pivoting topics until I fully explored what the heck was happening inside me. The shock of seeing Lon again had worn off. My southern manners kicked in. I needed to get drinks.

"We did, or we'll see if we did." Dash's hands went to my hips, trailing behind me outside.

"Everyone wash your hands," I called, pivoting one direction while Dash headed in the other.

I felt like my whole plan for the next couple of hours was to avoid Lon. The music that had been quiet inside our house for months began playing overhead.

The relief was instant. The sounds changed everything. If the tunes were back, then we were back.

One week later

"Babe, I'm going three-piece and adding the tie bar," Dash called from the inside of our closet. "Which means you need to wear this warm taupe suit to blend with me. We'll appear to coordinate effortlessly."

I was lying on the mattress, back against the headboard, my leg bent at the knee. My thumb rested on the channel search option on the remote, clicking until I found HGTV. We had two days before we left for Chicago. I didn't know how long we were going to be gone, but Dash wanted me there with him. Not for show, only for support. We were down to the wire, every second of every minute was planned with only room for a few unexpected twists and turns. Except those weren't afforded to me too. My whole game plan for the trial was to stay quiet and glare at the Richmonds any chance I got.

"Stone said he can send someone over tomorrow to dress us," I murmured somewhat distractedly, happy to see David Bromstad's gorgeous smile light up the screen. I tapped the increase volume button, letting that be the indicator that our favorite show was on. "If you win, let's use *My Lottery Dream*

Home to buy us a side place. What's that called—a vacation home?"

"How're you so relaxed?" Dash asked, poking his head out of the closet. "I'm the one who's done this before, and I'm a wreck."

"The anxiety medicine I started takin' last week," I said. How I hadn't started taking it years ago was beyond me. Man, did it help me put distance between me and the problem. Unlike my emotional wreck of a husband. Dash had taken the abuse he'd been handed straight to heart. I saw remnants of a young boy, seeking his parents' approval, and never getting it quite right. Those fuckers kept messing with my guy... The anger shot forward but then eased off. That's why I loved the medicine. "It's kicked in. I might take it forever."

"Yeah, I should too since it turns out, I'm the one who should be jealous of Lon," Dash said, persnickety as he crossed the bedroom, heading for the bathroom and its mirror.

What a revelation that had been. Apparently, I was the one who saw Lon in such a captivating way. Dash thought I was crazy when I described my feelings. He didn't see any of those traits in Lon, even going so far to say, Lon was entirely too high maintenance for his tastes. My guy was attracted to down-to-earth guys. The ones with a small amount of grit on them.

Still, it had been a solid week since my revelation, and he wasn't letting the jealousy go. Maybe it was a diversion for his brain. He hung on to the Lon effect for the same reason I sought the doctor out. We'd bitten off more than we could emotionally chew by going after his family. The stress was too much.

"Severe and persistent sexual abuse." They weren't words I'd ever agree to hear on repeat in our bathroom, but Dash needed to practice his courtroom voice. He had all his catchphrases ready to pull out of his back pocket.

"Boorish and sexist behavior. Predator in wait."

Sometimes the words led into sentences. Every once in a while, I heard a full paragraph. Dash was leaving nothing to chance, and honestly, damned good at his job.

When Dash's cell phone rang, I glanced at the clock while reaching across the bed for Dash's phone. Almost ten o'clock at night. Stone's name appeared on the screen. The fear of what that might mean penetrated the calm inside me. I swiped over the answer option. With a fluid sweep of my arm, I never stopped until I rolled to the other side of the bed to give Dash the cell.

"Hang on, Stone," I said.

He and I stared at one another, the intensity we shared was palpable. My hand went to his hip, as I sat on the edge of the bed, waiting. "What?" Dash asked into the cell phone.

The harsh tone reminded me that Dash was living on a thin line, trying his best to keep the savage attorney tucked away while home. The one barked word flipped him to the other side of patient in less than a second. "Why?"

My love's gaze shifted quickly back and forth. Although he focused in mostly my direction, he didn't see me—lost in the conversation.

"Meet me at the office," Dash finally said and swung around, heading back to the closet. Instinct had me dressing too. "Stone, I'm tired of being led around by my nose. They deserve nothing from me. It's too late."

I went to stand by the bedroom door, toeing on my runners, waiting for Dash. My ball cap came last to hide my bedhead. I scraped my fingers down my beard, combing it into shape.

"If it's not a plea, what would it be?"

Dash came out of his closet with the presence of power, much like a bull, searching for the matador. He wore a pair of pressed walking shorts with a collared polo shirt stretched over his chest. He had a key fob and wallet in one hand, cell phone still stuck to his ear.

"Where are you going?" Dash asked me, irritated. "I have to go to the office."

"I'm goin' with you."

My guy looked momentarily perplexed then nodded, walking past me toward the front door.

"I don't like secrecy. I'm not giving a single inch. They've lost the right to a code of conduct for the trial. I'm dying on this sword they created. Call Brianne. Have her call Lon and Penny."

He disconnected the call.

Dash dropped his chin to chest and worked the phone's keypad, never losing his direction, heading out the front door, ignoring me all the way to the Tahoe.

"Drive."

"Text Amelia. I left my phone inside," I said, climbing behind the wheel. It didn't matter what was happening. I sensed that Dash was going to lose it on someone tonight. I rarely saw him this way. Whatever happened, I hoped it was worth it.

26: The Free Fall Dash

Something akin to a fresh breeze blew through my mind as I stared at the small black-and-white photo of my family. Not a family completely made by blood, but by people who had picked me up and dusted me off after my foundation crumbled into rubble underneath me.

Where would I be today without these people in the photo?

If I had a skill, it was recognizing the one important person who'd be strong enough to walk through life with me. Beau. The rock who stood like a sentry in the waiting area, making sure he stayed between me and anything that might hurt me. That included Collin, the blood brother currently waiting in the conference room for my return. He was the sibling closest to my age. The weight of his worry caused him to appear much older.

Beau had no idea what was happening, but he waited quietly, ready to pick up whatever pieces shattered around me. My tears ebbed and flowed, never spilling over. After this was all said and done, I'd have to once again put my life back together.

The tears of my lost life, and the relief that this was almost over, had me rolling my neck and shoulders, trying to relieve the tightness there.

I sat with Stone inside my closed-door office, waiting on Lon to review the settlement offer my brother had delivered in person.

Without Beau's influence, I wouldn't know Lon or Stone. I rested my head against the headrest of my ridiculously comfortable desk chair.

I took for granted the way Beau had carefully documented our lives. The walls and shelves, end tables and credenza had strategically placed framed snapshots of us over the last twenty-four years. Such a special existence. It wasn't as if I hadn't seen the collection of photos, but today they drove their message home.

Collin had perused the candid snaps, briefly setting aside the tense, challenging meeting to show me his two beautiful children. They were toddler boys. Twins, who looked very much like Fisher.

I drummed my fingers against the armrest.

Maybe tonight represented the moment my mind had finally allowed its last thought to penetrate. The constantly pistoning cylinders had locked in place.

Through it all, this had been the most challenging time of my life.

"Carter's on his way here. I told him that you weren't available to talk until we finished, but he follows his own rules," Stone said from the other side of my desk. "On his way means flying home from Canada." A big toothy grin broke through the tension-filled wait. "Lon agrees with the terms. Teresa sent her approval to Brianne. We've reached an agreement."

Stone turned the screen of his laptop toward me. Lon's image showed him jumping up, driving his fist forward. Every ounce of fatigue Stone wore on his otherwise worry-free expression lifted. The tortuous journey had come to an end with swift, surprising finality.

Overwhelming sentiment assailed me. The fight and overload of emotional baggage was over. A tear built enough steam to trickle down my cheek. I was fucking crying when I should have been preening throughout the room. A cock of the walk. Instead, all I wanted was to fill my guy in and thank Stone. There was probably going to be a hearty hug between the two of us before this night ended.

"Let's get some signatures, then we'll have a proper celebration. I need to talk to Beau."

"Sure thing, buddy." Lon pointed his finger at me, the screen split into three with Penny, Brianne, and Lon. "Richmond-Brooks, I knew you were worth the effort. Excellent job. The student has officially outpaced the instructor."

"Oh, Lord," I chuckled. "Finish this up before you've realized what you said and take it all back."

"Beau," Stone called from the doorway to my office, laptop in hand, motioning Beau inside.

He went from appearing ass-kicking to drained in seconds when he caught sight of my tears. I wiped them away and came around my desk. "We're very close to done. We've accepted their settlement."

"Why're you cryin'?" Beau asked, unsure how to proceed. I had to reach for a tissue as I went for him. He stayed rooted just a foot inside my office. "I feel like I have to prove the kids right and go kick your brother's ass. Are those bodyguards flankin' his sides? He probably heard about my reputation and got scared."

"Oh yeah, I'm sure," I said, appreciative for the teasing words. I leaned my ass against the edge of the reception desk. "The text messages we found gave Collin what he needed to back up the Stuart Intelligence internal investigation. Richmond Holdings hasn't been a unified company for many years. The board has officially voted my father and his allies out of the company. That means the entire senior executive team. As of a few hours ago, they've all been removed. Collin's in a temporary CEO position. It's chaos over there."

I drew Beau between my parted thighs, giving Stone enough room to close the door behind him. "Did you get the settlement you wanted?" Beau asked.

"We did. Quite a bit more." As much as I wanted to say the amount, jump into his arms and celebrate our victory, I stayed in this weird, otherworldly place. I reached behind me for the printed settlement.

Beau glanced at the page, then up again, confused. "It's less than."

"Look closer."

His eyes dropped. Confusion turned into bug-eyed wonder. I almost laughed because it was probably my exact expression when I saw the total.

"Dash, is it billions?"

I nodded. With my share of this settlement, for all the work and pain that had gone into achieving this result, I no longer had to file bankruptcy. My children were going to be able to continue at their private school. Beau no longer had to work so damned hard to cover my slack. I could take care of my husband like I had always wanted to do.

The women hurt and abused by my family would have their day, and a public apology.

Their lives, which had been so negatively impacted by those heinous crimes, had now been changed forever as a direct result of their strength and conviction.

Beau tossed the paper on the desk and grabbed me into his arms. The tight embrace radiated relief, devotion, and something more. My love believed in me. My arms circled him, clinging to my life's preserver. We'd weathered the storm together.

"We're takin' time off," I said against his ear, but I didn't want to leave home. I needed to be put back into the day to day of my life. Make sure Beau and I were settling in for the long haul of peace and tranquility.

A quick rap on the door broke us apart. Well, inches apart. "Come in."

Collin surprised me by stepping inside as if it were the most normal thing in the world. He stared at Beau. "I wanted to meet you. The apology I extended to Dasham needs to be given to you as well. I also offer appreciation. Richmond Holdings has been in the fight of its life over the last few years. The leadership needed to leave the helm years before."

"What happens now?" Beau asked, threading our hands together.

I was certain none of my siblings had ever had a partner show such a sweet gesture like taking my hand and keeping me near. I recognized Collin taking us in, seemingly curious.

"We'll get the settlement offer in front of the judge," Collin answered for me.

"When its approved. We celebrate," I concluded. "Collin has his work cut out for him. My father won't be easy to deal with."

Collin's expression didn't change, but he offered one decisive nod at my statement.

"Dash, we're ready," Stone called.

"Let's get this done," Collin said. "I have a flight waiting." He left the room. When Beau tried to loosen his handhold, I tightened mine. We had only minutes left before I requested an amendment to our marriage contract, I wanted to add a twenty-four-seven clause, meaning I wanted to be with Beau every second of every day for the rest of our lives.

April 2025

"I feel like I've done this before," I murmured to myself. The salty breeze off the ocean teased my hair and added an extra layer of serenity to this monumental occasion. The rhythmic back and forth of the waves against the shore provided the perfect peaceful soundtrack for the day. The calm inside me was a significant contrast to the emotional upheaval of the last year.

Of course, this time was different. My clean-shaven husband stood beside me, looking like a million bucks in his linen button-up, tailored shorts, and expensive slide-on Italian loafers. And our beautiful children were here with us. Their laughter mingled with the squawks of the seagulls.

Who'd have thought that twenty-five years ago, being forced to come to Sea Springs, Texas would set such a far-reaching trajectory for my life?

The family I'd made were all here too. Joy and her family had come to celebrate the day. Scott, Lauren, Carter, Linda, and Kailey stood with me in front of the oceanfront hotel, a relic of its former glory. Even Amelia, who had fought me tooth and nail, was here with me. As much as anyone, she belonged on this day. That sweet woman had stayed by my side through the entirety of my life. She loved me and this family unconditionally. I felt the same in return.

The twenty-seven women who'd officially become multi-millionaires this morning were also in attendance. I had bankers and financial planners available as the settlement was distributed a few hours ago. Their joy, not just for the money but for the acknowledgement of what had happened to them, was palpable as they sipped champagne, waiting for the party to begin.

Somehow, everyone involved had managed to put the brutal bullshit, years in the making, behind them. Turns out, "fake it until you make it" worked.

How had this special moment come to be? Me standing in front of the former Richmond hotel complex was nothing short of being in the right moment at the right time. My firm had acquired the hotel and surrounding properties for pennies on the dollar. Plans for an office park, apartments suites, and my firm's new headquarters were already in motion. The building was large enough to fit every employee who worked for me, including a new office for Stone, and a new assistant for him while he assisted me. That was a firm must-have on the new contractual list of conditions he'd given me to live by these days.

"It's time," Stone announced, bullhorn in hand. His voice cut through the loud chatter, drawing everyone's attention. From our vantage point on the other side of the parking lot, we watched men work from the scaffolding, hanging from the top of the building.

The ocean breeze carried the chant that started with Beau and my rambunctious children. "Bring it down, bring it down..." Soon, everyone joined them in unison.

The previous exterior signage, the Richmond Resorts omen that always hung over my head, was removed from the building. Shooting streamers bombarded us from every direction and loud dance music added to the complete joy of the occasion. My firm's logo signage would replace it soon enough. Beau slipped an arm around my waist, drawing me close.

"I never thought I'd see the day," he yelled, his voice barely audible over the cheers. He pressed a kiss on my lips, and for the briefest of moments, the world around us faded.

"How did we make it through?" I said, rearing no more than an inch from Beau's handsome face. I marveled at the obstacles he and I had overcome. My hand cupped Beau's neck, drawing him in and down for another kiss. Smaller arms circled my knee. Fisher was there.

"He got you too?" Beau asked playfully.

"Yup."

Beau and I glanced down together to see Fisher's ever-smiling face. Then he placed a kiss on my knee, then on Beau's. His newest way of joining in our affection. Beau scooped our boy up into his arms. "You've been particularly good today."

"Yup. Daddy said if I was good, we could go to the trampoline park tomorrow," Fisher stated proudly.

"Next weekend," I corrected, smiling.

"I like the loud pop of the bombs." Fisher bounced off Beau's side, mimicking the sudden burst of the streamers. "But it scared Hunter."

"Margaritas and lunch in the foyer!" Stone interrupted again, the bullhorn still on blast. The throng of people began walking through the parking lot toward the grand foyer that had been transformed into a seascape of food and fun. Every woman of the twenty-six was given a hotel room for the weekend. The last guests to stay before the remodel began next week.

"Daddy, can we go inside?" Livie asked, tugging at the bottom of my shirt.

Linda swooped in, taking Fisher from Beau's arms and corralling the kids with practiced ease. "Best sons," she said, putting Fisher on his feet, who took off running. "After today, it's time for some quiet, easy years. Leave the drama behind."

"I'm into her idea," Beau said, lifting a hand to motion any stragglers toward the building. "I was thinkin' about becomin' a house husband."

His unexpected words stopped me in my tracks. I was stunned speechless. This same man who had given me hell over the years about paying his own way in the world was suggesting a slower pace? I searched his face for sincerity.

Beau and I had spent the last several months on a perpetual vacation, rediscovering who we were and how devoted each of us were to our family. I'd learned again about the effortless commitment, friendship, and understanding he and I had shared since day one.

The best part of the case ending successfully was my win also being my family's win. It took a village to get here. All of us had mucked through the scum to be standing here together.

Beau extended a hand, and I readily took it, separating the space between us. "I'd love you becoming a house husband. It's all I've ever wanted."

"Come on, guy," Beau said, chuckling at me, not with me. He released my hand to wrap an arm around my back, walking side by side with me to the front. "I don't wanna be a house husband like the *Real Housewives*, but I do want to permanently slow down. I want you to too. We lived way too much life on the front end of our relationship, let's keep the backend low-key."

Before I could respond, Hunter's triumphant yell drew our attention. He stood atop a mound of flowers, fists raised high, while Fisher lay face down, trapped under Hunter's tennis shoe.

Ava stood to the side, glaring at Beau and I, her finger pointing at the boys. "See what they do? You can't go anywhere with them. Why do we keep trying?"

"What's wrong with those boys?" Beau muttered, quickening his pace toward the kids. To my surprise, Amelia appeared beside me, keeping stride with me.

"You did it, Dasham," she said, her voice soft and encouraging. "You made a better life. We know love."

My arm anchored around her shoulders, slowing our way to the entrance. "You were always my strength, Amelia. I wouldn't be here without you. You keep this life moving for us. Especially over the last couple years. You kept me emotionally afloat."

"All that sweetness, and you're still good at keeping secrets." Not necessarily the conversational direction I'd expected. I ran through the words again before turning my head to her. Based on all that accusation on her face, the sweet moment I thought we shared, turned darker.

Okay.

She knew.

Dammit.

Amelia was the secret-whisperer. She read me like a book, a toddler-level read. "Don't tell Beau. I will after the party. I don't know that he knows we've moved past the figuring it out stage."

"How far along is she?" Amelia asked, her eyes twinkling with excitement.

"Six weeks," I lied, but Amelia wasn't fooled. "I've been waiting because Beau's nervous about handling the load. He doesn't understand I'm almost forty-one years old, and we need to wrap all this up."

With only a look, she suddenly reduced me into a young boy, explaining why I wasn't wrong.

"Seven weeks and three days," she said and pulled the sonogram picture out of her bag. "Don't leave things lying around if you don't want them seen."

The way she held the picture to her heart zipped my lips. The photo was an email attachment which meant she was poking around where she shouldn't have been and printing things that definitely needed to stay hidden. It didn't matter. Amelia loved my newest little nugget just like I did, just as Beau would after he finished freaking out.

"I was planning to tell Beau tonight," I called.

Every dream I'd had as a young man was a reality. My life partner, Beau, our beautiful children, the normal life with normal people we created, all happened for me. The overwhelming contentment squeezed my heart.

With belief, work, and nurturing, dreams did come true.

My lips quirked up in the corners as I tucked my hands into my pockets. She didn't catch my other lie. I figured forty-five years old was a good age to stop having children. We still had lots of time.

The End.

The Gravity series is over, I hope you enjoyed getting to know Dash and Beau, but the Richmond-Brooks family still has a long way to go. Look for more in 2027.

Please let me know what you think of this series. Email me at kindle@kindlealexander.com.

Other Books by Kindle Alexander

If you enjoyed Force then you won't want to miss 's bestselling
novels:

Breakaway
Reservations
It's Complicated
Painted On My Heart
The Current Between Us (with Bonus Material)
Closet Confession
Secret
Texas Pride
Full Disclosure
Double Full
Full Domain
Always
Forever
Havoc
Order
Chaos
Justice
Friction
Fusion

Force
A Wilder Inc. Story
Secret
Breakaway
Level Up
Reading Order Secret, Breakaway, Level Up
A Reservations Nightclub Story
Reservations Book 1
It's Complicated Book 2
Reading Order of all the characters mentioned in A
Reservation Story Series
Secret, Painted On My Heart, Reservations, It's Complicated
Always & Forever Duet
Always
Forever
A Nice Guys Novel
Double Full
Full Disclosure
Full Domain
Tattoos & Ties
Havoc
Order
Chaos
Justice
Tattoos & Tinsel
Layne Family Duet
The Current Between Us
Painted On My Heart
Gravity
Friction
Fusion
Force